CAFFEINE NIGHTS PUBLISHING

INCISIONS

CUT 1

Shaun Hutson

Fiction to die for…

Published by Caffeine Nights Publishing 2023

Copyright © Shaun Hutson 2023

Shaun Hutson has asserted his rights under the Copyright, Designs and Patents Act 1998 to be identified as the author of this work.

CONDITIONS OF SALE

All rights reserved. No part of this publication may be reproduced, stored in a retrieval system, or transmitted in any form or by any means, electronic, mechanical, photocopying, scanning, recording or otherwise, without the prior permission of the publisher.

This book has been sold subject to the condition that it shall not, by way of trade or otherwise, be lent, resold, hired out, or otherwise circulated without the publisher's prior consent in any form of binding or cover other than that in which it is published and without a similar condition including this condition being imposed on the subsequent purchaser.
All characters in this publication are fictitious and any resemblance to real persons, living or dead is purely coincidental.

Published in Great Britain by
Caffeine Nights Publishing
Amity House
71 Buckthorne Road
Minster on Sea
Isle of Sheppey
ME12 3RD

caffeinenightsbooks.com
British Library Cataloguing in Publication Data.
A CIP catalogue record for this book is available from the British Library

ISBN: 978-1-913200-29-9

Everything else by
Default, Luck and Accident

Also by Shaun Hutson:

ASSASSIN
BODY COUNT
BREEDING GROUND
CAPTIVES
CHASE
COMPULSION
DEADHEAD
DEATHDAY
DYING WORDS
EPITAPH
EREBUS
EXIT WOUNDS
HEATHEN
HELL TO PAY
HYBRID
KNIFE EDGE
LAST RITES
LUCY'S CHILD
MONOLITH
NECESSARY EVIL
NEMESIS
PROGENY
PURITY
RELICS
RENEGADES
SHADOWS
SLUGS
SPAWN
STOLEN ANGELS
TESTAMENT
THE SKULL
TWISTED SOULS
UNMARKED GRAVES
VICTIMS
WARHOL'S PROPHECY

WHITE GHOST

Hammer Novelizations
TWINS OF EVIL
X THE UNKNOWN
THE REVENGE OF FRANKENSTEIN

INCISIONS

CUT ONE

INCISIONS - CUT ONE	5
ACKNOWLEDGEMENTS	9
ON A STAR	21
SEA AIR	37
MAN'S BEST FRIEND	61
BOX	77
NIGHT GAMES	87
THE PICK UP	127
BATTLEFIELD	141
FROM THE LONG GRASS	163
OPEN FIELDS	181
THE THING IN THE TUNNEL	199
THE MISSION	213
THE INVADERS	229
A HOME OF ONE'S OWN	247
TROLL	267

ACKNOWLEDGEMENTS

The people who are mentioned in the acknowledgements of a novel are there for a reason. Be it support, encouragement or because they've begged me to be in… (just kidding).

Anyway, the list that follows is probably not exhaustive and it will probably seem familiar to people who read most of my books but here goes:

As always, I would like to thank my publisher, Darren Laws at Caffeine Nights. His continued faith in my work is both welcomed and greatly appreciated. Many thanks to everyone at Caffeine Nights.

My agent, Meg Davies, for her efforts and work.

I'd also like to thank Matt Shaw, Graeme Sayer, Michael Knight, Emma Dark and Mark Taylor. They should all know why.

A big thank you to everyone at Cineworld Milton Keynes where I seem to spend much of my spare time.

Thanks also to Claire, Dani, Leah, Belinda, Bruce, Steve, Dave, Adrian, Janick and Nicko and Rod Smallwood.

Thanks is far too inadequate a word for what I want to say to my daughter.

The most important people are, as ever, you lot. My readers. You support me, you challenge me, and you are one of the reasons I do this.

And now, I've probably been rambling for too long.

Let's go.

Shaun Hutson.

This book is dedicated to Claire, because I know how much it means to her.

"Think you're safe but you're wrong.
We are falling off the edge of the world."
                              Black Sabbath

"And if I close my mind in fear,
please pry it open…"
Metallica

AUTHOR'S INTRODUCTION

I always think that an author's introduction should more rightly be called author's intrusion. It wastes time when people just want to get on and read the book (you're probably doing that right now and proving me right) and it usually means the author has done something they're worried about and wants to apologise for it i.e., an "experimental" book that they've never tried before and are worried they've alienated their readers.

The reason *I've* chosen to do one on this collection is purely and simply because, in the past, I've always said I'd never do a short story collection. I'd like to explain why I have.

Most of these were written during the first bloody Lockdown. Christ knows where we'll all be by the time this is published. I just hope you're not all reading it during Lockdown 6.5!!!

The reason I did short stories is because lots of ideas simply don't have enough "legs" to be used as novels. An idea that sounds good when you first get it might not have the substance to turn into a 500-page book. Some of these stories were literally things I thought of and sat down to write, discovering that they were never going to be longer than twenty or thirty pages.

I've had short stories published in the past, usually in the Metal Magazines like Kerrang! and Metal Hammer. In fact, two of the stories in here (Soft Centre and Portraits) are "re-boots" of stories originally published back in the 80s or 90s in those very magazines.

I always thought that short stories fell into two categories. Namely those that genuinely were ideas not long enough to be novellas or novels and those that turned out to be little more than a long joke with a punchline. For example, the whole thing builds up to one single pay off line such as "but it was standing behind him" or "she tried to scream but it had already reached her." Something like that. I remember reading a complete pile of shit short story years ago that was about a guy in a bar with a giant toad and the whole thing existed solely so the author (and I use the word loosely) could use the pay off line "give me one for my baby and one for the toad." Yes, it was that bad.

Hopefully I've avoided anything as dire as that in this collection. Some of the stories are build ups to a payoff, I freely admit that. Even the stories I read when I was a kid in The Pan Books of Horror Stories (is there a horror writer working now of a certain age who wasn't influenced by them?) had that. Sometimes you can't avoid it. The whole *raison d'être* of the story is finding some way of using that payoff line. It might not be preferable but that's just the way it goes sometimes. I've got notebooks and pieces of paper all over the place with ideas scribbled on them going back years. Some are not useable at all. Some are only fit to be short stories. Some may become novels one day. There's no way of knowing. What appealed to me, what I wanted to write about a year ago, can change from day to day. My primary purpose with a book is to exorcise some kind of crap from my mind, it always has been. That's why I've saved a fortune on therapy over the years. The fact that my readers seem to want to share that self-flagellation and find it entertaining is even better. There's not really much point in writing if no one's going to read it.

I think another of the reasons I did this collection was that I'd always loved the old Amicus Films compendium horror films like *Vault of Horror, From Beyond the Grave,*

Torture Garden, Dr Terror's House of Horrors and the like. I wanted to do something similar. I even wrote another collection of short stories and linked them with one central main story like those films had. Whether that is published depends on the success of this volume, I suppose.

Another reason short stories appealed to me (from the reading or watching standpoint rather than the writing side) was the fact that I grew up with stuff like *The Twilight Zone*, *The Dark Room* and also reading horror comics like *Eerie* and *Creepy*. Sometimes the short, sharp shock kind of story just works better than a novel. It's easier to put a powerful punch in a short story, sometimes, than it is in a 500-page novel.

They also give you the chance to go off at a tangent if you want to. There are several stories in the collection that are me just ranting about things I dislike or feel strongly about. If you do that in a novel, then you have to put those thoughts in the mouths of a character and that doesn't always work. It sometimes seems like an author intrusion (a bit like a bloody introduction, I hear you cry). And that is the most unforgivable thing that any writer can do. It makes the reader suddenly aware that they're reading, and it breaks the spell that you've hopefully created.

Anyway, I should stop rambling and let you get on with reading these stories.

I hope you like them. If you do, let me know. In fact, if you *don't* then let me know too. I want to know what I did wrong.

Some are not what you might expect from my novels. Not all are blood-drenched. Not all are what you would immediately call "horror." But then again what the hell *is* horror? I think we've all been struggling with that definition for years now.

So, ignore my ramblings, dim the lights, curl up on the sofa or in bed or wherever the hell you read and dive in.

Hopefully some of these will stay with you. They might disturb you. They might make you smile. They might disgust you. But as long as they entertain you, I've done my job.

> Let's go.

Shaun Hutson.

ON A STAR

"How much for that?"

Carlie Rogers held up the small, red-tinted glass.

The woman standing behind the stall told her it was two pounds.

Carlie immediately dug in her purse and found the required change, dropping the little vase into her jacket pocket.

"Another bargain," she said, smiling.

"It's not a bargain, Mum," her fifteen-year-old daughter Casey grunted. "It's tacky crap. That's why it's cheap."

"Well, it's going in your bedroom so you'd better start liking it," Carlie said, chuckling when she saw the look of disgust on Casey's face. "It'll look nice on your windowsill."

Carlie, her daughter, her husband, and her son had been wandering around the car boot sale for more than an hour now. It was a huge gathering, sellers displaying their wares either directly from the boots of their cars or, more usually, from tables they had set up like display counters. All manner of items were on show, from electrical equipment to clothes. From toys to hand made mugs.

"You can pick up some real bargains at these places," Carlie said, wandering towards a table displaying a selection of tea towels and dusters.

"Yeah," Harvey Greaves murmured. "And some real crap too."

"Now, now," Stephen Greaves said, feigning reproach. "Your mum loves these places. She's an expert."

Carlie jabbed him playfully in the ribs.

"You've bought things today," she reminded him.

"A book about cars," Stephen admitted, nodding.

They were heading towards another display of goods when Carlie reached for her phone. She checked the caller ID and rolled her eyes, pressing the phone to her ear.

"Hello Mum," she said, wearily.

Stephen smiled, realising how much she disliked talking to her mother. As his wife wandered away to try and get a better reception, he and the two youngsters continued their way across the large open area where the cars and stalls were set up.

"Mum doesn't like talking to grandma, does she?" Casey offered.

"They don't always see eye to eye, let's put it that way," Stephen confirmed, guiding the children towards another display of crockery and ornaments.

He noticed a small blue ceramic vase with a gold pattern on it and pointed to it.

"How much?" he wanted to know.

"Just take it," the stall holder urged, picking up the vase and shoving it into his hand.

"A couple of quid?" Stephen suggested.

"Just take it," the woman continued. "I don't want it any more. Just take it."

Stephen frowned as he thought he heard concern in her voice. Or something stronger?

"Why are you selling it?" he asked. "It's a really nice piece."

"She's not *selling* it, Dad," Casey murmured. "She's trying to *give* it to you. Just take it."

"I haven't got the room for it any more," the woman insisted. "I need to get rid of it."

Stephen shrugged, smiled, and picked up the vase, inspecting it more closely before watching as the woman wrapped it in a sheet of tissue paper and put it into a bag.

He took it from her, sliding it into his pocket. Then he and the children walked away from the woman.

"Your mum will like that," he said. "It might cheer her up after her conversation with Grandma." He smiled, noticing that Carlie was heading back towards them now, her expression somewhat darker than it had been earlier. She sighed.

"If I had a pound for every time my mum told me that Chloe's kid is being christened on Sunday I wouldn't need to work again," Carlie announced. "I mean, does she think I'm going to forget?"

"She's just excited because it's her grandchild," Stephen offered.

"They're her grandchildren too," Carlie said, gesturing towards Harvey and Casey. "She never gets very excited about *them*."

"Never mind that," Stephen interjected, digging his hand in his pocket to produce the little vase. "What do you think?"

Carlie's eyes lit up.

"It's lovely," she beamed.

"And a real bargain," chuckled Stephen.

"Can we go to McDonald's now?" Harvey groaned and the others laughed. In five minutes, they were in the car and driving away from the car boot sale.

"So do we have to go to the christening on Sunday then, Mum?" Casey enquired, barely looking up from her phone.

"We'll see," Carlie answered.

"All that's going to happen is that you'll get more stressed out," Stephen offered as he drove.

Carlie didn't answer.

"But if you want to go, we'll go," Stephen continued, but then he shouted as a car cut in front of them, forcing him to slam on his brakes sharply. He hit his hooter hard. "Fucking idiot," he rasped, glaring at the vehicle ahead.

Carlie swallowed hard.

"Where did he come from?" she murmured. "He could have hit us."

"Bloody boy racer," Stephen snarled, trailing the other car and sounding his hooter once again.

He saw the driver of the car ahead lower his window and then raise his hand in several abusive gestures.

"Little bastard," Stephen snapped.

The car in front sped off but Stephen followed, keeping ten or fifteen yards behind. He muttered something under his breath when he saw the leading car turn into the lane leading to the drive-through window of the fast-food place they'd been heading for.

"Looks like he's hungry too," Carlie said, quietly, watching as the car in front pulled up to the window.

"I should get out and have a word with him," Stephen suggested, but Carlie shook her head.

"Just let it go," she told him, gripping his arm.

"I hate people like that," Stephen said. "No consideration for others."

The car in front suddenly reversed, stopping only inches from the front bumper of Stephen's car. They all watched as the driver jumped out, ran towards them and spat on their windscreen. He then raised two fingers, clambered back in and sped off.

"That's disgusting," Carlie shouted angrily, watching as the other car roared off. "I hope he crashes," she added.

The car ahead exploded.

A shrieking ball of red and yellow flame erupted from the vehicle, transforming it into an inferno in seconds. A tyre spiralled into the air, hurtling skyward as lumps of blazing metal and rubber flew in all directions, propelled by the blast. A thick, choking mushroom cloud of black smoke rose from the blazing wreck.

"Jesus," murmured Carlie, gazing blankly at the dancing flames and what remained of the other car.

Stephen too looked at the remnants of the vehicle as if mesmerised but then he drove on, guiding his own car past the wreckage, wanting nothing more than to be away from this place now.

From somewhere in the distance they all heard approaching sirens.

***

Carlie put down the phone and sighed.

As Stephen emerged from the bathroom, she looked at him and shook her head.

"What's wrong?" he wanted to know, wiping some toothpaste from the corner of his mouth.

"Chloe again," Carlie told him. "More about the christening."

"So, are we going?"

"It looks like it."

Stephen climbed into bed beside her and squeezed her hand.

"If that's what she wants then we'll go," he said. "Anything to avoid even more family arguments."

"I sometimes wish I was like you," Carlie told him. "An only child."

She kissed him gently, turning her head in the direction of the window when she heard the sound again. The barking of a dog cut through the stillness of the night. Loud and insistent as it had been for the past thirty minutes. Carlie frowned as the noise continued.

"There was something on the news earlier about that car, you know," Stephen informed her.

"What did they say?"

"The driver was killed."

"Well, it serves him right. Acting like that. Did they say what might have caused it?"

"Fuel leak or something," he told her.

"Well, I'm sorry but I just don't understand people like that," Carlie announced.

Stephen nodded sagely, his own attention now drawn

to the continual barking of the dog.

He walked across to the window and peered out towards the house next door.

"Jake said they were getting a dog, but he didn't say it'd be barking all night," he noted. "It must be keeping him and Michelle awake too, surely."

"It must be keeping half the bloody street awake," Carlie offered. "Why don't they see to it?"

Stephen walked back across the room and climbed into bed again, nodding towards the small blue ceramic vase that he now noticed was standing on Carlie's bedside table. She saw that he was looking at it and smiled.

"It looks nice, doesn't it?" she said, smiling.

"I thought you'd like it," Stephen told her.

"You know me so well," she chuckled.

The barking outside seemed to intensify and Carlie sighed again.

"I wish that bloody dog would shut up," she muttered.

There was another short burst of loud barking and then silence. Stephen smiled. He clambered out of bed and crossed to the window, looking out once again.

There was no sound from the dog.

"About time," Carlie announced.

"It looks like you got your wish," Stephen grinned.

***

The early morning frost had well and truly melted away by the time Carlie finished her housework. The sun was out and bathing the land with its welcome warmth.

A day off gave her the opportunity to run around the house with the hoover, do a bit of dusting and take care of the laundry (something she didn't like doing at the weekend) and even park herself in front of the TV for an hour or two watching the crap that passed for daytime television. She made herself a cup of tea and wandered out into the garden to peg a couple more items onto the washing line.

She was halfway down the garden when she heard the sound coming from the adjacent garden.

A sound that reminded her of soft crying.

Carlie crossed to the low fence and looked over.

Michelle Piper was hunched over something that Carlie couldn't make out, her body quivering slightly. She called the other woman's name, watching as she turned, straightening up at the same time. It was then that Carlie saw what lay at her feet.

It was the body of a large dog.

"I found him like this," Michelle announced, gesturing towards the dead dog.

Carlie gasped as she gazed at the motionless animal. Its muzzle was covered with blood, as was most of its head, but that wasn't the most startling thing about its appearance.

The jaws looked as if they'd been stitched together. Carlie could see something glistening and thought it looked like wire that had been used to fasten the animal's upper and lower mandibles together. It was difficult to tell because there was so much blood, but the sight made her recoil and she swallowed hard, shocked by the scene before her.

She exchanged a few consoling words with Michelle and then retreated back inside the house. She waited a moment, shaken by what she'd seen, then pulled on her coat and left the house, clambering into her car and driving away from the house, trying to banish the image of the dead dog from her mind.

Even walking around the town centre, she had trouble trying to force the vision of the animal from her head. Who could have done something like that to it? And why?

She walked into the baker's shop, still troubled. There was a queue in the shop, there always was. But Carlie took up her position and waited patiently, looking at the huge array of cakes, pastries and bread on display in the glass-fronted cabinets.

The man in front was muttering under his breath, occasionally looking at his watch and then gesturing to the staff who were run off their feet with the influx of customers.

"Come on, come on," the man grunted.

Carlie looked at him but ignored his frustrated mutterings, aware that he was turning to look her up and down every now and then.

"This is hopeless," the man snapped. "They need more staff."

"They're doing their best," Carlie reminded him.

"Well, their best isn't good enough," the man insisted. "I'm going to go somewhere else if they don't sort this out."

He looked at Carlie and smiled.

"Want to join me?" he enquired. "We could go and get a coffee or something."

"No thanks," she said.

"Yeah, come on," he persisted. "We'll get out of this queue and go for a coffee."

Carlie shook her head.

"It'll be fun," he assured her.

"I'm married."

"So am I. Who cares?"

He patted her gently on the thigh and Carlie moved a pace or two away from him.

"What's your name?" he asked.

"Does it matter?" Carlie countered, sighing. She kept her gaze fixed firmly on the cakes displayed before her, determined not to look at the man now.

"You're really pretty," the man went on. "Tell me your name."

"Just leave it, will you?" she said, softly, aware that some other people in the queue were now looking in their direction.

"Come on," the man demanded. "Why not? You think you're better than me or something? I'm just trying to be friendly."

Carlie felt her cheeks flush with embarrassment as more people glanced in her direction.

"Typical," the man sneered. "You good looking tarts, you always think you're something special. I'm just trying to be friendly, and you're all stuck up about it."

"Please, just leave it."

"Fuck you," he snapped. "I'll talk to you if I want. Fucking jumped up bitch. I bet you love the attention, don't you?"

Carlie was on the verge of turning and walking out now.

"All I did was ask for your name," the man hissed. "You fucking slag."

"Oh, drop dead," Carlie whispered.

The man went down like a stone.

He hit the floor in front of her and lay motionless, his eyes gaping wide, his mouth open and dripping saliva onto the polished wood beneath him.

Someone near the back of the queue shouted in surprise and shock. A woman in front stifled a scream. From behind the counter two of the staff hurried to help the fallen man. Carlie heard someone shout out something about calling an ambulance.

She looked down again at the fallen man, noticing his skin now looked slightly blue. She could see the bulging red veins in the whites of his eyes, his tongue lolling from his open mouth. Carlie was convinced he was dead. She spun around and hurried out of the shop, accusatory glances following her.

When Stephen got home that night, he found her sitting on the sofa, still shaken and still shaking.

The little blue ceramic vase was on the coffee table in front of her.

She told him about the dog next door, then about the man in the baker's and Stephen listened intently as she recounted the stories, finally sighing and shaking his head.

"How the hell could *you* have been to blame for either

of those things that happened?" he wanted to know.

"I wanted them to happen," Carlie explained. "Just like I wanted that guy to crash yesterday."

"We both wanted that," he reminded her. "And why should only your wishes or desires come true? And why only bad things?"

"I don't know."

Stephen shook his head and reached for the vase. "So, you think this is some kind magic charm that grants wishes? You might as well rub it and wait for a genie to come out."

"It's all happened since you brought me that vase."

"It's a coincidence."

"What if it's not?"

"Alright, go on then. Wish for something. Wish for the winning lottery ticket. Wish for a suitcase full of money to appear."

"It doesn't work like that."

"It doesn't work at *all*. A little ornament that grants wishes? Give me a break. It's a vase not a monkey's paw." He laughed.

"What do you mean?"

"The Monkey's Paw. It's a famous old story. A couple get three wishes because of a monkey's paw. The wife wishes for money and they get it because their son dies in an accident. She wishes him back to life and he comes back but in the same mangled state he died in. The husband uses the last wish to wish him dead again. This kind of thing only happens in horror stories, Carlie. Not in real life." He put the vase down again.

"I want to talk to the woman who gave it to you," she insisted.

"Why?"

"She might be able to tell us something about it."

"What's to tell? It's a vase. Nothing more and besides how are you going to find out who that woman is?"

"The organisers of the car boot sale will have a list of

stall holders. I can find out from them."

Stephen shook his head dismissively. "If that woman experienced the same thing why not just smash the vase up? Drop it in a river or something? Why try to pass it on?"

Carlie sighed.

"I'm overreacting, aren't I?" she said, softly.

Stephen smiled.

"I wish that we had got some wishes to use," he said. "But it's coincidence, nothing more." He leaned forward and kissed her gently on the forehead.

"What would we wish for if we could really have anything?" Carlie pondered, smiling. "Ten million pounds? Immortality?"

"Sounds like a good start," Stephen chuckled. "Make it twenty million, just to be on the safe side."

"Perfect health for us and the kids forever?" she went on.

"Never getting fat," he added. "Never going bald. Never being impotent."

They both laughed.

Carlie got to her feet and walked off into the kitchen to retrieve her ringing phone. Stephen waited a moment then followed her, watching as she snatched it up.

She rolled her eyes and he realised immediately who she was speaking to.

"Yes, Mum," he heard her say and he retreated from the room, heading upstairs where he showered and then changed.

When he returned to the kitchen, Carlie was still on the phone.

"Yes, I know Mum," she said, wearily into the device. "You've told me. Yes. You've told me that too."

Carlie shook her head.

"We'll be there about three, just like I said," she went on. "Yes, I'll ring Chloe and sort that out too."

She finally finished speaking and terminated the call,

putting the phone down on the worktop.

"I swear to God she doesn't listen to a word I say," Carlie exclaimed, spooning chilli and rice onto plates from the saucepans on the stove. "All she's bothered about is this bloody christening." Again, she shook her head, placing a plateful of food in front of Stephen. "I wish Chloe had never had that baby."

They ate hungrily, the food washed down with half a bottle of wine they had left. They were almost finished when Carlie's phone rang again. She picked it up.

"Hello," she murmured.

Stephen watched her face as the voice at the other end of the line spoke. He could see the colour draining from his wife's face. When she put the phone down, she was as white as milk. She looked straight at him, her lips barely moving when she spoke.

"That was Chloe's boyfriend," she said, her voice little more than a whisper. "The christening is off." She swallowed hard. "Chloe's baby died less than an hour ago."

Stephen felt a cold lump in his stomach that seemed to grow like a swiftly swelling tumour.

"This is my fault, isn't it?" Carlie mumbled. "Because of what I said. Because of the vase."

Stephen got to his feet and hurried into the sitting room. When he returned he was carrying the little blue ceramic vase. Carlie watched as he walked across to the back door and wrenched it open.

"What are you doing?" she wanted to know.

"I'm getting rid of this bloody thing," he snarled, drawing back his arm, ready to fling the vase away forever. "I hope none of us ever see it again."

Carlie froze then watched as he hurled it away down the garden, the little vase sailing through the air into the hedge at the bottom of the garden.

Only as Stephen turned back to face her did she hear his gasps of pain and horror.

Where his eyes had been there were now only two

gaping holes, choked with blood, some of which poured down his cheeks like crimson tears.

He staggered helplessly for a second then fell forward, slamming into the table.

His words suddenly echoed in her ears: *"I hope none of us ever see it again."*

She clapped hands to her face, feeling rapidly growing pain in and around her eyes.

And she knew those words were prophetic. None of them would ever see the vase, or anything else, ever again.

Carlie screamed.

SEA AIR

The sea crashed against the old pier with such ferocity sometimes that many of the locals expected it to simply collapse and drop into the water.

A fire had destroyed most of the buildings on it two years earlier, but it stood defiantly in the dark water, jutting out from the beach into the sea. The thick wooden supports that held it up were covered in moss and barnacles that also seemed to be eating into the wood itself. It appeared as if the elements were conspiring against the pier to drag it down into the ocean, but somehow it resisted.

The businesses that had been situated on the pier before the fire had re-located, but many had left behind equipment that still remained on the jutting promontory as if to remind those who looked upon them that it had once been a thriving little community in itself. A helter skelter poked upwards into the night sky like an accusatory finger. The remains of an amusement arcade (where authorities thought the fire had started) stood next to what was left of the theatre, and that faced what had once been a dodgem car rink. The cars had been left in place and looked as if they were simply waiting for customers to arrive and use them once again.

The pier had once been one of the focal points along the beach front of Little Granby but now it was merely a reminder of better days. Of days gone by when the town was a flourishing holiday resort. Before foreign holidays became more attractive to people. The town still did a fair bit of business during the season but, in the off season, it was dead. It was as if the entire place sank into a state of suspended animation until the first tourists began to arrive in May.

In these winter months the whole town was as gloomy and forbidding as the dark sea that crashed up on its beach.

In addition to the spray of the sea that was sweeping across the pier, there was also a light drizzle falling but as Polly Dean moved quickly and effortlessly along the pier in the darkness she seemed not to notice either.

She left the concrete ramp that formed the first part of the pier and made her way onto the wooden part of the structure, her feet beating out a tattoo on the slats. As she walked she ensured that the holdall she carried was held well clear of the ground and, every now and then, she would glance down at it.

When she reached the end of the pier she stopped to recover her breath then dug in her coat pocket for a torch.

She flicked it on and off two or three times, the light cutting through the blackness and across the rough sea.

Then Polly waited.

She glanced out over the churning waves, thinking how dark and forbidding the sea looked tonight. She could hear it lashing against the pier and, more than once, she fancied she felt the structure beneath her move slightly. She reached down slowly and unzipped the holdall.

Inside there were towels and pieces of rag. Inside those was a baby.

No older than six weeks, the child was crying softly and it continued to do so even when Polly picked it up and held it before her. She swallowed hard and held the child higher, advancing again towards the wooden rail that surrounded the walkways of the pier. The only thing that separated her from the sea.

She held the child over the rail for a second, its cries lost beneath the raging sound of the waves.

Polly dropped the baby.

She closed her eyes for a moment then looked down.

The man who was standing on the deck of the boat beneath the pier had caught the child in his gnarled hands.

He looked up in Polly's direction and then she heard the roar of an outboard motor as the boat moved away, disappearing into the blackness.

Polly waited a moment longer then snatched up the holdall, turned and hurried back down the pier towards the shore.

***

In the confines of his small hotel room, Carl Jennings sat at the writing desk in one corner and gazed at the laptop before him.

The cursor was winking on the blank screen, but Carl merely got to his feet and crossed to the French windows that opened out onto a small balcony. From there he could see out across the seafront to the beach and the dark sea beyond. Even this far away (and he estimated he must be a full eight hundred yards from the water) he could hear the roar of the surf as it slammed down onto the beach.

Arrayed up and down the beachfront on what was known locally as The Golden Mile, were amusement arcades, crazy golf courses, a covered swimming pool and an assortment of restaurants, most of which were closed with it being the off season. The whole front looked as if it needed a coat of paint.

The occasional car drove up or down and Carl watched the vehicles disappear into the early morning gloom. It would be dawn in less than twenty minutes. He finished his cigarette then finally turned away from the balcony and headed towards the large wardrobe in the room.

From inside he selected a jacket and slid his hand into the inside pocket, pulling a newspaper cutting from that hidden compartment.

FIFTH CHILD GOES MISSING

the headline proclaimed.

Below it was a photograph of a young girl. No more than three. She was smiling happily at the camera. Carl traced the outline of her face with one index finger, tears filling his eyes. He gazed at the picture for what seemed like an eternity then he pushed it back into the jacket and shut the wardrobe door. One single tear rolled down his cheek and he brushed it away before turning towards the door of the room.

Carl made his way down from his room on the first floor of the Royal Hotel and out onto the seafront that it overlooked. Every morning he walked for about half an hour before breakfast, enjoying the stillness of the deserted seafront and the scent of the air at such an early hour. He had trouble sleeping and was invariably up at some ungodly hour of the morning, so the little stroll was a way of alleviating this problem and also helped him build an appetite before he had his breakfast.

He took his usual route, down the wide pavement past the other hotels and guest houses (most of which were closed for the off season). Then across the road to the walkway that ran parallel with the beach itself. Beneath the old, deserted pier and then down past the jetty towards the boating lake at the far end of the Golden Mile. Once he reached it, Carl turned around and headed back in the same direction. When he got back to the hotel he made his way straight into the dining room, the smell of freshly cooked food reaching his nostrils as he sat down at his usual table.

The dining room was large but only three of the tables were laid for guests and there was someone sitting at the table nearest to Carl's. He was a man in his late forties. Slightly overweight, balding and with a moustache that resembled a slug clinging to his upper lip. The man nodded to Carl as he walked in then he returned to his laptop that he had placed on the table beside his breakfast.

"Gives whole new meaning to the word desolate, doesn't it?" the man said.

"What does?" Carl wanted to know.

"This place," Nigel Thomas said. "This town when there are no tourists here. I mean, it's bad enough when there *are* people here." He smiled at his own joke.

"Why are you here?" Carl asked.

"For work," Nigel told him. "I sell cutlery."

"Don't people buy that kind of stuff online these days?"

"They like to feel it in their hands before they buy it. I sell to the hotels, restaurants and guest houses here. What about yourself? What brings you here? Not exactly the fanciest hotel in town, is it?"

"My parents brought me here every year for fifteen years when I was a kid," Carl explained. "I brought my own daughter here and..." He finished his sentence hurriedly, lowering his gaze. "I like it here," he went on, his voice lower. "It's comfortable."

Nigel raised his eyebrows.

"How long are you here for?" he wanted to know.

"Another few days," Carl informed him.

"We should have a drink later. Beat the boredom."

Carl smiled but it was a mechanical gesture. He watched as Nigel gathered up his things and got to his feet. He apologised that he was going to have to leave and then disappeared from the dining room. Carl poured himself another cup of coffee from the pot that had been left on his table.

"What else can I get you, Mister Jennings?"

He turned as he heard the woman's voice, smiling as Polly Dean emerged from the kitchen. Carl ordered his usual breakfast, chatting amiably with the woman as she scribbled down what he wanted on a small pad.

"Why do you stay open in the off season?" he asked.

"There's always someone who wants a room," she told him. "Like you."

Carl smiled.

"How long have you had this place?" he enquired.

"My parents ran it for thirty-five years," Polly informed him. "I took it over twelve years ago. I didn't really want to. I wanted to get out of here. Out of this town."

"Why?"

"You've heard the stories."

Carl sighed. "Yes I have," he murmured.

"There's something wrong with this town," Polly said, quietly.

"The missing children?"

She turned away abruptly.

"I've got to get on," she told him, heading back towards the kitchen.

Carl watched her disappear through the door. He thought about following her and trying to pursue the conversation. He wanted to find out more. He needed to know as much as possible about the town and the things that happened here, but no one would talk to him. He was an outsider. He was to be shunned not welcomed.

Carl finished his breakfast and made his way back to his room where he slipped on a jacket before setting off once again, this time into the town.

Little Granby town centre seemed to consist of four streets and a town square. As with the seafront many of the businesses were closed for the off season, or at least only open half days, but life had to go on whether there were tourists present or not. As Carl walked through the town centre he found that it was busier than usual. He made his way up the main street, turning off to his right towards the building he sought.

The structure that housed the Wax Museum looked like a large terraced house from the outside.

It had been there for as long as Carl could remember, certainly for all the years his parents had brought him to Little Granby for family holidays. A visit to the Wax Museum had been a special event for him as a young boy. The figures, the atmosphere, the gloomy surroundings.

There was that combination of excitement and apprehension that made any adventure so intriguing. And, once inside, he remembered how the motionless wax figures fascinated him and scared him. Now, as he dug in his pocket for the entrance fee, those same feelings resurfaced in him. Carl paid, got his ticket from a woman in the cash box who looked as if she'd once been an exhibit in the waxworks, and walked into the building.

Due to the time of the day and the fact that it was off season, the building was deserted.

As far as he was aware, the wax museum was privately run and nothing to do with the more famous chains of similar attractions run by Madame Tussauds or Ripley's. He moved slowly around the building, gazing at each of the figures, either impressed by their likenesses or amused by how little they resembled the people they were meant to be.

Figures from history, from showbiz, so called celebrities and sporting figures seemed to have been jammed into the museum with barely a foot or two between them. Some were arranged in tableaux, others merely stood gazing out blankly at visitors from behind glass partitions.

Carl made his way down some narrow stairs and towards an open hallway. To his right was a small amusement arcade but, straight ahead of him, a sign above a stone arch proclaimed: CHAMBER OF HORRORS.

He remembered that the amusement arcade was an alternative to the rigours of the Chamber of Horrors, a way out for those of more delicate sensibilities who didn't wish to sample the frightful sights beyond the archway. Carl smiled as he remembered how exciting this part of the tour of the waxworks had been for him as a youngster. He remembered practically begging his mother to let him go into the chamber when he was nine and how terrified he'd been once he'd entered it. Now, he walked towards it slowly, all those childhood fears crowding in on him once again. He knew that what lay beyond that archway was only wax figures and yet his heart was still hammering against his ribs as he took the first few footsteps down the short flight of stone steps leading into the darkened area beyond.

The smell that met his nostrils was one of neglect. A fusty odour that seemed to have been impregnated into the figures themselves.

Carl moved slowly into the chamber, glancing at the first exhibit. Arranged behind iron bars, it showed various torture methods through the ages. Eye gouging, pulling out the fingernails, tearing off the nose with red hot pliers, racking and strappado vied for space with an iron maiden, a spiked chair and electric shock torture. Carl looked at each figure with the usual mixture of fascination and revulsion before moving past the famous murderers section where he saw Jack the Ripper, Charles Manson, Christie, Haigh and Dennis Nilsen amongst others.

He was reading one of the newspaper pages from 1969 (framed in glass) telling of the horrors perpetrated by the Manson family when one of the lights behind the exhibits went out.

The darkness that descended was total and Carl gasped, unable to see a foot ahead of him.

He shot out one hand and gripped the cold metal bars that separated the exhibits from the public and, as he did, the light came back on again. He wondered if it was triggered by some kind of electric eye. A shock designed to induce even more fear in an already nervous visitor?

He was still considering this when he felt the hand close on his shoulder.

Carl spun around, his heart racing.

"Jesus," he hissed, his breath coming in gasps. "You scared the shit out of me."

Jack Fraser smiled.

"Why the hell did you want to meet up in here?" Fraser wanted to know. "We could have met in a cafe or somewhere like that, like normal people."

"I wanted somewhere less...public," Carl explained.

"Why are you back here, Carl?" Fraser asked. "I've told you all I know. If I had any more information about your daughter's disappearance I'd have given it to you."

"There's been two more kids taken since my daughter. What the fuck is going on?"

"It's under investigation, you know that."

"You're the detective in charge and that's all you've got to say?"

"Three more have gone missing since your daughter, not two. A baby was taken a day or two ago."

Carl swallowed hard.

"And you know nothing about those either?" he grunted.

"I can't discuss the investigation with you," Fraser announced. "You know that."

"Can't or *won't*? You've got a child. Imagine how you'd feel."

The two men walked slowly through the chamber, heading towards the steps that led upwards and out of it.

"If I tell you anything it better not appear in any articles or on your bloody show," Fraser snapped.

"I'm a journalist, I'm supposed to report facts."

"Not *these* facts," Fraser said, placing a hand forcefully against Carl's chest. "Not *this* case."

"What makes you think the latest disappearance is linked to the others?"

"The child was taken from a quiet location, no CCTV and we found grains of sand in the pushchair he was taken from."

"You believe the stories then?"

Fraser walked on ahead, eager to be out of the confines of the dungeon-like room.

"End of conversation, Carl," he called without turning his head.

"There'll be others," Carl shouted after him. "You know that."

He watched as the policeman walked out, his footsteps echoing away on the cold stone floor.

Carl waited a moment then strode off the same way, heading back through the town towards the seafront. A light breeze had sprung up and it ruffled his hair as he walked, glancing up at the seagulls whirling overhead. He walked across the wide road and headed onto the walkway beside the beach, finally settling himself on a bench close to one of the few beachfront cafes that remained open. Carl reached into his pocket for his phone, glancing at the screensaver. At the little girl there. His daughter. He swallowed hard and slid the phone back into his pocket again, shifting his attention towards the gleaming sand and the rough sea beyond.

The scent of the salty air was invigorating and Carl sat there for a long time enjoying the peacefulness of the scene, mesmerised by the churning waves. Since recorded time people had spoken of the power of the sea, regarding it with awe and respect and also with fear.

With so much of the ocean depths unexplored who knew what lay beneath the surface? Who could imagine the limitless life forms that lived in the deep? The thought made him shudder slightly.

He walked to the cafe and got himself a coffee, settling down on the bench once more with his beverage and his thoughts, his gaze again fixed on the water. His vigil was only interrupted when he saw the woman walking along the sea front with her young son.

He recognised her immediately. It wasn't difficult. He'd been following her for two days now.

Same routine. Same route. Same time.

She was wheeling a pushchair along and, every now and then, her young son would cross to it and clamber in, choosing to ride for a few yards before scrambling out once again so that he could dash back and forth across the wide path above the sand. Every time he got too close to the edge (it was only a three-foot drop, but she was cautious) she would call his name or hurry across to prevent him falling.

The woman finally took her son's hand and walked into the cafe, emerging a moment later with a coffee. She sat down at one of the outside tables while the little boy eagerly chewed his way through a small cake.

Carl waited a moment longer then got to his feet, walking past the cafe and the woman then turning. He walked back and sat down at the table next to her.

"Hazel Wilson?" he said, smiling.

She regarded him warily but then nodded.

"I don't mean to disturb you," Carl went on. "I just wondered if I could have a quick chat with you."

"Who are you?" she wanted to know.

"My name is Carl Jennings, I'm an investigative reporter," he announced. "I'd like to speak to you about your daughter."

"I don't want to talk to the press," she told him, sternly.

"My daughter was taken, just like yours was."

Hazel lowered her gaze, her expression darkening.

"How do you know me?" she wanted to know.

"I've been following you. I thought I might be able to help."

"Unless you can tell me who took my daughter there's nothing you can do."

"What did the police tell you?"

"Only that they had no clue who kidnapped her or why."

"I've spoken to some of the parents of the other missing children and they were told the same thing."

"What about you? When was your daughter taken?"

"Two years ago, almost to the day," Carl said, placing his phone on the table top so Hazel could see the screensaver. She regarded the little girl in the picture for a moment then smiled.

"She's beautiful," Hazel murmured.

Carl slid the phone back into his pocket.

"What do you know about the Cult of Persa?" he asked.

The colour drained rapidly from Hazel's face and she got to her feet but Carl shot out a hand to restrain her.

"I think that was who took our children," he went on, his voice low.

"You believe in them too," Hazel murmured.

"A group that sacrifice children to a god of the sea? People who think that if those offerings aren't made something will rise from the sea and destroy them? I think they're insane. But I think *they* believe it and I think that belief makes them do things you and I can't understand."

"How do you know about them?" Hazel asked.

"I'd heard of them even before my daughter was taken, but after it happened I did as much research as I could about them."

"All the knowledge in the world won't get our children back."

"It might, and besides, we can't allow them to carry on like this. They've got to be stopped."

He pulled a card from inside his jacket and pushed it across the table to her.

"If you want to talk, call me," he said, getting to his feet.

Hazel nodded, looking at the card and then watching Carl as he walked off along the sea front.

He walked the full length of the wide walkway beside the sand, passing the model village and a couple of crazy golf courses, more cafes and finally the large area of amusements and rides known as The Pleasure Beach. It was dominated by a huge rollercoaster that Carl glanced up at as he passed by. Like so much of Little Granby, the Pleasure Beach closed for the winter months and the only people moving within its high walls were some engineers who were working on another of the rides.

Another few hundred yards along the beachside pathway and he'd reached the small harbour.

There was a sign on a high wire fence and Carl read the words: BOATS FOR HIRE.

He walked along one of the short quays, glancing down at the various vessels moored there. Small motor boats mainly, but there were larger craft bobbing about on the rough sea on the far side of the harbour. Carl remained close to the smaller boats.

There was a small whitewashed wooden office standing at the end of the quay that looked as if it was about to be blown into the water by the steadily growing wind. Carl walked slowly towards it, hands dug into his pockets. He tapped on the door and, when he got no answer, he stuck his head inside but the office was empty. Carl turned and walked back down the quay noticing that someone was heading in his direction.

The man was in his fifties. His face so tanned and leathery it looked as if he'd spent his life on or near the sea. His hands were covered with oil that he was wiping off with a dirty rag.

"Do you work here?" Carl asked.

"Sometimes," the man told him. "When there's work about."

"I wanted to hire a boat," Carl informed him.

"You're talking to the right person then." The man introduced himself as Clive Harris. "I'm sure we've got something here to suit you." He motioned to the bobbing line of vessels below them.

"I need someone to take me out. I'm not really much of a sailor," Carl said, smiling.

"I could do that. I own most of the boats here. Where do you want to go? Fishing?"

"I want to go out to the wind turbines."

"Why?" Harris snapped, his expression darkening

rapidly. "What the hell do you want to go messing about out there for?"

"I just want to have a look around."

"It isn't the sort of place to go pleasure boating you know. There's nothing to see that you can't see from the shore."

"How much to take me out there?"

The man considered the offer for a moment then said, "One hundred and fifty," thinking that would put Carl off.

It didn't.

Twenty minutes later they were speeding over the churning waves, Carl standing beside Harris as he guided the boat across the surface.

"Is it always this rough?" Carl asked, steadying himself against the guard rail that ran around the deck of the boat.

"Storm coming," Harris told him. "I can tell. I've worked on the sea all my life. You get to know her ways. My grandfather was a fisherman. My father too."

"But not you?"

"No money in it now. I rent the boats instead. That pays better."

"If you've always been connected with the sea then you must know all the stories about it," Carl offered. "About this town."

"What do you mean?"

"The legends. The stories about the Cult of Persa. You must have heard those."

"You hear a lot of things. Most of them are rubbish."

"So you've heard about them then? What they believe? What they do?"

Harris eyed him briefly then returned his attention to the sea ahead of them, guiding the boat over the waves, barely reacting when sea water splashed the deck.

"You can't blame the people who live here," he said, quietly. "It isn't their fault, it was the people who built the wind turbines. They caused the trouble. They drilled too deep. They disturbed something."

"Like what?"

Harris didn't answer.

"I need to know," Carl insisted. "My daughter was taken by those maniacs. I have to find her."

"Man has been exploring space for the last fifty years but they still don't know what's in the sea," Harris said, grinning. "There's things down there no one understands."

"Make me understand," he said.

Harris merely continued to smile.

Carl glared at him but the other man kept his gaze fixed ahead, finally jabbing a finger in the direction of the huge wind turbines that were towering above them. Like massive windmills they turned slowly, blades cutting effortlessly through the air, their enormous size quite awe-inspiring. Carl looked up towards the nearest one as it thrust upwards from the surf.

There was a building on a raised platform about two hundred yards away and Carl gestured towards it.

"Take me over to the substation," he said, raising his voice to make himself heard above the sound of the sea.

Harris nodded and brought the boat to a halt beside a ladder that stretched up the side of the construction.

"Engineers used it when they were working on the turbines," Carl told him and the other man nodded disinterestedly, watching as Carl climbed up the ladder, finally emerging onto the platform at the top. It was metal and Carl had to ensure he didn't slip as he walked across it towards a block-like structure twenty or thirty yards away. He moved up to one of the windows and tried to peer through but the glass was too dirty, grimy with long months of neglect and exposure to the savage elements.

"What are you looking for?"

Carl turned as he heard the voice of Harris behind him.

"Anything," he told the grizzled-looking man.

"You'd be better off just going home and leaving things alone," Harris insisted, glancing around the platform. "It's none of your business."

"They made it my business when they took my daughter," Carl rasped. As he finished speaking he drove his foot against the door of the building before him and it swung open.

Harris looked on quizzically, watching as Carl disappeared inside. He waited a moment then followed, glancing around him at the dark interior of the building. Metal pipes and girders criss-crossed the roof and higher reaches of the substation, the whole space dull and forbidding as is the way of long-abandoned buildings. The floor was metal and slippery and Harris walked carefully as he followed Carl towards a flight of metal steps that led down into a lower level of the building.

"Five have been taken so far," Carl said as he walked.

"That's the way of it," Harris intoned. "That's what the legends say. Five must be given up every thirty-six years or all lives will end."

"Given up?"

"Offered."

"Sacrifices, you mean?"

Harris shrugged. "I'm only telling you what the legend says."

"Do *you* believe it?"

"Doesn't matter what I believe. There are enough that do believe."

Carl was about to say something else when he heard a sound from ahead of them. An unmistakeable noise that made him quicken his pace.

It was the soft crying of a child.

He hurried along the corridor, his footsteps echoing as his feet connected with the metal.

He dashed on, using the sound as a guide and a beacon and came to another flight of steps. Carl hurried down those too, almost stumbling as he reached the bottom. Harris laboured along behind him, stopping once to gasp for breath such was the breakneck pace of their journey.

Carl came to the end of a corridor, the sound ahead of him now. There was a single metal door before him and he walked to it and put his ear against the steel partition.

Sure enough, the plaintive sound of a child's crying drifted to him on the cold air. Without hesitating he grabbed the large handle of the door and jammed it up and down using all his strength. It opened immediately and Carl pulled it wide, gazing into the room beyond.

He murmured something under his breath as he caught sight of the five children within.

None was older than seven or eight and the youngest he guessed was less than a year. There were metal plates and bowls near to the children holding scraps of food, and Carl shuddered as he thought what these poor kids must have been through. The baby was in a rudimentary wicker carrycot and it was gurgling quietly. The child that was crying was about two and she looked up at him as he stepped into the room. The other children also turned to gaze at him, wondering who this newcomer was but two of them also got to their feet, moving towards him.

"Come on," Carl urged. "We're going. Come with me. I'm going to get you out of here."

"You can't do that," Harris said, appearing behind him. "You don't know what you're doing. They have to stay here."

"You knew about this," Carl snarled.

"We all did. That's why they were brought here. Five lives to save *all* lives." As he raised his hands, Carl could see that the skin was thicker at the base of the digits. The thick fingers almost webbed with gnarled flesh.

"You're insane," Carl snapped. "I won't let you hurt them."

He snatched up one of the metal plates that was lying nearby and hurled it at Harris who tried to duck but was a little too slow. The plate hit him in the forehead with enough force to stagger him. Carl grabbed him, hurling him to one side. Harris slammed into the wall and went down heavily.

"Come on," Carl called to the children. He himself snatched up the baby's carrycot and all of them hurried out of the room, clambering up the metal steps until they finally emerged on the platform above.

The children looked frightened but their fear and the desire to escape from this place drove them on and they followed Carl to the ladder that led down from the substation to the waiting boat.

He held another of them, the girl snaking her arms around his neck, the others managing to get down the ladder.

"Stop."

The shout came from above them and Carl looked up to see Harris stagger into view.

"Bring them back," he roared angrily but Carl and the children were already in the boat and Carl gunned the engine, swinging the boat away from the foot of the ladder. He turned it towards the shore and coaxed as much speed as he could from it, the vessel skidding across the waves.

Behind him, Harris bellowed something unintelligible, silhouetted as he was against a rapidly darkening sky.

***

The interview room was small.

Empty but for a wooden table and a couple of chairs. Carl Jennings glanced around at the bare walls, his mind wandering.

When the only door into the room finally opened he looked up quizzically and saw that Jack Fraser had walked in.

"Can I go now?" Carl said. "I've been here for hours."

Fraser sat down opposite him, glancing through some sheets of paper he had in a thin manilla file.

"Yes, you can go," the detective told Carl. "But don't go too far, we might need to talk again."

"What about the children?"

"They'll be returned to their families."

Carl nodded. "What about my daughter? She wasn't with them," he murmured.

"I know, I'm sorry. All we can do is keep looking."

Carl let out a long breath then got to his feet. He walked across to the door then turned.

"It would have been tonight you know," he said, softly. "The children would have been sacrificed tonight. I saved them."

"I know," Fraser told him, watching as he walked out. As Carl left the room, the detective rubbed his hands together gently, glancing down at them. Near the base of each finger, joined by a thin membrane of flesh, they were webbed.

Carl left the police station and caught a taxi back to the hotel where he packed hurriedly.

He dropped the last item into his small suitcase, closed it up and was about to make his way down to reception when his phone rang. He didn't recognise the number but answered anyway.

"Hello," he murmured.

"Mister Jennings?" the voice at the other end asked and he thought he recognised it.

"Who's this?" Carl wanted to know.

"It's Hazel Wilson," the voice said. "You found my daughter. You brought her back."

Carl smiled. "Yes I did. I'm glad I could help."

"You should have left her where she was," Hazel snapped. "You don't know what you've done." She hung up.

Carl glanced at the phone for a moment in puzzlement then he slid it into his pocket and made his way downstairs to reception.

As the elevator doors slid open he was surprised to see that the reception area was full of people. Even more puzzled to see that he recognised some of them. As well as Polly Dean he could see the gnarled features of Clive Harris. Just ahead of him was Hazel Wilson. They were all looking in his direction, their faces set in hard lines.

"Why did you have to interfere?" Polly snapped.

"It was none of your business," Hazel added.

"You don't know what you've done," Clive Harris told him, jabbing an accusatory finger in his direction. It was a gesture they all imitated and, as they did, Carl could see that every person in the reception area, all those glaring so angrily at him all seemed to carry the same deformity. All their fingers were slightly webbed close to the base of the digits.

Carl swallowed hard and took a couple of steps backward.

"Five lives offered to save *all* lives," Hazel Wilson shouted. "But you've spoiled that."

"You should not have interfered," another woman told him.

"It was none of your business," a man close to him rasped.

Carl moved back again and, as he did he felt a crashing blow to the back of his neck. It floored him and, as he lay there, unconsciousness rushing in around him, he saw that the blow had been delivered by Jack Fraser. The detective was standing over him, looking down contemptuously.

Carl blacked out.

"We have to hurry," Fraser said.

"He won't be enough," Harris protested.

"He might," Fraser countered. "He might. We've got to try."

Outside, the storm was growing ever more powerful, lightning now lashing across the dark sky, the boiling clouds merging into one icy grey mass above the sea and the town.

When Carl eventually woke, he was gazing directly up at the blackened heavens.

The first droplets of rain mingled with the sea spray that spattered him as waves broke with increasing ferocity upon the sand. He twisted his head back and forth, trying to get up but the more he struggled the quicker he realised why he couldn't move. He'd been tied down. Secured to the wet sand by strong bonds around his ankles, wrists and waist. Thick rope had been used to pin him as helplessly to the sand as an insect to a collector's board.

Carl tried to pull himself free but it was impossible. He strained against the bonds but couldn't loosen them, just as he couldn't slip free. The knots that secured them were too expertly tied. He was helpless. Nonetheless he continued to struggle frantically against the ropes, desperate to be free of them.

That desperation increased when he heard the sound.

The loud roar that came from the sea. A growing cacophony of noise that melded together into one bone-chilling wail. A sound unlike anything he'd ever heard before. It wasn't human and he could only imagine what kind of animal might make that blood-freezing ululation.

Something huge. Something unspeakable. Something monstrous.

And it was growing closer by the second.

Carl struggled even more frenziedly now and, as he turned his head, he saw something silhouetted against the dark skies. Something that seemed to be so huge it penetrated the low-lying cloud.

Whatever it was seemed to be hundreds of feet tall. Easily as tall as one of the wind turbines out to sea.

Carl screamed. He didn't know who would hear him. He didn't know what his shriek of terror and desperation would achieve but he could see that massive shape drawing closer to shore, the sea almost parting before it as it strode onwards.

Carl's screams grew louder, competing with the roar of the storm and the deafening bellow coming from the sea.

Whatever had emerged from the depths lowered over him and, in that split second he felt the sharp pain in his chest. He had trouble breathing. Each breath caused white hot agony, as if someone were stabbing him with a heated blade directly in the heart.

The pain grew to intolerable levels as the shape above him came closer.

He was almost grateful for the unconsciousness that swept over him and his last thought was of his daughter.

The storm raged around him.

MAN'S BEST FRIEND

From the twelfth-floor office in The Crystal Tower, Martin Johnson had a wonderful view of London as it stretched away before him but, right now, his mind wasn't on the splendour of the panoramic view he had. It was firmly fixed on business. It was always on business. On *his* business. And if the two men seated at the long, polished wood table behind him would make up their minds about what he was proposing then that would be another giant step forward for his business.

Martin continued to gaze out of the window, collecting his thoughts and preparing himself for the next round of questions that he knew would come from the two older men in the room.

They were both in their early fifties, twenty years older than him and although Martin appreciated they must weigh up every possibility before committing themselves, he was also anxious for an answer from them. As long as that answer was in the affirmative of course.

"Just run over the costs of the scheme again for us will you, Mr Johnson?" John Parkinson asked, shifting position in his seat.

Martin turned back to face the two immaculately dressed men, ensuring that his best practised smile was in place.

"To provide CCTV coverage on a building this size," he began. "Adding in the manpower needed to service and monitor that system, you're looking at over one million pounds initially and then another fifty thousand a month. What my company are proposing will cost you a fraction of that."

Martin paused, allowing that information to register with his customers.

"The phrase 'you get what you pay for' springs to mind, Mr Johnson," Maurice Dobbs observed. "I'm not resistant to this idea as you know, particularly from a financial point of view, but it's just that quality seldom comes cut-price."

Martin smiled even more broadly.

"You need to protect the contents of this building and I'm telling you that my company can do that for less than fifty thousand a year," he intoned. "And our presence here will be far less intrusive."

"I agree with my colleague, Mr Johnson," Parkinson added. "Your credentials are impeccable, we've spoken to other firms you supply your services for and they've been full of praise for you and what you do."

"So do yourselves a favour and hire my company to protect *your* building too," Martin interjected.

He looked at each man in turn.

Say yes, just say yes.

"I think we need to see how tonight's demonstration goes first," Parkinson offered. "If that is satisfactory then we can move forward."

"Is that acceptable to you, Mr Johnson?" Dobbs added. "If we're satisfied with the situation after your demonstration then the contract is yours."

Martin nodded.

"Your employees leave in an hour," he said. "As soon as the building is empty we'll begin."

Martin began collecting up the brochures and promotional material that was spread out on the table before him, slipping it into his briefcase when he was finished.

He said the necessary goodbyes, shook hands with the two men once again and made his way out of the office, letting out a long sigh as he closed the door behind him. He hoped it was a sigh of relief.

Martin walked along the corridor to a bank of elevators and pressed the 'Call' button. As he waited for the elevator to arrive he reached for his phone, muttering to himself when he saw that he couldn't get a signal.

"You can never get a signal in here."

Martin turned as he heard the voice and he discovered its source was a young woman in her later twenties who was smiling happily at him.

"You might as well wait until you get outside," she persisted.

She was also carrying a briefcase that Martin noticed was virtually identical to his own. He wasn't slow to point that out and they both laughed, stepping inside the elevator when it arrived.

"Ground floor?" he asked and she nodded.

The lift doors slid shut and the car began to descend.

"Do you work here, in the building?" Martin asked. "I wondered if you'd had problems with getting a signal on a regular basis."

Cathy Webster smiled and shook her head.

"No, I sell vending machines," she explained. "I was just checking on the ones we'd installed here. What about you?"

"Security."

Cathy's smile widened. "I thought all Security Guards had shaved heads, were six feet across and covered in tattoos."

"Well... normally," he said, grinning. "It is dress down day today."

Again they both laughed.

"The guys who own the building are thinking of taking on our security system," Martin went on. "We don't use CCTV cameras or men on the premises."

"What do you use then? Sharp sticks and harsh language?"

Martin smiled.

"We use dogs," he announced. "Attack dogs.

Dobermanns usually. They're the easiest to train."

"And the most dangerous?"

"You don't mess with them if you've got any sense, let's put it that way."

"So how does it work? You wait until the building is empty and then release attack dogs into it?"

"They've got the run of the place until the morning when our handlers arrive to take them away again. They patrol the reception area, the stairwells, the corridors. God help anyone who breaks in."

"What about... the mess? Dogs have to...er...relieve themselves, don't they?"

"We guarantee a 'crap free' environment," Martin told her, feigning indignation. "Our dogs do *not* shit where they work."

Cathy laughed and Martin thought what an infectious sound it was. He looked at her, hoping he hadn't allowed his gaze to linger for longer than it should have. When the elevator bumped to a halt on the ground floor Martin stepped back allowing his companion to walk out first. She smiled demurely at his gallantry.

"We could get a coffee," Martin offered, gesturing to the area on the far side of the reception. "If you're not in too much of a hurry."

"I've got other clients to see," Cathy told him.

Martin's smile fell away.

"But, if you're still around later we could get a drink or something," she went on. "If you like."

Martin found his smile again and nodded.

"That would be great," he told her, attempting to hide his relief that she'd agreed to meet him again. "What time?"

"I'll meet you in the reception here at six. How's that?"

Martin nodded.

"Sounds good to me," he told her, smiling. He watched her as she walked away, glancing down at his watch. Another four hours. The time, he hoped, would fly.

***

Russell Wells guided the Land Rover along the dirt track, wincing every time the vehicle encountered a pothole. The narrow thoroughfare was flanked on both sides by high and unkempt hedges. On one side fields stretched away into the distance, on the other a collection of buildings were surrounded by tall fences and Wells turned the wheel, ensuring that the Land Rover approached a set of metal gates. They opened into a wide and muddy forecourt area that led up to several sheds and outbuildings, some with flat concrete roofs others with sloping corrugated iron coverings.

Once he'd passed through the gates, Wells brought the vehicle to a halt and swung himself out of the Land Rover. He stepped straight into a deep puddle, wincing when cold, dirty water splashed up his leg as far as his calf. Muttering to himself he continued across the open area towards what looked like a large wooden garage.

Wells took a key ring from his belt and selected a key to fit the padlock that secured the garage. He swung both doors open and looked in at the blue and white painted trailer inside.

Working quickly and efficiently, he attached the trailer to the tow bar of the Land Rover and then headed off across the open area again towards another building.

He could hear the dogs barking as he approached.

They must have heard him.

They never barked until he was close and Wells always had the feeling that they were watching him. Holding their howls until they were sure he was near enough to hear them.

He found another key on the ring and opened this newest door, stepping into the building beyond.

It was filled with cages, each one housing a dog. And every animal within seemed to be barking frenziedly at him. The sound reverberated inside the building and also in his ears. Some of them hurled themselves at the bars, teeth bared and spittle-covered. Even though they saw him every day they still reacted as if he were a stranger, and he walked slowly up and down the first line of cages studying each animal in turn.

The Dobermanns were sleek, elegant-looking animals, their appearance almost giving lie to their savagery.

Wells stood motionless for a moment, the barking of the dogs ringing in his ears, then he began his work.

***

Martin Johnson looked once more at his watch as he stood in the reception of The Crystal Tower. He smiled briefly at the receptionist as she passed him, hurrying across the gleaming floor to join her friends who were also leaving.

Most of the staff had vacated the building now, Martin noted. Another thirty minutes and the entire place would be deserted.

He glanced towards the main entrance then checked his watch again. Still no sign of Cathy. He hoped she hadn't changed her mind about meeting him and fumbled for his phone just to ensure there were no apologetic messages telling him that 'something had come up.' He needn't to have worried. There were no such messages and within minutes, he saw her approaching.

A feeling that combined delight and relief swept through him.

"Sorry I'm late," Cathy said. "You know what customers are like."

"They say the only problem with customer service is the customers," Martin joked.

"I've got one job to do before we leave," she went on. "Up on the twelfth floor. One of the vending machines is on the fritz. My boss asked me to have a look at it while I was here."

"You can fix it?"

"I repair them as well as sell them," Cathy informed him. "Come on, come and watch a master at work."

Martin walked with her to the elevator and they rode it to the desired floor. They chatted as they walked along the deserted corridors of the Crystal Tower, the conversation flowing easily. Martin watched as Cathy flipped open a panel on the side of the vending machine, running an expert eye over the wires and switches within. He watched her for a moment or two then wandered towards the end of the corridor, glancing out of the large window there as he reached for his phone.

There were a couple of messages including one from Russell Wells informing him that everything was running on time (despite heavy traffic). Martin nodded and tried to reply but there was no signal and he eventually turned away and walked back to where Cathy was just finishing her work on the vending machine.

"All done," she exclaimed. "Let's go and get that drink."

They walked back to the elevator and got in, chatting as it descended.

"Where do you want to go for drinks? Or do you trust me?" Martin asked.

"I'll trust you," Cathy told him, smiling.

The elevator stopped dead.

Lights flickered on and off for brief seconds, creating a strobe-like effect inside the small car then they glowed brightly once more.

Martin jabbed the 'G' button and the elevator began to descend once again.

"That's a relief," Cathy said. "I was stuck inside one of these for forty-five minutes once. I hate enclosed spaces."

"I suppose it depends who you're enclosed with," Martin offered.

Cathy shook her head and grinned.

"Do you specialise in cheesy lines?" she chuckled and they both laughed.

That happy sound ceased abruptly when the elevator jerked to a halt once again.

This time, when Martin pressed the buttons on the control panel, nothing happened. They remained stationary. The lights flickered on and off then sputtered into life again. They both looked up towards the lights then at each other.

Martin pressed the emergency button on the panel.

"Someone will come," he said, not sure if he was trying to reassure Cathy or himself.

"But the building's empty, isn't it?" she protested.

"Someone will be watching on CCTV," Martin said. "Security will know."

"But there is no security tonight, is there? I thought your company were taking care of that tonight."

Martin reached for his phone.

"No signal," he murmured.

"I told you," Cathy confirmed, checking her own device. "There's never a signal in here. How are we going to let anyone know we're in here?"

"It's probably just a mechanical fault. It'll right itself in a minute."

Cathy raised her eyebrows.

"I wish I had your faith," she said, quietly.

"Well, all we can do now is wait," Martin offered. He glanced at his watch and saw that it was 6.47.

On the other side of the elevator car, Cathy sat down. She was still sitting there an hour later.

She reached into her handbag and pulled out a bottle of water. Cathy sipped from it then offered it to Martin who accepted it gratefully.

"It's a hell of a first date, isn't it?" he said, forcing a smile.

Cathy also managed to grin.

"Do you think we'll look back on this in years to come

and laugh?" she asked.

"No," Martin exclaimed. He got to his feet once again, crossing to the elevator doors. He dug his fingers between them, straining to try and open the metal partitions.

"Leave it," Cathy called. "You can't open them. If there *is* a mechanical fault you're wasting your time."

The elevator moved.

It juddered slightly then began to descend.

Cathy jumped to her feet in hope and surprise. Martin murmured something under his breath. *Encouragement? A prayer?*

The elevator continued on its downward journey, slowing slightly as it reached the sixth floor but then it moved lower. Martin glanced at Cathy, hardly daring to believe that their ordeal might be over.

The elevator stopped again and the doors slid open.

"Fourth floor," Martin exclaimed.

"We should get out now," Cathy urged and they both hurried towards the doors, stepping out into the corridor beyond, relieved to be free of the elevator.

"Thank God for that," Martin breathed, glancing back into the now empty elevator car.

"At least we can walk down from here," Cathy added. "I'm never using a lift again."

Smiling with relief, they set off for the end of the corridor and the exit that would lead them to the stairs. They were halfway there when Martin suddenly froze. He glanced at his watch, the colour draining from his cheeks.

"What's wrong?" Cathy wanted to know.

"The time," he stuttered. "It's after eight o'clock…"

He didn't finish the sentence because his gaze was suddenly drawn to the two dark shapes that had padded into view at the end of the corridor ahead of them.

Two Dobermanns stood stiffly before them, their lips sliding back to reveal long teeth.

"Oh God," Cathy murmured, staring at the dogs as if hypnotised.

It seemed that time had been momentarily frozen. Nothing moved. And then one of the dogs barked.

It was like a signal. Martin hurled his briefcase at the animals in a futile gesture designed to startle them, then he and Cathy turned and ran back down the corridor, the dogs pursuing them barking wildly now.

Martin reached the elevator first and dashed in, hitting the door close button as Cathy joined him.

The doors began to slide shut but with such agonising slowness Martin was convinced they wouldn't shut the pursuing dogs out in time.

He hit the button again and again, the frenzied barking of the dogs growing louder by the second as they drew nearer.

Cathy pressed herself against the back wall, her eyes bulging wide in terror as, finally, the doors began to close.

"Come on," Martin gasped. "Come on."

The barking was much louder now. The Dobermanns were only a matter of feet from the slowly closing elevator doors that were still three or four inches from shutting completely. The leading dog even managed to get its long snout through the gap before the doors slid closed, shutting it out.

The elevator began to rise.

Martin breathed a huge sigh of relief and turned towards Cathy who still had a hand clapped to her mouth, her body shaking.

"What now?" she gasped.

"If we can get to the roof we can get a signal," Martin said. "Call for help."

"If the elevator doesn't break down again."

"We're safer in here than we are out there with the dogs."

The lights inside the car flashed on and off as if to remind them of the precariousness of their situation, and the illuminated numbers that denoted floors were now blank. When it finally bumped to a halt, they had no idea which floor they were on. Martin moved closer to the doors, straining his ears to try and detect any sounds. For all he knew there were dogs right outside just waiting for them to step out.

He finally reached out and pressed the 'door open' button, stepping back as the metal partitions widened.

He glanced out into the corridor beyond, relieved to see that it was empty and also anxious to find out which floor they were on.

There was a sign to the right that proclaimed: ACCESS TO ROOF.

Martin breathed a sigh of relief and motioned for Cathy to follow him out of the elevator towards the door they sought. Moving as quickly and quietly as they could, they hurried towards the door, Cathy turning to look back into the corridor as Martin attempted to open the door. He pushed the bar up but it wouldn't budge.

"It's locked," he hissed, trying again to force a way through the door but it remained stuck firm.

Cathy spun around and ran a few yards down the corridor, pulling a fire extinguisher from the wall. She returned and, wielding the red cylinder like a weapon, she struck the bar that was holding the door shut.

From somewhere nearby the sound of dogs barking began to filter through to them. Alerted by the noise, the animals were now approaching them, but exactly how far away they were Martin could only guess. They could be on the same floor, they could be just around the corner.

Cathy struck the door again and this time it opened a fraction. Encouraged by her efforts she struck harder, aided by Martin driving his foot against the wood. It swung open, swinging back on its hinges and smashing into the wall behind. Cathy dropped the fire extinguisher and dashed through, heading for a small flight of stone steps that led up to another door which offered direct access to the roof.

As Martin was about to join her he heard the barking at the end of the corridor and spun around to see three of the Dobermanns hurtling towards them.

The damage to the fire door was so severe that it was barely hanging on its hinges now, and Martin realised that it wouldn't keep the dogs back for more than a moment or two even if it was shut again. He slammed it shut and threw his weight against it, feeling one of the animals crash into the wooden partition as it tried to get through.

Cathy was already trying to open the door that led out onto the roof and, when she had, she gestured to Martin who realised he'd have about five seconds to get across the open area between the door he was now guarding and the one he needed to pass through. Would it be long enough? Would the dogs overtake him in that time?

There was only one way to find out.

He watched as Cathy disappeared through the door onto the roof then he put both hands against the door he was supporting, his back also wedged against it keeping it upright. He could feel the impact as the dogs slammed against it, trying to force their way through, their barking frenzied just beyond the wooden partition.

He closed his eyes momentarily as he felt another crash against the door but then he realised he had no choice. It was now or never. He could stand there all night and the dogs wouldn't give up. Martin launched himself away from the door and ran for his life, hurtling towards the short flight of steps and the door to the roof.

As he stumbled up the first of them the dogs crashed through behind him.

Cathy shouted something he couldn't hear as he stumbled towards her, the barking of the dogs filling his ears.

One of them launched itself at him but he hurried on, reaching the door and blundering through it as another of the dogs bit wildly at him.

It missed his calf by inches and Cathy slammed the door shut in the animals' faces, wrenching the bar upwards to lock it.

Martin sucked in several deep breaths.

Cathy was already reaching for her phone.

She dialled three nines and waited.

The voice at the other end was a welcome sound and asked which emergency service she required.

"Police, Fire Brigade and Ambulance," she panted. "Send them all."

Martin fumbled for his own phone but then realised he hadn't got it on him, but that didn't seem to matter at this precise second. He listened to Cathy relaying details of their predicament and saw her smile as she terminated the call.

"The police are on the way," she said, gratefully.

They embraced and held each other for what seemed like an eternity. Already they could hear the sound of approaching sirens.

It was another forty minutes before they were escorted safely from the roof and down to the foyer of the building.

"There are paramedics outside," one of the firemen told them. "You should get yourselves checked out."

"No one was bitten," Cathy said.

"I mean for shock," the uniformed man went on. "It's quite an ordeal you've been through. Something like that can creep up on you, you know."

They both nodded.

"Are we still on for that drink?" Cathy asked Martin. "I wanted one before, I actually *need* one now." She smiled thinly.

"You bet," he said, also managing a smile. "But I've got to get my phone first. It's up on the fourth floor. It was in my case when I threw it at the bloody dogs."

"Leave it, Martin," Cathy insisted.

"I need it," he told her then, looking at the nearest

policeman, he went on, "Is it okay for me to go up?"

"Yes," the constable told him. "The building's been cleared. It's safe. A colleague of yours helped us clear the dogs out."

"None of them were injured, were they?" Martin wanted to know. "They're worth money you know."

"Your colleague knew how to handle them," the policeman assured him. "They're fine, which is more than you two would have been if they'd got to you."

"They were only doing what they've been trained for," Martin said.

Martin squeezed Cathy's arm lightly, assured her he wouldn't be long and set off up the stairs. He found his briefcase there and his phone inside it then he turned around in the corridor intent on returning to the ground floor. The elevator was close by and, almost against his better judgement, Martin moved towards it. His legs ached, particularly the area around his left hamstring and, he reasoned, if the elevator should stop working again at least he wasn't alone in the building now. He decided to ride it to the ground floor and pressed the door open button, smiling to himself as the metal barriers slid back.

He stepped inside.

There was one single Dobermann inside the elevator.

It was sitting in one corner, out of sight and silent. As Martin stepped into view it stood, its hackles rising, its lips sliding back to reveal razor-sharp teeth.

Martin tried to turn, tried to escape the elevator but the doors were already almost shut and the dog was too quick for him. It was on him in a heartbeat. Fast and powerful. It aimed its first attack at his throat and Martin knew he had no chance. The sheer power of its attack knocked him to the ground, its jaws clamping around his throat.

The elevator continued to descend.

BOX

The silence was almost oppressive.

Laura Reese took a tray of watches from the nearest glass display cabinet and set them down on the piece of black velvet she'd just laid out there. She took the watches from the tray one by one and wiped each one with a cloth before replacing it, then she repeated the procedure with a number of crystal paperweights. All through her tasks she was aware of the stifling stillness inside the jeweller's shop.

She'd only worked there for a week (it was her first full-time job since leaving school) and already it was starting to get her down. She didn't mind having to wear a blouse, skirt and jacket, in fact she quite enjoyed getting "dressed up" for work, but it was just the silence inside the small shop that wore her down day in, day out.

"Can't we put the radio on or something?" she asked, glancing across the small shop to where her boss was trying to fit a battery into a watch.

Alex Patterson glanced up from his task and shook his head.

"We might not be able to hear the customers when we're talking to them," he explained.

"What customers?" Laura mused, looking around at the empty shop.

"It's not always as quiet as this," Alex told her. "But while they're doing the building work in the rest of the precinct people don't come in so much. When they've finished it'll be fine."

Laura continued polishing the paperweights and nodded, not too convinced by Alex's words.

"The clothes shop where I used to work on a Saturday was...livelier," she said.

"Don't worry about it, you've only been here a week, things will pick up."

"How long have you been here?"

"Eighteen years," Alex told her.

Laura sighed. The prospect of spending eighteen years working in this place was enough to crush her soul. She looked on as Alex started cleaning a tray of rings and bracelets.

When she saw someone walk into the doorway of the shop she almost shouted for joy. She watched him as he looked at the offerings on display and then he pushed the large glass door open and walked in. He was in his mid-twenties, tall, unshaven and wearing what looked like expensive clothes. Laura wasn't sure what excited her most, the fact they'd got a customer or that he was so attractive. She smiled to herself then beamed at him as he walked in, nodding a greeting, but it was Alex he moved towards.

"Good morning," Alex said, getting off the stool he'd been perched on. "How can I help you?"

"Good morning," the younger man replied, smiling. "I'd like to see some rings please."

"Certainly sir," Alex gushed. "Anything in particular? Engagement? Wedding? Eternity?"

"Diamonds," the younger man announced. "Just diamonds."

As he spoke he dug his hand inside his jacket and pulled something large and metallic free, pointing it at Alex.

It took both Alex and Laura only a second to realise that what he'd produced was an automatic pistol. The barrel looked huge, yawning wide as the man swung it so that it was pointing at Alex's chest.

"Fill the fucking bag with rings," he barked, turning briefly to look at Laura. "You, come over here so I can see you. And keep your fucking mouth shut or I'll kill both of you." He pushed the weapon closer towards Alex. "And if you even think about touching your alarm button, I'll kill you. Got it?"

Alex nodded, his hands shaking madly as he pushed items of jewellery into the canvas bag the younger man had slammed down on the counter. Laura began to cry softly.

"Please don't hurt us," Alex stammered.

Frank Parker looked briefly around the shop, the gun still gripped in his fist. He spotted some gold and silver bracelets on a revolving stand and motioned towards them, watching as Laura unlocked the cabinet and began removing the merchandise, bringing it back to the counter where Alex was still pushing items into the bag.

Laura kept her eyes low, reluctant to look at Parker as if that simple action would somehow make him vanish.

He finally grabbed the bag from Alex and turned towards the door.

"If you call the police, I'll come back here and kill both of you," Parker snarled.

And then he was gone, running out into the street.

He dashed across the road and headed down a narrow passageway between shops, fumbling for his phone in the process.

He found the number he wanted and waited for the call to be answered.

"Where the fuck are you?" he snapped. "You were supposed to be waiting for me."

"A cop car kept driving past," the voice on the other end of the line told him. "I moved."

"Where the hell are you?" Parker demanded. "Come and get me."

As he spoke he heard sirens approaching and, as he emerged from the end of the alleyway, Parker saw several uniformed policemen walking around. Another police car pulled up and more of the men clambered out. Were they after him? How the hell did they know? He pushed his phone back into his pocket and felt his heart hammering against his ribs as he walked on, deciding that it was probably the best policy to pass by the nearest of the uniformed men. If he ran it would only draw attention. *Bluff it out.*

When another police car pulled up, Parker had trouble controlling his breathing. He turned, wondered if it might be prudent to head back the way he'd come, but then decided against it. He had to get off the street, he decided. As he ducked down another narrow alleyway he found that it brought him past the back yard of a whitewashed building bearing the sign MASON AND MASON: UNDERTAKERS.

Parker stepped into the yard and moved towards the black-painted rear door of the building.

As he moved furtively into the building he saw a middle-aged man poring over one of two coffins that were set up on trestles in the large room. One of the coffins was sealed, the other still open revealing the white satin lining. As Parker watched he saw the man turn away and move back to a work bench where he consulted a computer screen for information before scribbling down some notes on a large pad.

Parker moved nearer to him and gently pressed the gun against the back of his head.

"Don't move," he hissed.

Gary Mason raised his hands instinctively.

"There's nothing in here for you to steal," he breathed.

"Where are the other people who work here?" Parker rasped.

"There's no one else here," Gary told him. "My wife runs the outer office but she's nipped out and my son drives the hearse and he's out too but he'll be back very soon. They help me run the business. It's been in my family for two hundred years."

"Bullshit," Parker snapped, pushing the pistol harder

against Mason's head. "I don't care about your fucking business. It's your *help* I want, not your money. Do as I tell you and no one will get hurt."

"What do you want?"

"I want to get out of here. I want *you* to get me out of here. There are coppers everywhere out there and they're looking for me." He swallowed hard. "There's a hearse parked out the back of your building, I can get away in that, with your help."

Mason looked warily at him.

"Where's it going?" Parker went on.

"To a funeral at St. Angela's church. The body is there." He pointed at the sealed coffin. "It's a pauper's funeral, the only people there will be myself and my son, the pall bearers and the vicar."

Parker nodded, smiling slightly.

"Coppers aren't going to search a hearse, are they?" he chuckled. "You get me away from here, get me out again and we'll call it quits. You try to fuck me around and I'll kill you and your fucking family. Got that?"

Mason nodded.

It took less than fifteen minutes for Parker to clamber inside the empty coffin and for Mason to close the lid securely. Once that was done it was just a matter of waiting for his son to return so they could load the coffin into the back of the hearse. That done, Mason and his son checked their suits for any stray flecks of hair or dust then they clambered into the vehicle and set off.

Once inside the coffin, Parker fumbled for his phone, the only source of light inside the blackness of the box.

He put up a hand and felt the satin on the interior of the coffin, thinking how smooth it felt. When his phone vibrated he snatched it up.

"Right, listen to me," he said into the device. "Get to St. Angela's church, right. The one out on the road near to the Two Chimneys pub. You know it, right?"

"Yes, I know it," Peter Wright told him.

"Just make sure you're there. Don't fuck it up again. If you'd been waiting for me like you should have been I wouldn't be stuck in here now."

"How much do you reckon the stuff is worth?" Wright enquired.

"At least twenty-five grand, maybe more," Parker said.

"Cool," Wright said. "Does Carla know you were doing the job?"

"Why the fuck would I tell her?" Parker asked. "All that matters is that I get the money to pay for her abortion. We get this lot fenced as quick as possible and we're sorted."

He lay back in the coffin for a moment, listening to the low rumble of the engine as the hearse drove on.

"Where are you?" Wright wanted to know.

"How the fuck do I know?" Parker grunted. "I can't see anything. They've been driving for about ten minutes. We should be at the church soon. You just make sure you're there."

"I will, I will," Wright assured him. "How do you know the guy driving the hearse won't tell the law what happened?"

"Because I told him I'd kill him and his fucking family if he did," Parker grunted. "He doesn't know any different, does he? He didn't even know the gun was a replica." He laughed throatily, turning his head slightly as the hearse slowed down momentarily. Parker wondered if they had finally reached their destination but, when the vehicle increased its speed a moment later, he realised that they hadn't. He was starting to feel a little warm inside the box and the sooner he could get out of it the better. He was sure there was plenty of air inside but he was already beginning to feel a tightness in his chest that he disliked. Parker tried to take more shallow breaths, fearing that he might run out of oxygen before he could be freed from the coffin.

"Do I need a screwdriver?" Wright asked.

"What?" Parker grunted.

"To undo the coffin lid?" Wright went on.

"No, you dickhead, he didn't seal it like they usually do. How close are you to the church?"

"About ten minutes away," Wright told him.

"Good," Parker said. "I want to get out of here."

He pushed against the lid of the coffin, beads of perspiration now forming on his forehead and top lip. When he tried to breathe it was with difficulty.

Had the undertaker lied to him? Was there really very little oxygen inside the coffin? Was he running out already?

He was suddenly gripped by uncontrollable fear. The thought of being encased in this wooden box was intolerable. The image of gradually running out of breathable air tormented him. Each inhalation now tasted stale or bitter to him.

Get a grip. You'll be out soon.

What also struck him was the sudden silence. He'd been able to hear the low drone of the engine before. It had been strangely comforting, but this new and total silence was unnerving. What if they'd already unloaded the coffin? What if he was at the graveside? Even worse, what if they were lowering him into the grave?

He gritted his teeth and tried to push the thoughts from his mind, instead reaching for his phone.

"Where are you?" he barked into the device.

There was a hiss of static by way of an answer.

"They've been moving the coffin, I could feel it," Parker went on. "And I could hear voices. You need to get here now and get me out of here."

"I'm nearly there." Wright's voice sounded as if it was coming from inside a vacuum.

"Hurry up," Parker hissed. "You said you were close when we spoke earlier. What the fuck is keeping you? Have you got the right church?"

"I'm outside the church now. But I can't see anyone. There's no one here. No hearse. No mourners. No vicar.

Nothing."

"There aren't any mourners," Parker snapped. "There's no funeral here."

"Are you sure you're at the right church? It's St. Angela's."

"That's where I am," Wright protested.

"I can feel the coffin moving," Parker told him.

Sure enough, he felt a slight vibration as the box began to shift almost imperceptibly. They must be taking him to the graveside now. Carrying him. He thought about calling out but then decided against it. If Wright was at the church now it would only be a matter of moments before he found him and got him out.

The coffin juddered to a halt and Parker placed both hands against its sides as if bracing himself.

"I just realised why I can't see you," Wright said, cheerfully. "I'm on the wrong side of the church. There's a little chapel near to the church, isn't there? You must be there, not at the church itself."

"Chapel?" Parker grunted, puzzled.

"Yeah, where they do the cremations," Wright informed him.

Parker froze.

And now he realised why the coffin had begun to move slowly again. Why it was gliding so easily. Even as that horrific realisation swept over him he felt heat at the bottom of the box, where his feet were. He screamed but no one heard him over the roaring of the flames.

"I'll have you out in no time," Wright chuckled. There was a loud blast of static from the phone. Then nothing. Wright looked dumbly at it and shook it as if that simple act would cure it. It was as well he couldn't hear the sounds from the other end of the line.

Parker screamed again as the doors of the crematorium furnace opened to welcome him.

NIGHT GAMES

There were large trees outside each of the houses on Kirby Lane. Vying for space with the street lights and arranged as evenly as if they'd been put there using mathematical implements.

Tom Norton suspected that some streets were designed in just this way, but the trees and houses in Kirby Lane had been standing for hundreds of years. Long before town planners and designers began forcing their carefully formulated blueprints onto living arrangements. He was thinking just those thoughts as he and his wife walked slowly along the street, feeling the warm sunshine on them and enjoying the stillness of the late afternoon.

Hannah Norton moved closer to her husband, allowing him to snake an arm around her waist. He kissed her on the bare shoulder as they walked and she giggled.

"Perhaps we'd better get back," Norton suggested, raising his eyebrows.

"That's all you ever think about," Hannah chuckled.

"Of course it is. Why do you think I married you?"

He slapped her backside, also smiling.

Hannah moved towards the nearest of the large trees, her attention caught by a large piece of yellow paper that had been stapled to the bark.

On the paper, in large black letters were the following words:
VILLAGE FETE. VILLAGE GAMES.
COMMEMORATION SERVICE.

"I wonder what they're commemorating," Norton asked, also glancing at the flier. "The most inbred baby? The first cow born with two heads?"

Hannah slapped him playfully.

"It might be fun," she suggested.

"Excuse me while I fight to contain my excitement."

She slapped him again.

"Oh, come on, Tom," she protested. "If we're going to live here we should take more interest in what goes on locally. Join in with village life. That kind of thing."

Norton shrugged.

"Villages can be pretty tight-knit you know," Hannah went on. "They don't always take to outsiders."

"That's because they're all inbred."

They looked at the flier once more.

"Village games?" Norton mused. "I wonder what they are. Pin the tail on the farmer? Hide the tractor?"

"I'll ask Malena tonight. Her and David have lived here for five years and they seem to have fitted in well enough."

"The locals probably don't trust us. We're the newcomers from the big city."

"It's a good job they don't know why we moved here."

"Don't start that, Hannah."

"Just saying. I don't want to have to keep uprooting every few years."

"And it's my fault, is it?"

"You're the one with the gambling problem."

Norton glared at her for a moment then walked on, moving across to the next large tree where there was another flier stuck to the trunk.

Hannah touched his back, stroking it gently until he turned to face her.

"I just want us to be able to settle here," she said, softly.

Norton nodded.

"Overcome our outsider status?" he said, smiling.

"It's so beautiful too."

"And expensive. Some of these people must have worked or do work in the big bad city. You don't make enough money to buy places like this shovelling shit in the countryside."

"It's old money around here."

"Right back to the Domesday Book."

They walked on.

***

The sound of laughter filled the dining room.

Tom Norton reached for the bottle nearest to him,

preparing to re-fill his own glass and those of his wife and guests but, as he picked it up, he realised that it was empty. Just like the other three bottles on the table. That might, he mused, explain the volume of the laughter in the room. All four of them were a little tipsy to say the least, and it wasn't really surprising. As Norton watched, David Roberts lit his cigar, puffing out great clouds of smoke into the room.

"That's revolting," said his wife, Malena, her American accent immediately recognisable. "You shouldn't smoke. It's bad for you."

Malena was in her late twenties and stunning. Norton had tried to find other words to describe her but that one seemed particularly apt. She was nearly five feet ten in her high heels (which were presently on the floor beneath the table, kicked off an hour or two ago). Dark haired and slender with a perpetual smile on her finely chiselled features. It was all Norton could do to prevent his gaze lingering on her longer than it should have.

Hannah had seen him gazing at her more than once during the evening and he'd been rewarded with a sharp kick under the table for his rather intense interest in this statuesque creature. The persistent rumour that she had made several hardcore porn films before leaving LA with David four years earlier only served to make her more attractive as far as Norton was concerned. He'd found some stills of her on the internet during one of his exhaustive searches but there had been no sign of any of the videos he regretted to say. Now he glanced at her once more then looked briefly at his wife, noticing that she was also smiling, shaking her head gently at him.

Norton smiled back, aware that he'd been caught red-handed but he merely reached out and squeezed Hannah's hand, relieved when she returned the gesture then got up and crossed to him, seating herself on his lap.

"So tell us about these village games," she said, gazing at Malena who sipped her wine and ran a hand through her thick brown hair.

"Oh God, it's like their Olympics," the other woman said, smiling. "Every two years. Sometimes they compete against other villages from around here."

"What do they do?" Norton enquired.

"Everything," Malena told him. "Welly throwing. Quoits. Bat and Trap. Skittles. Aunt Sally. It's all traditional stuff, they've been doing it for years. Everyone gets involved. If you're not competing, you're fixing food for the spectators."

"Spectators?" Hannah chuckled.

"I told you, if you're not competing, you're watching," Malena told her, sipping her wine again.

"And then there's the highlight of the whole event," David interjected. "On the Saturday night, they use it as a closer." He laughed. "The whole village gets involved in the biggest game of the lot."

"What is it?" Norton wanted to know.

"They call it 'By Darkness Hidden'," Malena offered.

"That sounds ominous," Hannah said, taking a swig of her own wine.

"What is it?" Norton wanted to know.

Malena hesitated for a moment then looked at her husband who nodded almost imperceptibly. Only then did she continue.

"There are so many stories," she said, quietly. "The game is played to commemorate the death of a local farmer. A man called Bennett." She took another sip of her wine. "Supposedly his wife left him and took their three children. She couldn't stand his drinking and he was violent too. He hit her *and* the kids. He was so distraught he used to sit in his bedroom window every night just looking out over the fields trying to catch sight of her. One night he thought he saw her so he grabbed a lantern and rushed out into the fields. He hadn't seen her of course. He was drunk. He fell over, dropped the lantern and it set fire to his coat. He was burned alive."

"And the people in the village commemorate *that?*" Norton grunted.

"When did it happen?" Hannah asked.

"Farmer Bennett burned to death one hundred years ago" Malena announced. "That's why the games this year are even more important. When we play the game on that last night it will be one hundred years to the day that he died."

"She's a mine of information, isn't she?" David said, nodding towards his wife.

Malena picked up a piece of food from her plate and threw it at him.

"How do you know all this stuff, Malena?" Hannah wanted to know.

"I read about some of it but just talking to the locals, you find out things," the American exclaimed, placing her feet on her husband's lap. He began to gently rub them.

"Every village in this country must have stories like that," Hannah said, finishing what was left in her glass.

"Oh yeah, right," Norton grunted. "About people being burned alive, I'm not so sure."

"There were witches executed in this area too," David reminded him. "Some of those were burned."

"All in the name of religion," Norton smiled.

"Didn't someone say that there's never been a kingdom given to so much bloodshed as that of Christ?" David mused.

"Montesquieu, I think," Norton said, nodding.

"You're not as dumb as you look, are you?" Hannah said, kissing her husband on the cheek. Laughter filled the room.

"This country has so much history," Malena chuckled. "And it's so beautiful around here."

"You've only lived here for three or four years, haven't you?" Hannah said. "Did you find it easy to fit in?"

"You have to adapt, don't you?" David offered. "As soon as we knew we wanted to live around here we knew we were going to have to, I don't know, change our ways if you like. Learn to live by different rules."

"You make it sound like a little club," Norton said, sipping his drink. "Don't you miss the city life sometimes?"

"Not at all," Malena interjected. "We both love it here. We'd do anything to stay here."

Norton raised his glass in salute, a smile on his face.

"You said there were lots of stories," he added. "What did you mean?"

"Stories about the village. Myths. Legends. Hearsay," David exclaimed.

"But what about the game you mentioned?" Hannah pressed.

"The game is played in the fields around the farm where Bennett lived but he's not the only one who died there,"

Malena began. "Supposedly during the Second World War a German fighter plane crashed. The pilot was thrown clear but the villagers had seen him come down. About a hundred of them went to look for him."

"Did they find him?" Hannah wanted to know.

"Oh, yeah, they found him," Malena went on. "He was beaten to death and then decapitated. His body was buried in an unmarked grave in the churchyard. There are still two or three people living here who can remember that night, apparently."

"And these are the people you want to live with?" Norton said to his wife, a smile on his face. "The descendants of murderers?"

"They'd probably say they were just defending themselves against the enemy," Hannah offered. "After all, they were at war, weren't they?"

"That's no excuse to decapitate the poor bastard, is it?" Norton said.

David Roberts chuckled.

"War is hell," he said.

Norton laughed.

"It was a long time ago, Tom," Malena offered. "Even if it *was* on your land."

"*Our* land. What do you mean?" Norton wanted to know.

Malena took a sip of her wine before she spoke again as if waiting to build up the drama of her words.

"Farmer Bennett burned to death and the German pilot was killed in the fields at the bottom of your garden."

***

Tom Norton stood beside the bedroom window gazing out into the night, squinting to see through the blackness that enveloped the land.

It was pitch black. The sky was thick with clouds and had been since they came to bed, and that seemed to cut out any natural light that might normally brighten the gloom a little. Even the stars were hidden from view by the rolling banks and try as he might, Norton could see no lights at all in any direction as he peered towards the bottom of their garden and into the fields beyond. The bulk of the village lay nearly a mile across those fields but, at such a late hour, there were no lights gleaming to offer respite from the blackness. At least none that he could see. He glanced at his watch, groaning when he saw that it was almost 3.10 am.

He'd thought the amount of food he'd eaten and booze he'd drunk might have aided sleep but it hadn't. He was as wide awake now as he had been when Malena and David had left, Malena kissing him drunkenly on the lips upon their departure. Mind you, David had done the same to Hannah and it was all Norton could do now to suppress his fantasies about a foursome with their friends.

In your fucking dreams.

He smiled to himself, administering a swift mental rebuke. Things like that happened only in his fevered imagination, not in real life. Norton shook his head and stepped away from the window, wondering if he should perhaps make himself a warm drink. It might help him sleep, seeing as nothing else had done so far.

In the large double bed to his left he could hear Hannah breathing slowly and rhythmically and, before he made his way to the bedroom door, he bent over her and kissed her lightly on the cheek.

She stirred slightly but then rolled onto her stomach and continued her own blissful slumber. Norton walked slowly out of the room, not wanting to disturb her.

He made his way downstairs, moving assuredly through the dark house and only turning on lights when he finally reached the kitchen.

The plates from their dinner party earlier were still piled up on the worktops and Norton smiled to himself, thinking how much easier it would have been to simply shove them into the dishwasher, but they had both been too drunk to care about things like that.

Norton switched on the kettle and rummaged through the cupboard nearby looking for some camomile tea. There were all sorts of different flavours in there. Herbal tea. Fruit tea. Christ knows what but he knew that camomile was supposed to help the onset of sleep so he selected a bag, dropped it into a mug and waited for the kettle to boil.

As he did he walked across to one of the windows, wondering why the blinds hadn't been pulled down. He could see out into the back garden, at least as much of it as the black night allowed him to see. One of the trees close to the house was swaying gently in the strong breeze that had grown during the night, and Norton watched the skeletal branches dancing for a moment before he reached for the cord that would allow him to lower the blinds.

He was about to begin his task when he saw something glowing out in the darkness.

Didn't he?

Norton was sure he could see a small pinprick of yellow light close to the bottom of the garden.

There was a low privet hedge separating the garden from the fields beyond and he was certain that the tiny ray of brilliance was hanging there, just above the unkempt hedge. But, he reasoned, it wasn't as if there was a short cut across the field or some previously undiscovered footpath that would lead to nearby houses. Who the hell would be walking about in that field at three in the morning?

Norton moved closer to the window, cupping his hand over his eyes in an effort to see better but it did little to help.

And then the point of light vanished.

As quickly as it had come it was gone and he frowned, continued to gaze at the spot outside for a moment longer and then turned away from the window as he heard the kettle was on the verge of boiling. Norton turned towards it, glancing at the small red light on it close to the handle. The red light that signified it was on.

It had been a red light he'd seen outside in the field.

Could it, he wondered, have been nothing more than the light on the kettle reflected in the glass of the window?

As the steam began to pour from the spout the red light clicked off and Norton glanced again at the window behind him. There was no red light. No light of any colour. He smiled to himself. The stories told at the dinner table earlier must, he convinced himself, have made him think he was seeing something more than he actually witnessed.

Your mind is playing tricks. Get a grip.

He poured boiling water on the teabag and stirred it around, sitting down at the kitchen table for a moment, glancing occasionally at the window once more. Unable to shake the thought that he had actually seen a light beyond the garden but then thinking once more that it was nothing more than reflected luminescence from the kettle. He sipped the tea and decided to take it back upstairs with him.

Hannah was awake when he walked into the bedroom, but he didn't realise until she spoke.

"I wondered where you'd gone."

Her words startled him and he spilled some of his tea, muttering under his breath as he headed back towards the bed where she was sitting up, the duvet held across her chest.

"I couldn't sleep," he told her.

"I figured."

"I think it must be Malena's stupid bloody stories," Norton chuckled, sliding into bed beside his wife.

"I think it's just Malena," she told him, moving closer to him. "I know you want to fuck her. Most guys would."

She moved closer and Norton snaked an arm around her.

"How dare you?" he said, pretending to be insulted by her comment.

"I don't mind, you know," she purred, closing her fingers gently around his penis. "She is very cute."

Norton chuckled.

"And you're very horny, aren't you?" he said, softly.

"How did you guess?" she giggled.

She kissed him then looked at him in the darkness of the room.

"If you ever touch her," Hannah breathed, the hint of a smile on her lips. "I'll kill you."

"I believe you," Norton told her.

The sound of laughter filled the room.

***

There must have been thirty or forty tents on the village green, Norton thought. All of varying sizes and colours. Some just plain white, others blue and white or red and white or yellow and a multitude of other shades designed purely, it seemed, to look inviting.

They were arranged in a haphazard manner around a central area that featured smaller stalls manned by people from the village. Some were dressed in costumes which ranged from the immediately recognisable to the downright obscure and, as Norton and Hannah walked around the fair, they tried their best to identify the outfits with varying degrees of success. There were a party of morris dancers prancing around, going through their paces while a small band (none of whom seemed to be less than about seventy years old) played with an enviable gusto and enthusiasm.

People moved around among the tents and stalls, stopping to inspect the contents or the offerings there. Sometimes buying the jars of homemade jam or inspecting the specially created items of clothing. Everything from jumpers to dresses were on display, each of them fashioned by someone in the village for sale or simply so others living nearby could admire the craftsmanship.

It was, Norton thought with a smile, like every cliché of village life in rural England had been brought to life in one small area of Buckinghamshire.

"What are you smiling at?" Hannah asked, as she noticed his expression.

"Just enjoying myself," he told her. "Do you think we're fitting in?"

"You were great in the welly throwing and I think I did really well winning the Jenga competition," Hannah said, laughing.

"Perhaps they'll let us stay," Norton added.

They were about to walk away when a tall, heavily built man in his late seventies approached them. He raised one hand in greeting then extended that same hand towards Norton who took it and shook it, surprised at the strength in the grip that enclosed his own offered appendage.

The older man smiled broadly then rubbed his large and extremely red nose with one finger.

"Mr and Mrs Norton, isn't it?" he said.

"Tom and Hannah," Norton corrected him, smiling.

"I'm John Gormley, I'm one of the organisers. Are you enjoying yourselves?"

"It's great," Hannah beamed.

"We're just wondering what to do next," Norton told him.

"Coconut shy or bat and ball."

"Have you signed up for tonight?" Gormley wanted to know.

"Not yet," Norton told him.

Gormley looked shocked and immediately moved between them, sliding arms around both their shoulders, guiding them inside the nearest tent.

It felt humid inside, due mostly to the number of people gathered in there, peering at the cakes arrayed on some trestle tables or sipping the small glasses of fluid also on display. At the far end of the tent there was a small wooden desk and seated behind it was a woman in her fifties with the largest shock of curly hair Norton had ever seen. Most of it was held in check by some hair bands and grips but he was sure that if they should come loose, the entire mass of hair would spring outwards and fill the tent to its extremities. As they approached, the woman looked up, a welcoming smile on her pinched features.

"Stella, my darling," Gormley said to the small woman behind the desk. "This is Tom and Hannah. Tom and Hannah, this is Stella Waites. A woman of such exceptional organisational abilities that words truly fail me. She…"

"Ignore John," Stella said, waving a hand dismissively in the direction of the older man. "He never learned the meaning of restraint."

They all laughed.

"Tom and Hannah would like to sign up for the game tonight," Gormley said. "If that's all right with you, Stella. They're not too late, are they?"

"Goodness me, no," the small woman remarked. "Have you played before?"

"No," Hannah said. "We only moved in…"

"Seven months ago," Stella said. "You bought the old farm, didn't you?"

"You noticed?" Norton smiled.

"Not much goes unnoticed in a village like this," Stella said. "Why did you leave London?"

Norton looked a little taken aback at first.

"We got fed up with city life," he said, quietly.

"My husband and I lived in Bristol for a time," Stella

announced. "I hate cities. It's more friendly here."

"Why did you choose to live here?" Hannah enquired.

"We felt at home as soon as we looked around," Stella beamed. "And I think if you find a place where you feel you belong, it's important to go with your feelings. We'd never leave here now."

She looked at Hannah and smiled.

"While you two girls chat, I'm going to whisk Tom off to my favourite tent," Gormley announced, putting his arm around Norton's shoulder again.

"The homemade wine tent?" Stella said.

"You know me so well," Gormley chuckled, guiding Norton away.

Hannah watched them go.

"He's full of it but he's a nice man," Stella announced as the two men departed. "He used to be a GP. He delivered my son. He's retired now. He just keeps himself busy organising things in the village."

"Is there a lot to organise then?"

"We're very community-minded. You'll find that out. I missed that when I moved out of the village. My husband's job meant we had to move around quite a bit, but I was just happy when we could come back here. I was born in the village, you know."

"You must have played the games a lot then."

"Sometimes once is enough," Stella said, her smile fading slightly.

***

The smell inside the tent reminded Tom Norton more of a urinal than a place where wine was being purveyed.

It was warm inside the tent and, combined with the four or five very strong glasses of homemade wine that he'd already consumed, he was beginning to feel a little light-headed.

John Gormley seemed less bothered both by the growing heat and also by the effects of the domestically created wines. He was laughing and joking constantly, occasionally stopping to talk to people who passed him or caught his attention. Norton had to admit, he was a very strong personality and a likeable man who was obviously very popular among his neighbours.

"It's good," Norton said, raising the latest of the glasses he'd been sipping from. "And it's strong, too." He smiled and blew out his cheeks.

"It is pretty powerful stuff," Gormley admitted. "I think the trick is not to ask what went into it." He drained what was left in his glass and reached for another from the many standing on a table nearby.

"Why does it smell so bad in here?" Norton wanted to know.

"Some of the wine is still fermenting," the older man told him. "It has a very distinctive aroma."

"You can say that again."

They both laughed.

Gormley noticed that Norton's glass was empty and handed him another.

"I think I've had enough," the younger man told him.

"Nonsense. You'll get used to it. Live a little. Life's too short to worry about things like that."

Norton took a sip.

"How long have you lived in the village?" he wanted to know.

"All my life," Gormley informed him. "The only time I was away was when I was at university and I couldn't wait to get back here. My parents and grandparents lived here too. There have been Gormleys in this village as far back as the 1850s. We're something of a fixture here. Many of the families here are the same."

"It seems like a very tight-knit community."

"It is, but that isn't a bad thing."

"It is if you're an outsider."

"If people are ready to become one of us then we welcome all. Give it time. We have our ways but you'll get used to them."

Norton nodded.

"There isn't much to do for younger people though is there?" he mused.

"It depends what they want out of life. There are plenty distractions here if you look for them." Gormley smiled. "There's one now." He nodded in the direction of a young girl who had just entered the tent. She couldn't have been more than eighteen or nineteen, Norton guessed. Petite and extremely pretty, her blonde hair pinned up on the top of her head, her slender figure accentuated by the tight jeans and black top she wore. She was arm in arm with a young man about the same age, who was wearing a look on his face that combined pride with the complete disbelief that he was actually walking around with a girl as beautiful and desirable as this one.

"Young Rhiannon Morgan," Gormley said, smiling, his gaze now fixed on the girl. "Now there's something to distract any man." He cracked out laughing and slapped Norton on the shoulder. "Don't you agree?"

"She's beautiful," Norton conceded, trying not to look too closely at the teenage girl.

"And her boyfriend, Josh Cutler," Gormley went on. "Lovely young people."

Gormley was still gazing at the young couple, occasionally taking sips of his wine but never allowing himself to look away from the two youngsters as they moved through the tent also sampling some of the wine on offer.

"They look even better naked," Gormley said, flatly.

Norton wondered if he'd misheard the words for a moment and he glanced at the older man as if waiting for him to qualify the statement in some way. To correct or excuse himself for what he'd just said.

"Their bodies are perfect," the older man breathed. "At that age they're unblemished, you see. Untainted. Her skin is like velvet. His body is hard and firm." Gormley was breathing more heavily now, his gaze still fixed on the young couple. "Imagine her wrapping those slender legs around his back as he fucks her, squeezing her little tits."

"Shall we get back to the other tent and find out what Hannah's up to?" Norton asked, feeling distinctly uncomfortable now.

"There's plenty of time for that," Gormley told him, one hand now pulling furtively at his groin as he continued to watch Rhiannon and Josh. "I'm still enjoying the scenery." He grinned widely.

"I know what you're looking at."

The voice startled Norton and he turned to see another man,

a tall dark-haired individual in his early forties dressed in baggy jeans and a crumpled shirt, standing behind them.

Gormley turned briefly to find the source of the voice, laughed, and then fixed his stare on Rhiannon and Josh once more.

"This is Mike Holding," the older man said. "Mike, meet Tom Norton. He's new here. Just moved in to the old farm."

The dark-haired man nodded and extended a hand which Norton shook.

"Enjoying the view?" Holding said, guffawing. "She's stunning, isn't she?"

"Very nice," Norton agreed.

"Tight as hell I bet," Holding continued, his own breathing heavy.

"Tight and wet," Gormley added and he and Holding laughed.

Norton looked at both of them, wanting nothing more than to be away from these men now.

"She'd need to be wet to take his huge cock," Holding chuckled. "Imagine it stretching that tight little cunt."

"Or sliding into that little mouth of hers," the older man grunted.

"But you just know she swallows," Holding intoned.

Both men laughed.

Norton put down his glass and glared at Gormley.

"I've got to go," he said, sharply. "Hannah will wonder where I am."

"Nonsense, my boy," Gormley said, grabbing his arm. "She knows you're in good hands. Have another drink."

"I think I've had enough," snapped Norton. "I think you have too."

Gormley eyed him warily.

"What do you mean?" the older man challenged.

"Well, talking like that about that young girl and her boyfriend," Norton murmured. "It's not…it's not very pleasant, is it?"

Holding grunted.

"What's your problem?" he said.

"I just don't think it's right," Norton explained.

"Because we're older?" Gormley said. "Is that why it's

wrong? Would it be acceptable if we were in our twenties or thirties? Just because we're older doesn't stop us thinking about things like that."

"Fair enough," Norton sighed. "But I'm not comfortable with it."

"Why?" Holding wanted to know. "Are you gay?"

"No I'm not gay," Norton snapped.

"Would you rather have Josh's stiff cock in your mouth than taste Rhiannon's slippery cunt?" Holding went on, his face fixed in hard lines now. "I'd try both."

Norton shook his head.

"He's not gay," Gormley added. "His wife is in one of the other tents with Stella Waites. Lovely young thing."

"I suppose you want to fuck *her* too," Norton snapped, angrily.

"If you're offering, my friend," Gormley chuckled. "I wouldn't say no."

Norton shook his head, shot both men a final withering gaze and headed for the exit.

Gormley and Holding watched him go and so did several other pairs of eyes. Only when he was clear of the tent did the others inside begin to laugh.

***

Tom Norton moved briskly through the maze of tents on the village green, occasionally bumping into people in his haste to get back to his wife. He apologised with each small collision, seeing either bewilderment or irritation on the faces of those he collided with.

He felt unaccountably angry. Desperate to be away from John Gormley and Mike Holding. Not wanting to hear their conversation any longer. He was thinking of suggesting to Hannah that they actually return home instead of taking part in the pathetic little games this village seemed so obsessed with.

Games.

They need to grow up a bit, he thought.

He was still thinking that when he turned a corner and almost bumped into Malena Roberts.

The American was talking to an older man who Norton didn't recognise but, as soon as she saw him, she whooped loudly and threw her arms around his neck as if they'd just been reunited after twenty years. She smelled amazing, Norton noted. Freshly washed hair and just a hint of a perfume he didn't recognise. It was an intoxicating aroma. He held her tightly, his hands closing around her slim waist. He could feel the warmth of her body through her thin top and, the longer she held herself against him, the more Norton tried to resist the fact that he was becoming aroused.

Too much homemade wine.

Malena pushed against him slightly and Norton now felt the unmistakeable beginnings of an erection as she held him.

She looked deeply into his eyes for a second then allowed him to move back from her slightly.

"Tom," Malena trilled. "Hey, you. Isn't this cool?" She motioned around her at the other tents.

Norton nodded.

"This is Peter," Malena went on, gesturing to the man who was standing beside her.

"Peter Ridley," the man elaborated, shaking hands warmly with Norton who guessed that he was in his fifties.

"Tom Norton," the younger man said.

"What do you do?" Ridley enquired.

"Tom's a photographer," Malena told the older man.

"That's interesting," Ridley said, nodding. "What kind of things do you photograph?"

"Fashion mainly," Norton told him. "But I've done some glamour stuff too."

Ridley nodded again. In fact he kept nodding as they spoke, regardless of the subject they were discussing. He was a small, slightly built man with glasses, thinning hair and rheumy eyes. When he spoke and leaned too close, Norton noticed that his breath smelled particularly rank and he tried not to make it obvious that he had detected the odour.

"Peter's a writer," Malena announced. "Isn't that cool?"

"What do you write?" Norton asked.

"Novels mainly but I've done a couple of scripts for TV shows for Netflix and Amazon," Ridley said.

"That's good," Norton told him, then he turned to Malena.

"I was looking for Hannah. I left her in one of the tents."

"She's with David," the American told him. "We bumped into her about ten minutes ago. Don't worry, he's taking good care of her."

"I bet he is," Norton chuckled.

"Are you taking part in the game tonight?" Ridley wanted to know.

"I think so," Norton told him, stepping back slightly to avoid Ridley's noxious breath.

"Well, everyone does," Ridley went on. "It's best to." He took a bite of the sausage roll he was holding.

Norton frowned and looked at the sausage roll. His own stomach rumbled.

"I need to get something to eat," he murmured. "We haven't had anything since breakfast and I think I had a drop too much of the old homemade wine."

Ridley laughed.

"Some of it is pretty potent," he agreed.

"Come on then," Malena said, pulling at Norton's arm. "We'll go and get some food." She then turned towards Ridley who stepped forward, arms outstretched. Norton watched as they embraced, Ridley pushing his face towards Malena's. Their lips met and she pressed closer to him.

Norton saw one of Ridley's hands close on Malena's taut buttocks, squeezing and kneading the flesh there. Then he saw her open her mouth, her own tongue sliding forward into Ridley's mouth.

Norton wasn't sure what to do. His head was already spinning slightly from the effects of the wine and now this. He wasn't sure what he should be feeling. The emotions he was experiencing at this precise second felt like confusion, revulsion and dismay. He saw Malena drop her hand to Ridley's crotch, her fingers gliding over the material of his jeans, squeezing more tightly when she found his stiffening penis.

Norton coughed theatrically and glared at them.

When he saw Malena squeezing the outline of Ridley's hardness he began to feel envy as well as the other emotions coursing through him. He blinked hard, wondering if the wine was causing him to hallucinate. Was he really seeing what he thought he was witnessing? Was this stunning, statuesque American woman now sliding her hand inside the older man's jeans as they continued to kiss? It certainly looked like it.

No fucking way.

Norton sucked in a deep breath and shook his head, unable to believe what was happening in front of him. When Malena finally broke the kiss she smiled at Ridley, her hand still buried deep inside his jeans and now moving rhythmically. She continued to look deeply into the older man's eyes, her hand still moving agitatedly inside his jeans. He gasped loudly but Malena let out a deep sigh then pulled her hand free, waving happily at the older man before turning once again to Norton.

"Let's go and find some food," she said, happily.

Norton didn't speak.

***

Hannah Norton looked at her husband as they sat outside the tent at one of the dozen or so plastic tables, eating from the Styrofoam trays they'd been given earlier.

Norton was pushing pieces of food into his mouth and chewing slowly, his gaze fixed ahead but not trained on anything specific. Every now and then he would glance at David Roberts who was also eating, or more particularly at Malena who was sitting next to her husband, alternately sipping from a plastic cup and nibbling on a pasty.

"Are you okay?" Hannah asked, squeezing Norton's thigh.

He nodded distractedly and looked at Malena again, his gaze fixed on her right hand. The one she'd pushed inside Peter Ridley's jeans. The one that had been wrapped around his penis.

Norton coughed and cleared his throat.

"You sure you're okay?" Hannah whispered again.

"I was just thinking about something," Norton told her.

"Anything you want to share?" Malena called, winking at him and laughing.

Norton shook his head.

You dirty, sexy bitch, he thought. Why the fuck couldn't you have done that to me? Why couldn't you have stuck your hand down my jeans? Why couldn't you have closed your fingers around my dick?

He took a deep breath and glanced at David.

Do you know what your wife is really like?

David Roberts was chewing on a chip, one hand gently massaging the back of Malena's neck beneath her long dark brown hair.

"I think everyone in the village must be here," Hannah said, glancing around at the throng of people around them, all going about their business happily. From nearby there was the sound of fiddles and drums. A melody that no one seemed to recognise was drifting on the wind along with the scent of food, alcohol and warm bodies. It was late afternoon now and the sun was a burnished gold circlet in the sky. Clouds of midges buzzed around here and there and, close to the large village pond, the centrepiece of the green, dragonflies dived and wheeled over the discoloured water.

"I feel like I've met so many people today," Hannah went on. "I'm sure I'll never remember all their names."

"You will in time," David told her, smiling. "We were just the same when we first got here, but you get used to them all eventually."

"Have you met Peter Ridley?" Norton said, glancing quickly at Malena but directing his question to his wife.

"No," Hannah said.

"He's a writer, apparently," Norton went on. "Malena introduced us earlier."

Again he shot Malena a glance and this time she met it with a small grin on her pursed lips.

"We've known Peter since we moved in," David said. "He helped us settle in. He was very welcoming to us."

"I bet he was," Norton murmured under his breath.

"Everyone all right?"

The voice cut through the still, late afternoon air and Norton turned to see that John Gormley had joined them. He looked up at the older man warily, ignoring the hand that slapped his shoulder as Gormley smiled down at him.

"Are you all having fun?" the older man wanted to know.

Like some sort of bizarre chorus line they all nodded. Malena got to her feet and took a couple of paces across to Gormley, kissing him lightly on each cheek.

"Oh, I am privileged," he said, smiling, slapping Malena's backside as she turned away from him, returning to sit beside her husband.

Norton glanced at Malena and then at Gormley.

"I'll see you all later on when the game starts," he beamed.

"You might not, John," David told him. "After all, if you do see us we've lost the game."

They all laughed.

Except Norton, he merely glanced at his companions one by one then returned his attention to his food.

Gormley moved off, welcomed by other visitors to the fair.

"He's a character," David chuckled.

"That's one word for him," Norton muttered.

"I thought you liked him," Hannah said, catching the tone of her husband's voice.

"He's okay but you should have heard the way he was going on earlier when we were in the wine tent," Norton persisted. "Him and some guy called Holding."

"Mike Holding," Malena said. "Dark hair. Tall."

"Yeah, that's him," Norton said, dismissively. "They were talking about some young girl and..." He allowed the words to trail away.

"What?" Hannah insisted.

"It was just the things they were saying," Norton continued. "I thought it was disgusting. Guys of their age talking like that about a young girl. Fuck me, she's only eighteen. I mean..."

"What were they saying?" Malena wanted to know.

"Have a guess." Norton grunted. "They were saying what they wanted to do to her. Imagining what her and her boyfriend got up to. It was revolting."

"You should lighten up, Tom," Malena told him, her eyes fixed on him.

"Do you agree with it then?" Norton challenged.

"Who was the girl they were talking about?" David enquired.

"Rhiannon Morton or Morgan. Something like that."

David grinned.

"No wonder they were talking about her, she's fucking gorgeous," he said, quietly.

"A real little cutie," Malena added, resting her hand gently on David's thigh. "So is her boyfriend. What we used to call a 'horny honey' when I was younger." She giggled girlishly.

Norton regarded them both with a look that combined confusion with distaste, then he saw that Hannah too was laughing.

"I saw them earlier," she told him, grinning. "Malena's right. Her boyfriend is pretty hot."

"Jesus, not you too," Norton grunted.

"Tom, chill out. It's only a bit of fun," David told him. "And don't tell me you wouldn't if you got the chance. Rhiannon is stunning."

"She's eighteen years old for fuck's sake," Norton protested.

"Old enough to bleed, old enough to fuck," Malena said, her tone flat and expressionless. "And I bet her boyfriend could keep going all night. Guys that age are like fucking machines." She raised her eyebrows in Norton's direction, squeezing David's thigh a little more tightly, her hand sliding higher up his leg.

Norton exhaled wearily and returned his attention to his food.

"So what were John Gormley and Mike Holding saying about Rhiannon?" David wanted to know.

"I told you," Norton insisted. "They were saying they wanted to fuck her. Stuff like that."

"Would you have been so offended if they hadn't been old?" Malena wanted to know.

"That's what Gormley said," Norton informed her.

"If it had been two guys of twenty talking about her like that you wouldn't have batted an eyelid," Malena went on.

"Well, I don't mind saying, I'd fuck her," David said, grinning.

"So would I," Malena added.

They both laughed.

Hannah too joined them as they continued to chuckle and Norton looked at her angrily.

"You think this is right?" he said, his anger barely concealed.

"Like David said, it's just a bit of fun," Hannah protested. "You've seen other women you want to fuck, don't pretend you haven't."

"Women. Not kids. Rhiannon Morgan is a *kid*."

"She's legal," David said, smiling. "She has been for two

years now. I bet she's not a virgin."

"And I imagine she knows how to handle a cock," Malena added, her hand now almost resting on her husband's groin.

"You're a fucking expert on that then, are you?" Norton snapped, glaring at the American.

"I have my moments," Malena giggled.

An uneasy silence descended, broken only by the sound of the music drifting on the air and the many voices around them chattering away excitedly.

Hannah took Norton's hand and squeezed it gently.

"I'm sorry," he grunted. "Maybe I was a bit oversensitive."

"No problem," David told him. "Everyone has different views on things like that, don't they?" He sipped his drink. "Personally, I'd still fuck her."

They all burst out laughing once again. This time, even Norton managed a smile. As he looked up, Malena winked at him and, once again, he felt a stirring in his groin.

Hannah glanced at her watch.

"We have to go and get our torches soon," she noted. "As soon as it gets dark, the game starts."

***

The sun was bleeding to death on the horizon, deep red and orange staining the sky as evening finally took a hold and shook the last vestiges of light from the heavens. As the growing darkness spread further and further over the sky, shadows lengthened until they eventually became just a tiny part of the all-enveloping gloom. A chill that had been building for the last couple of hours also became stronger and, as he walked across the huge open field, Tom Norton shivered slightly and rubbed his bare arms.

Beside him, Hannah also picked her way across the field, stumbling once or twice on the rutted ground, laughing good naturedly when a supportive hand shot out to support her.

Malena and David Roberts accompanied them too, Malena moving less steadily than the others due to the amount of alcohol she'd consumed before they'd finally left the fair and trekked out to the open spaces that surrounded the village.

"I can't believe we're doing this," Norton grunted,

stumbling on a clump of grass he hadn't spotted in the darkness.

"It's called having fun," Malena cooed. "Remember what that is?"

"It's called fitting in," Hannah reminded her husband.

"It's called acting like a twat," Norton added, wearily.

"It'll be cool," Malena said, reaching out to pull him along, her slender fingers closing around his forearm. She flicked on her torch, aiming it below her chin so that her face was bathed in shadows. She laughed.

"We won't be able to see a hand in front of us soon," Norton commented, looking up again at a sky that was now almost totally black and, he felt, unforgiving. There weren't even any stars to be seen and banks of thick cloud that were scudding across the heavens, propelled by the growing wind, helped to complete the gloom.

"I hope it doesn't start raining," Norton offered again.

"It won't," Malena told him.

"You're an expert on the weather too, are you?" Norton grunted.

"I have absorbed country ways," Malena giggled, almost dragging him over as she too tripped on something unseen in the blackness before her.

"Are you all right?" Hannah called.

Malena merely laughed by way of reply, steadying herself before walking on.

"So when can we turn the torches on?" Norton wanted to know.

"You can't," David told him. "That's the idea. Not until you find someone else, then you point your torch at them and shout "I Can See You," just like Farmer Bennett did all those years ago." He laughed.

"Just before he caught fire?" Norton added.

The two men laughed once more.

"Stop it, you two," Malena rebuked. "This means a lot to the people in the village. If you want to become a part of it you have to get involved."

"I'm all for that," Hannah called.

They walked on, down slopes in the ground and along beside an almost dried-up stream.

"What happens when someone gets spotted?" Norton wanted to know.

"They put on their torch to show they've been seen," David announced. "Then they go back to the village. To the pub if they've got any sense."

"Sounds good to me," Norton grunted. "I hope I get found first."

"If you do then you won't get your prize," Malena told him. "The last ones to be found win."

"What do they get?" Hannah wanted to know.

"That's a surprise," Malena purred.

"Perhaps they get to spend a night with Rhiannon and her boyfriend," Norton said, a trace of scorn in his voice.

"Sounds good to me," David told him, laughing.

"Oh, don't start that again," Norton snapped, steadying himself as he felt the ground sloping away beneath his feet. There were trees close to them now too. Gnarled and mostly leafless despite the time of year, they stood like sentinels in this part of the field. How old they were was anyone's guess, but Norton thought they'd probably been standing for hundreds of years.

"Where are we going, anyway?" he wanted to know. "We're all following Malena as if she knows where the fuck she's going."

"We're going to our starting point," the American told him. "Just above Compton Brook. Everyone has a different starting position."

"How long does it all take?" Hannah wanted to know.

"It depends how long it takes for everyone to be found," Malena explained.

"Oh, Christ, we could be out here all night," Norton grunted. "We're missing out on valuable drinking time."

David chuckled.

"We're here," Malena announced, flicking her torch on and off, the powerful beam illuminating more of the twisted and blackened trees that Norton had seen earlier. "We start from here."

"And do what?" Norton asked.

"Find our way back to the village without anyone seeing us," Malena informed him. "There's an old dried-up stream bed that runs from here nearly all the way to the village, lots of people use that. If we avoid it we can stay out of the way, but we'll still spot others."

Hannah flicked on her torch but it glowed weakly and then died.

"You should have checked the batteries before we left the village," Norton told her.

"It's okay," Malena said. "If we all stick together we'll be fine. We can work like a team."

David tested his own torch and then Norton did the same, nodding when they saw the bulbs glow white.

Norton turned and glanced around, squinting in the gloom. He suddenly caught sight of two pinpricks of light about two hundred yards away and ducked down instinctively, motioning towards the other lights he'd seen. There were obviously others in the field now. Those same torches began to flash now.

"Someone must have been found already," Hannah observed.

"Good," Norton said. "That means we can get back to the pub quicker."

"How far are we from the village now?" Hannah wanted to know.

"About two miles," David told her.

The breeze blew powerfully across the open field, ruffling their hair and making them shiver and Norton wrinkled his nose, detecting a faint odour on the wind. It reminded him of burning, as if material had been scorched or singed. However, the smell disappeared as quickly as it had come and Norton was convinced he had imagined it.

"Everyone ready?" Malena cooed, keeping her voice low. "Let's go."

They moved off towards the distant lights of the village.

***

It was, Norton imagined, something like being blind.

The darkness was total out here in the fields and meadows that surrounded the village, and the lack of natural light was startling. It was really quite unnerving he found and, with the uneven ground too, it was becoming more hazardous even trying to walk across the countryside. More than once they'd had to negotiate their way over or through wooden fences or hedges. The others had accepted these obstacles and even laughed as they'd clambered over them or squeezed through them, but Norton just found that this added to his discomfort and irritation.

As he eased himself down from a battered stone wall he sucked in a deep breath, surprised at his own lack of fitness. They'd only been walking for thirty minutes or so and he was close to being out of breath. He made a mental note to take up jogging as soon as possible.

Ahead of them there were more torches, flashing on and off briefly then cutting through the gloom as more people made their way back to the village, their presence discovered by someone.

The ground sloped away before them once more, this time covered with slippery grass, and Norton had trouble keeping his feet as they descended. They had barely reached the bottom of the gentle slope when the figure loomed out of the blackness above them.

They froze, all eyes turned towards the shape that had come from the night. It seemed to have detached itself from the blackness, growing out of it to form a new entity that stood motionless at the crest of the slope, standing looking around, trying to pinpoint where they were.

Norton could hear breathing.

Nasal inhalations and exhalations that seemed to indicate the person above them was having trouble breathing even in this clear atmosphere.

Hannah squeezed his arm, excited by what was happening and Norton himself, almost despite his own best efforts, did find the situation quite thrilling in a weird kind of way. He knew the whole thing was ridiculous but he was attempting to enjoy himself and apparently almost being found by someone else from the village contributed to this.

The figure stood motionless for a moment longer then turned and set off across the field, footsteps gradually fading in the blackness.

Norton was about to get up when Malena shot out a hand

and held him down, ensuring that whoever had been at the top of the slope was well out of earshot. They both remained immobile there until Malena finally rose, crawled up the slope and looked around as best she could in the blackness. She slithered back down the slope, giggling.

"That was close," she said, leading them on further down the dried-up stream bed.

Again Norton wrinkled his nose, and again he detected the odour of charred material he thought he'd smelled earlier.

"Can you smell that?" he whispered to Hannah who also took a sniff.

"Something burning?" she muttered.

"That's what I thought," Norton agreed.

Slightly ahead of them, Malena tripped over a fallen branch, dropping to her knees. She could see a dark shape close to her on the ground and reached out her hand to touch it, feeling the heat as she moved her fingers closer.

Norton joined her, aiming his torch at the object and flicking the light on briefly.

"It's a glove," he said, softly. "A child's glove."

The material was indeed scorched. As if the woollen garment had been held in the flame of a blow torch for several seconds before being dropped. There was even a slight whisp of smoke rising from it.

"Who the fuck left this here?" Norton breathed.

"Farmer Bennett," David chuckled. "It must have belonged to one of his kids."

Norton shot the other man an irritated glance and walked on, stepping over the singed glove.

They moved on through the night. Over more fields. Through more hedges. Over more fences. All the time drawing closer to the sanctuary of the village. They saw torch beams cutting through the blackness occasionally and sometimes they ducked down to avoid being caught in those bright white rays. On other occasions they witnessed the flickering of lights as someone else was discovered hiding in the all-enveloping gloom. A number of times they even heard distant laughter as those who were really enjoying the night were discovered and illuminated by fellow hunters and hiders.

When they finally left the stream bed, Malena led them

towards a wider dirt track, flanked on both sides by a high privet hedge.

They made their way slowly along this thoroughfare, avoiding the branches of the hedges that sometimes snatched at them like skeletal fingers.

They were half-way along the track when they again heard thick, nasal breathing coming from close by.

Again they froze, not wanting to give away their position. Resisting the temptation to flick on their own torches and catch whoever was on the other side of the hedge. And the breathing continued. Rasping and rapid. It sounded as if the person above was taking breaths through a film of mucus, Norton thought with disgust. He too peered in the direction of the breaths but could not make out their source.

When the sound finally died away he crept further down the track, his nostrils again filled with the smell of burning.

This time he merely flicked on his torch.

"Jesus," he murmured as the beam picked something out in the darkness.

It was a torch.

The same in every way to the one that he and his companions held, except the one that lay on the dirt ahead of him was melted in several places, as if it had been exposed to some powerful source of heat.

"Turn it off," Malena snapped. "Someone will see us."

"I don't care," Norton told her. "I'm sick of this bloody game."

He kicked the burned torch with one foot, seeing smoke rise slowly from it.

It had obviously not been there very long.

A little further down the track, illuminated by the torch beam, he could see another object which, as he drew closer, he could see was also burned in several places.

It was a jacket.

The arms and back were both badly scorched.

"I suppose this belonged to Farmer Bennett, did it?" he snapped, nudging the jacket with his foot.

Hannah walked over to join him.

"This is fucking sick," Norton went on, his remark directed at Malena who was looking around her, anxious that either their voices or their lights would attract others. "So it's like this every year, is it? Commemorating the death of some poor bastard by doing shit like this?" He jabbed a finger in the direction of the jacket. "Who does this, Malena? You? One of your cronies from the village? Is that how you fit in, by trying to make idiots of the newcomers like us?"

"I don't know who put that there," the American protested.

"Perhaps it was John Gormley or one of his friends," Norton suggested. "Perhaps he did it while he was following Rhiannon, thinking about how much he wanted to fuck her."

"Don't be stupid," Malena chided.

"So now I'm the stupid one?" Norton hissed. "I'm not the one who believes these bullshit stories about ghosts and murders and men being burned alive when they try to find their family in the dark."

"They're just stories, Tom," the American continued.

"I know," Norton snapped. "It's all just a game, isn't it? Is all this talk about sex just a game too? Is everyone trying to find out how easy it is to shock us or humiliate us? Is that how these weirdos in the village get their fucking kicks?"

"No one was trying to shock you," Malena told him. "This is just the way things are here. You're an outsider. You wanted to become a part of it."

"We're outsiders because people keep telling us we are," said Norton, irritably. "And the more I see of this village and its people, the happier I am about that. I don't think I want to be a part of this fucking charade."

"That's your choice, but think about Hannah too," Malena told him. "She has to live here as well."

"Put the torch off," David insisted. "They'll see us."

"I couldn't give a fuck who sees us," Norton snapped. "I'm not playing your little games any more." He looked at Hannah. "I'm going back to the pub. If you want to come with me, that's great. If you want to stay with these two, that's up to you. Play along. Try and fit in."

"It doesn't have to be like this, Tom," Malena protested.

"Like what, Malena?" he countered.

"People in this village are good," she told him. "They don't ask much from those who come to live here. Why do you have to be such an asshole?"

Norton smiled and shook his head.

He set off down the track, waving his torch in front of him, the wide beam cutting effortlessly through the night.

Hannah was about to run after him when Malena caught her arm.

"Let him go," she murmured, watching as the light from Norton's torch gradually disappeared into the blackness. Swallowed by the enveloping night.

"I'm sorry," Hannah said. "He gets impatient sometimes."

"I noticed," Malena muttered.

"You can come back to ours if you like," David suggested. "Give him time to cool off."

Hannah smiled.

"I'd like that," she said. "Thank you."

David slipped a comforting arm around her waist.

"He won't get his prize now," Malena said, sighing. "We could have won. We're not that far from the village. We'd have made it without any one seeing us."

"Maybe next year," Hannah offered.

Malena nodded, watching as the light from Norton's torch finally disappeared completely in the impenetrable night.

"Maybe," she murmured, softly.

From somewhere above them, the sound of harsh, mucoid breathing began again and inquisitive eyes looked down at the dirt track and those upon it.

***

Tom Norton sat at one end of the sofa cradling a large whiskey in his hand, his attention veering between his watch and the front window of the sitting room.

From his vantage point he could see out into the dimly lit driveway and he kept glancing in that direction, watching for anyone who might approach the house. He had already downed two or three drinks since he got back an hour ago and he was feeling distinctly light-headed.

No. Actually, if he was honest, he was feeling drunk.

The whiskey, combined with the homemade wine he'd consumed earlier in the day, had contributed to his current state. He finished what was left in his glass then got to his feet and stumbled across the room to get himself another. His progress was a little unsteady and he had to stand still for a moment to prevent his dizziness overtaking him. Nonetheless he poured more whiskey into his glass then made his way back to the sofa where he slumped down again, his eyes moving once more to the driveway outside.

It was another twenty minutes before he saw the car's headlights cutting through the gloom as it moved up the driveway.

Norton took another sip of his drink as he listened to the sound of the key in the lock and, a moment later, as the taxi outside pulled away, Hannah walked into the room.

She looked at him and smiled and sat down on the opposite end of the sofa, regarding him silently.

"You took your fucking time," Norton grunted.

"I went back to David and Malena's," she told him, pulling off her trainers and dropping them on the floor beside the sofa.

"That's what I thought. Did you have fun?"

She wasn't slow to catch the derision in his tone.

"They're nice people, Tom," she told him. "You thought so too until today."

"Maybe I didn't know them as well as I thought."

"You didn't give them much of a chance, did you?"

"I listened to them talk about sex and then walked into the middle of a fucking field with them. What more did you want me to do?"

"We were supposed to be joining in."

"We can manage without them. Them or anyone else in this fucking village."

"I don't *want* to manage without them," Hannah snapped.

"Then you stay friends with them. I couldn't give a shit."

He got to his feet, swaying for a moment as he stood.

"Did you tell them all your fantasies tonight?" Norton said, his speech a little slurred. "Or did you show them?" He held her in his gaze for a moment.

"I'm going to bed," Hannah told him. She got to her feet, pushing past him.

Norton grabbed her arm.

"This village is obsessed with sex," he hissed. "Malena and

David are obsessed with it too. If that's how you get to belong then fair enough." He was already undoing his jeans with one hand.

Hannah looked at him dismissively.

"Come on then," he grunted, trying to pull his shirt off. "It's what you want, isn't it? It's what they *all* want."

"I just wanted to belong," she said and stepped past him, heading for the sitting room door.

Again Norton grabbed for her arm but she shook loose and looked angrily at him.

As she stood there she saw something outside.

It was a light.

It only flared for brief seconds but Hannah was sure she had seen it. Somewhere further down the driveway, towards the wooden gate that opened onto the approach to the house.

"Did you see that?" she said.

"See what?" Norton grunted, turning to watch her as she walked towards the sitting room window and peered out into the night.

"There was a light out there," Hannah told him.

"There can't be."

"I saw it."

"You're drunker than I am then."

She jabbed a finger towards the window and, this time, Norton himself saw the brief flare of white light. This time it was moving along the bottom of the garden, level with the field and road beyond.

"Is this part of the game too?" he grunted, heading for the door.

"Where are you going?"

"I'm going to find out which of these fucking idiots doesn't know when to stop playing."

As he moved towards the door he stopped at the large bureau and pulled open one of the drawers, tugging a heavy rubber torch free in the process. He flicked it on, checking that it worked, satisfied when he saw the bright beam explode from the top of the device. Now adequately equipped, he made his way to the front door and opened it noisily, finally stepping outside into the garden, the fresh cold air hitting him like a fist. He staggered for a second, wishing he hadn't had quite so much to drink.

"Hello," he called, swinging the torch back and forth. "I know there's someone there so you might as well come out now. Your little joke isn't funny."

When there was no response, Norton moved slowly across the grass of the lawn, shivering a little as the chill breeze nipped at the back of his neck and his bare arms. It had grown distinctly colder since he'd arrived back at the house and he winced as he felt the chill. He walked all the way down the garden as far as the hedge, moving the torch back and forth as if it were a searchlight, anxious to catch sight of anyone who might be skulking about in the blackness.

"I've got a torch too," he called. "In case you hadn't noticed. Also, this is private property. So you need to fuck off, right? I'm not playing your little games."

He moved across the lawn, shining the torch beam down at the slick grass.

Two or three patches of it were black and shrivelled. As if they'd been subjected to extreme heat.

Norton dropped to one knee, running his hand across the scorched grass and he could feel that the blades were indeed crisp and charred beneath his touch. He got up again slowly, his head spinning. Then he walked back up the garden towards the house, wondering why all the lights were now off and the front door was closed. He was sure he'd left it open when he first left the building.

He reached out, ready to push it open.

"Shit," he snarled, pulling his hand away quickly.

The handle was red hot, as if it had been heated from the inside until it was like a forgotten frying pan growing ever hotter on a cooker.

Norton looked down at it once more, puzzled and unsettled by this latest discovery. Touching only the wood of the door he now pushed it again, watching as it swung back on its hinges. He stepped forward into the dark hallway, wondering why all the lights were out. Had there been a power cut or something? He fumbled for the switch close to the door and flicked it.

It felt rough beneath his fingertips and he squinted in the gloom to see what was wrong, peering closer. He finally used his torch, shining it over the light switch.

The switch and the plastic panel around it was also scorched black in places, some of the plastic having melted. Norton tried the switch, moving it up and down.

Nothing. Only darkness.

"Hannah," he called, stepping further into the hallway.

And now silence too.

He sniffed and caught a familiar odour in the air. The smell of something charred and singed. Norton felt his heart thumping faster now.

He moved towards the sitting room.

"Hannah," he called as he reached the door.

Again he flicked at the light switches but nothing happened.

The room and the house remained in darkness.

Norton peered around in the gloom then ducked back out of the room and made his way to the kitchen then the dining room.

There was no sign of his wife in either of those rooms too.

He looked up towards the landing, suddenly struck by how silent the house seemed. The stillness seemed oppressive, almost palpable.

"Hannah," he called again but his voice merely echoed inside the hallway and there was no answer.

He began to ascend, his eyes on the top of the stairs, his ears alert for the slightest sound of movement, but there was none. All he could hear as he moved higher up the steps was his own footfalls and the occasional creaking of the wood beneath his weight as he moved closer to the darkened landing.

Only as he reached the very top of the stairs did he finally catch sight of the figure standing close to his bedroom door.

"I was calling you," Norton said, realising that it was Hannah. "Why the hell didn't you answer?"

As he took a pace towards her she flicked on the torch she was holding, shining it beneath her chin, the shadows it cast making her face look pale and skeletal.

She laughed softly.

"I can see you," she said. "You lose the game."

Norton frowned.

"What game?" he snapped.

"The game we were playing earlier. Farmer Bennett's game.

It was a special celebration tonight, Tom. One hundred years since Farmer Bennett died. One hundred years to the day. The villagers respect that. But you don't."

Norton hesitated a moment, looking intently at his wife who was still illuminated only by the white beam of torchlight. As he took a step forward he felt something wet around his foot and he glanced down at the puddle of liquid, also sniffing as he smelled something familiar. He pressed two fingers into the pungent fluid and swallowed hard as he finally identified the odour.

"Petrol," he murmured.

"It's everywhere," Hannah told him. "All over the house."

"Who did it?"

"*He* did. Farmer Bennett. He wanted to punish you."

Norton sucked in a deep breath.

"Hannah," he snapped. "Put the lights back on. This isn't funny any more."

"All I wanted to do was belong," she hissed. "I just wanted to be a part of something. Of this village. I wanted them to welcome us, Tom. But you couldn't even do that, could you? Well, *I* want to belong even if you *don't*."

She dug a hand in her pocket and pulled something from it.

Norton realised immediately that it was a lighter.

He swallowed hard, suddenly afraid when he saw her strike it and he saw the flame billow into life, glowing yellow and white at the end of the lighter.

"Hannah," he breathed, taking another step towards her.

She lifted the lighter above her head and he could see the flame reflecting in other wet patches on the landing carpet. He guessed that those other puddles were also petrol and he took a step backwards, wanting to reach the stairs, wanting to be out of here. He was convinced that she was going to drop the lighter at any moment and, if she did, the whole lot would ignite.

Norton began to move slowly down the stairs, gripping the hand rail as he backed away from his wife.

She moved forward, her face now bearing a thin smile.

"Put it down," he said, softly. "Please."

"I've never asked you for much, have I?" she said, advancing towards him. "And I don't think I was asking for too much this time."

Norton continued to back away, almost stumbling on the steps as he retreated, his eyes still fixed on the sickly yellow flame of the lighter.

He never even heard the sound of movement behind him. He didn't have time to turn or to defend himself.

The pitchfork was driven into his back with such incredible force that it almost lifted him off his feet.

The first of the two prongs pierced his back between the shoulder blades, tearing through muscle and bone as if it had been cardboard. The second ripped through his heart and punctured a lung before exploding from his chest where huge gouts of blood jetted from the wounds, spraying onto the carpet which was already soaked with petrol.

Norton remained upright for a moment, looking down blankly at the metal prongs of the pitchfork protruding from him, then he fell forward and lay still on the stairs.

He never saw the figure on the stairs. The dark shape that now moved swiftly back down the steps and across the landing.

Hannah aimed the torch at the fleeing image but saw nothing. Despite that she smiled slightly.

"I can see you," she whispered, the smile growing wider.

THE PICK UP

The rain was falling more heavily now. So much so that Paul Benton had to flick his wipers onto double speed to clear the windscreen.

The lights coming towards him also made driving more difficult and he winced as particularly bright headlamps momentarily blinded him.

He murmured something under his breath about turning them down. *Some people*. He shook his head.

Paul blinked hard, trying to clear his vision. He felt tired too and smoking countless cigarettes and downing several cans of energy drink hadn't helped him during the long drive. He knew the most sensible thing to do would be to pull over and get a coffee, but all he wanted to do now was get home. He wasn't that far away, and if he kept going then he could finally relax in his own bed instead of prolonging the discomfort, which he would if he paused for coffee at a service station.

He lowered his window slightly, hoping that the sudden rush of cold air might shock him into alertness, but all that happened was the rain spattered him and he closed the window again muttering under his breath.

Paul turned up the volume on the CD player but, after ten minutes of thunderous rock music, he didn't feel any more awake so he switched it off again.

It was then that his phone rang.

He saw that it was his wife and reached for it, smiling.

"Hey, you," he said into the device.

"How far are you from home?" Jo Benton wanted to know.

"Another hour or more, you should go to bed," he told

her.

"I'm already in bed but I can't settle down until you get back safely."

He slowed down slightly, moving across into the inside lane as the deluge grew even more intense.

"Are you tired?" she wanted to know.

"Very," he told her.

"Then pull over into a services and get a coffee. Clear your head."

"And then I'll be even later."

"I'd rather you were late than dead."

"Okay, you're the boss."

"And don't you ever forget it," she chuckled. "How did the meeting go?"

"It was brilliant. We got the contract."

"That's great. You deserve it."

"We deserve it. It just means I might have to be away from home a bit more."

"I do understand, you know," she reminded him.

"I know, that's one of the reasons I love you."

"What are the others? List them all. Tell me how amazing I am."

Paul could hear her giggling on the other end of the line and he smiled broadly.

"I'll *show* you when I get back," he said.

"You pull over and get that coffee first, right?" she insisted.

"All right, you win. Services coming up in about five miles. I love you."

"I love you too," she purred and hung up.

Paul smiled at the phone again then squinted through the driving rain in the direction of the sign that announced he was approaching a service station. He signalled and guided the car off the motorway, finding a parking space as close as possible to the complex of buildings that made up the stopover. The rain was still lashing down and he hesitated a moment longer before rushing from the car towards the nearest entrance, holding a magazine over his head to try and diminish the effect of the downpour.

It didn't help. He was soaked to the skin by the time he blundered into the building, glancing around for the cafe.

It was on the other side of the carriageway, accessible by a covered footbridge and Paul made his way up the steps towards the first of the many eateries housed within the services. Pizza, hamburgers, sushi and Italian all had their own outlets within the complex, but he walked on until he came to a place called The Greasy Spoon. It was obviously meant to be a copy of a classic, clichéd English cafe from the seventies and it was equally obvious that whoever had designed it had never set foot in any such establishment, but Paul walked in nonetheless, got himself a coffee and sat down at a table near the counter, sipping at the beverage and glancing around.

He was amazed at the amount of people milling about at this godforsaken hour of the night.

As well as the expected lorry drivers there were also many others seeking shelter and sustenance within the services.

He saw a couple in their thirties at a nearby table arguing quietly over something. A man in a grey suit sitting alone glancing at his tablet. Two women chattering happily as they ate fish and chips (even the thought of consuming food like that at this time of night made Paul feel queasy).

The young girl was sitting alone at a table near the door.

She couldn't have been more than eighteen or nineteen, Paul thought. Slim, pale skinned, her dishwater blonde hair pinned up beneath the hood of the grey zip-up sweatshirt she wore over impossibly tight black jeans and scuffed trainers. She had a small, battered rucksack with her that she kept touching gently with one foot as if fearing it was on the point of disappearing.

She was picking at a piece of cake, occasionally sipping

from a mug of tea. When she lifted it he could see that her hands were shaking slightly.

He tried to ensure she didn't see him looking at her. She looked wary enough already without knowing that a guy twice her age was running appraising eyes over her.

Yeah, stop looking you weirdo.

He sipped more of his coffee, noticing that the girl was getting to her feet. Careful not to look too closely, he watched as she pulled the rucksack onto her back and walked out, taking one last swallow of her tea.

Paul wondered where she, like everyone else in the place, was going at such a late hour. Were they going back to happy homes like he was? Back to people who loved them? He doubted if that was the case for all of them and he felt suddenly sad. He wanted everyone to feel the happiness he felt. He wished everyone could love and be loved as he did. He smiled at his own musings and drank more coffee, then he stretched, got to his feet and wandered back across the footbridge.

He bought more cigarettes in the shop near the exit, ensuring he put them in his inside pocket (he didn't want Jo worrying about his smoking – she'd nagged him enough times to give up). Paul glanced out again, noticed the rain had eased a little, and dashed back to his waiting car.

He slid behind the wheel, smoked a cigarette then drove off, guiding the car towards the slip road that would take him back onto the motorway.

As he swerved to avoid a particularly huge puddle on the tarmac he saw a familiar figure standing near the top of the slip road.

It was the young girl he'd seen earlier inside the cafe and he slowed down slightly, pulling across towards her. He rolled down the passenger side window and the girl walked towards the car, ducking down so he could see her face beneath the hood.

"You want a lift?" he asked.

"How far are you going?" she wanted to know, rain battering her as she stood there.

"Another hour on the motorway. Get in," he urged.

She hesitated a moment and then clambered into the car, dropping her rucksack onto the back seat.

"It's better than standing out there in the rain," Paul said, guiding the car down the slip road and onto the motorway once again. He smiled at her but she didn't return the gesture, instead contenting herself with peering out of the windscreen or the side window into the rain-blasted night.

"I saw you inside," he told her.

"I know. I could see you looking at me," she said, again without turning in his direction.

"I wasn't *looking* at you. I just wondered where you were going at this time of night. You look a bit young to be hanging around service stations at midnight."

"I'm seventeen."

"Then you *are* young to be hanging around service stations at midnight." Again he smiled and again she failed to meet his gaze.

"Is that why you picked me up? Because I'm a young girl?" she said, and Paul heard something in her tone that made him glance at her. What was it? Anger? Defiance?

"I fancied a bit of company," he told her. "I was feeling tired. Having trouble staying awake. Playing loud music, drinking coffee and Red Bull didn't seem to do the job. I thought conversation might help."

"What do you want to talk about?"

"You could start by telling me your name."

"Rhiannon. What's yours?"

"Nice to meet you, Rhiannon. I'm Paul."

She nodded almost imperceptibly.

"Have you got a cigarette?" she murmured.

Paul reached inside his jacket and passed her the packet. She took one and lit it.

"You probably think I'm too young to be smoking too,"

she said, a slight smile on her lips.

"It's your life, knock yourself out," he said, his eyes on the road ahead. "So, what were you doing at the services?"

"Waiting for another lift. The last guy wasn't going any further, and he was a bit creepy anyway."

Paul grinned. "Creepy? In what way?"

"He kept looking at me," she said, puffing on the cigarette. "Looking at my legs. He said he thought I was pretty."

"You *are* pretty. That doesn't make him creepy. Does it make me creepy too?"

She didn't answer but her smile broadened a little.

"Does it?" Paul persisted, also smiling. "You think I'm creepy now, don't you? Some creepy old bastard."

She chuckled and shrugged. Paul glanced at her as she slipped off her trainers and put her bare feet up on the dashboard. She looked briefly at him then continued gazing out of the window.

"What are you doing on the motorway so late at night? Where have you been?" he asked. "If you don't mind me asking," he added quickly, not wanting her to think he was grilling her.

"London," she murmured.

"To see your boyfriend?"

"I haven't got a boyfriend. Well…not really. We just split up."

"You're married, right?" she said, pointing at his wedding ring.

"For three years."

"Aw, that's nice," she purred. "Got any pictures of her?"

Paul reached for his phone and found the photos of Jo. He handed the device to the girl and she scrolled through several of the pictures, nodding.

"She's really nice," she murmured. "You got any kids?"

"Not yet," he announced. "I've got my own business so we want to get that sorted before we start thinking about kids. Myself and a friend have got a small production company. What about you? You working or are you still at school?"

"I left a few months ago."

"What do you want to do? For a living I mean?"

"I don't know, really. Something in music would be good. I want to be famous." She laughed.

"I think everybody does these days. Andy Warhol said that everyone would be famous for fifteen minutes."

"Who?"

"Andy Warhol. He was a famous artist in the sixties. He said that everybody would be famous..."

"Never heard of him," she interrupted, puffing on her cigarette. "I just want people to remember my name. Remember the things I did."

"So what are you going to do to make them remember you?"

"Kill someone," she told him, her tone perfectly flat and emotionless. Murderers always get remembered, don't they? People know who they are." She looked at Paul and saw the concern on his face. It made her smile. "I said that to the last guy I hitched with. He nearly shit himself."

Paul didn't answer.

"I bet you're wishing you hadn't picked me up now, aren't you?" she went on. "You only picked me up because I'm a young girl. Didn't you?"

"I told you, I wanted some company," he told her.

"Yeah, right," she sneered. "And if I'd been fat and ugly would you have picked me up? No, you wouldn't."

"Listen, I just wanted to help you."

"Of course you did. I bet you wanted to help me right onto your back seat didn't you? Or did you think I'd give you a blow job while you were driving? Just as a thank you for giving me a lift? Is that what you thought?"

"You're talking crap now," Paul snapped, indignantly. "I didn't think of any of that. I just thought..."

"Bullshit," she interrupted. "Every man thinks about

that when they see a nice-looking girl."

"Listen, Rhiannon, you've got me all wrong..." Paul countered, but once again she cut across him.

"You remembered my name? Well done. You think I'm impressed by that?" she barked.

"Look, I don't know what's going on here," he said, trying to stay calm. "I don't know why you're so angry with me. I haven't done anything to you, except try and help you."

"That's what the last guy said. You're all the same. He was married too."

"I can stop the car and you can get out if you like. I'm sure there'd be plenty of other people who'd give you a lift."

"Guys who want to fuck me, you mean?"

"You need to change your attitude, Rhiannon. Don't be so hostile."

"It keeps me safe. The day I start trusting people is the day I'm really in trouble."

"Who taught you that?"

"My dad," she hissed. "Just before he walked out on my mum."

"Is that why you hate men? Because of what your dad did?"

"I don't hate men."

"You said you'd kill a man."

"Not only a man."

"So you'd kill anyone just to get famous, is that it?"

"Pretty much." As she spoke she turned and looked at him and Paul heard a low metallic hiss as she pulled something from her jeans. Something that she now brandished before him.

The blade was more than six inches long. Wickedly sharp and double edged. He could see the light glinting on the razor like cutting edges. He tried to swallow but his throat was dry. His heart thudded a little harder against his ribs as he looked at the threatening steel.

Rhiannon smiled.

"You'd spend the rest of your life in prison," he muttered.

"Not if they didn't catch me."

"Then who'd know your name? They'd have to catch you for you to be famous."

"They never caught Jack the Ripper, did they?" She moved the blade a little closer to him then giggled and pulled it away again.

"Did you kill the last guy who picked you up?" he asked, glancing again at the knife.

Rhiannon merely smiled a little more broadly and raised the knife slightly, turning it gently in the air.

"I could cut your head off with this," she mused.

"Whatever you're thinking of doing, please don't," he said, his voice cracking. "I told you, I've got a wife... I..."

"Oh shut up," she snapped. "You'll be crying next. They're all really brave until they know I can protect myself. You're no better. You're all the same."

"I was trying to *help* you."

She faked a yawn.

They drove a little way in silence and then Paul spoke again, trying to keep his tone even.

"When did your dad leave?" he asked.

"Why do you care?" she sneered.

"I just wondered. If you wanted to talk...my parents divorced when I was your age. I know what you're going through."

"No you don't. You're just saying that. Trying to get on my good side. Trying to talk me down."

"I just don't want you to do anything stupid with that knife."

She suddenly pushed it towards his thigh, resting the gleaming metal blade against his crotch.

"Like cut you?" she hissed, holding the knife still against his testicles.

Paul gasped and sucked in a breath. He gripped the

wheel more tightly trying not to think about what might happen if she put just a little more pressure on that blade.

"And don't think because I'm smaller than you that you can grab this knife and get it away from me. I could cut your throat before you get it," she reminded him.

"I'm sure you could," he breathed, letting out an almost audible sigh when she pulled the blade away.

She eyed him, smiling thinly.

She's enjoying this. She's enjoying how much she's scaring you.

"If I take you where you want to go, will you let me go without hurting me?" Paul asked.

"You could identify me," she said.

"I wouldn't do that."

"Liar."

"I just want to get out of this in one piece." He continued to drive, keeping his eyes on the road, anxious not to meet her gaze in case she inferred too much from his looks and decided to use the knife anyway. He thought about telling her that if she stabbed him while he was driving that the car would go out of control and they'd both die but he thought better of it and just drove, aware that she was glaring at him for most of the time.

"You said you had a production company," she murmured. "You must be rich."

"Unfortunately, no."

"Liar. This is an expensive car. The clothes you're wearing are expensive. You've got money."

"How much do you want to let me go?"

"I don't want your fucking money."

"What *do* you want then?" he snapped. "To kill me? Is that it? Am I one of the ones who helps make you famous?"

When she laughed the sound raised the hairs on the back of his neck. She looked up ahead and saw the motorway exit sign looming.

"Get off here," she snapped.

Paul nodded and guided the car over into the inside

lane and then onto the slip road that led off the motorway. It quickly merged with another road that disappeared into some thick trees and bushes on either side of the carriageway. There were a few houses dotted around, he could see the lights inside them, but, for the most part, the area was dark and deserted apart from the industrial estate that loomed from the darkness to the right of where they were.

Rhiannon pointed to the first road that led into it, looking out at the monolithic buildings that now surrounded them.

There was a lay-by just ahead, almost shrouded from view by the trees and hedges on three sides of it, but Paul guided the car towards it, finally pulling in and turning off the engine.

"Now what?" he asked, reluctant to look at her.

"How much money have you got?" she wanted to know."

"You said you didn't want money."

"I lied," she hissed. "You're going to drive to the nearest cashpoint and you're going to get as much money out as you can, right? If you do that I might not hurt you."

"My card's in my coat. It's in the boot."

She pressed the knife against his side. "Get it then."

"Do you trust me to get it without running off?"

"I'll be right behind you," she said and they both clambered out of the vehicle, walking to the rear of it. Paul told her that his coat was in the boot and she nodded, watching as he opened it.

She stepped forward slightly as the lid swung upwards to reveal the contents.

There were three bodies in the boot. All young girls about Rhiannon's age. All covered in blood. She gaped blankly at them, shocked by the sudden appearance and the fact that one of them had been so badly mutilated that her eyes had been gouged from the sockets. The stench that rose from the three corpses was almost overpowering and Rhiannon put a hand to her mouth, caught completely off guard by the sight of the butchered remains.

Paul noticed her hesitation and he moved quickly, grabbing her arm and shaking it hard, using his other to wrestle the knife from her grip. He hit her hard across the face, the impact knocking her backwards against the car, splitting her bottom lip. As she staggered forward again she was already reeling and he snatched up the fallen knife and drove it three times into her stomach, wrenching the blade free in time to drag it across her throat.

Blood erupted from the savage gash and Paul was lucky to avoid the sprays of arterial blood that shot into the air.

He pushed her twitching body into the boot of the car, watching as she trembled there, her life fluid jetting from her severed arteries, her eyes slowly glazing over.

It took only a moment or two then he reached forward and gently touched her cheek.

"Stupid little bitch," he said under his breath, slamming the boot shut. "You should be careful who you ride with."

He walked back towards the driver's side of the car. A quick detour to dump the bodies in the usual place and then home.

He should be there in less than an hour.

Paul Benton smiled.

BATTLEFIELD

The light was blinding when he looked straight into it.

Richard Hill tilted the spotlight down slightly, aiming it at the small figure he held between his thumb and forefinger.

It was an officer of the French thirty-third line regiment and Richard used a small brush to put the last touches of colour to the plume on the officers' headgear, holding the lead miniature up again when he'd finished. The paint job was excellent as usual, Richard thought, admiring his own handiwork. It usually took him about three hours to complete each 28mm figure, from applying the first coat of primer to adding the finishing touches as he was doing now.

He always painted the faces of the figures first (a tip he'd picked up years ago), sometimes using oil paints to do their features rather than the acrylic paints he used for the rest of the uniforms and bases. The oil paints he normally used for larger models or for personality figures like Napoleon and his marshals, Wellington and other famous commanders.

There was a pile of reference books next to him and Richard gently turned the pages, re-checking uniform details with the illustration there, ensuring that all the colours were absolutely correct. The tunic buttons, the plume colours, the facings on the collar and cuffs. Satisfied that it was all perfect he flipped to another page of the uniform book, ready for his next task.

Richard set the officer down on his desk and nodded approvingly. There were several other painted and unpainted figures and pieces of equipment laid out before him, and in his hobby room he guessed there were thousands of the miniature figures lining the shelves or arrayed on the model battlefields he'd built over the years.

It was a hobby and had been since he was in his teens, but it was also very therapeutic for him. Richard found it quite easy to switch off from life's vagaries when he was in his hobby room painting and constructing.

He was about to reach for another figure when there was a knock on the door.

He called for the person to enter and glanced up briefly to see that it was his wife.

Francesca Hill wandered over to the desk, glancing down at the little soldiers with the same expression of bemusement and disdain she always reserved for Richard's hobby.

"Sometimes I think you'd rather spend time with your toys than you would with me," she said.

"They're not toys, Fran," he told her.

She reached for one but Richard stopped her.

"He's not dry yet," he told her.

Fran moved across the room towards some shelves where hundreds of miniature figures were arrayed. Each one was painted with scrupulous accuracy whether they were Roman legions, Ancient Britons, French knights, Cavalry of the New Model Army, Zulu warriors or Austrian grenadiers (the Napoleonic Wars were Richard's speciality, but he was also fascinated by many other conflicts and uniforms from history).

"How much longer are you going to be?" Fran wanted to know, picking up a British Lancer from the Crimean War section.

"I don't know," Richard told her. "I've still got a gun crew to finish." He watched with trepidation as she looked at the Lancer then set it back down again. "It could take me a couple of hours. I need to get my army finished before Saturday. It's the annual War Games convention you know."

"How could I forget?" Fran said, disinterestedly.

"It's important."

"It is to *you*, Richard."

She walked across to the far side of the room, looking down at a huge model battlefield (also constructed by Richard) that was covered with not only thousands of model figures but also with miniature buildings, trees, bushes, roads, dirt tracks, hills and streams. She even saw some small model sheep on one of the hills. Every part of the display had been created with love and care by her husband so that it formed a perfect reconstruction of the battlefield of Waterloo.

"Did you actually want something?" Richard enquired.

"I don't know why you don't involve Elliott in this," Fran said. "He'd love it."

"No he wouldn't. He's not interested in anything but his Xbox, his phone or his tablet."

"He's thirteen, what do you expect?"

"He's like a zombie unless he's staring at a screen. Why doesn't he ever read a book? The only thing he ever reads are the tweets by that porn actress he follows on Twitter."

"As a matter of fact he brought home a book today."

"Wonderful," Richard said, not attempting to hide the sarcasm in his tone. "What was it? Steve Jobs' autobiography? How to start your own porn site? The world according to Mark Zuckerberg?"

"It was about necromancy, as a matter of fact."

"Well, I'm sure there'll be plenty of witchcraft sites he can visit on his computer. Does he fancy himself as a wizard?"

"Just because you hate technology doesn't mean it'll go away."

"Unfortunately. I preferred a more sedate time when there was no internet, no mobile phones, no computers, no social media. Like when these guys lived." He motioned to the miniature soldiers before him.

"No, just war."

"You still haven't told me why you came up here," Richard reminded her.

"I want to know if you're taking Elliott with you on Saturday. You know, to your little convention thing."

"Why would I want to do that?"

"Because he's your son."

"He's not *my* son, he's *your* son. And he's never slow to remind me of that. It's been the same since you and I got married."

"He's still adjusting."

Richard rolled his eyes.

"I don't want him left here alone on Saturday and I have to go and visit my mother," Fran reminded him.

"He's not interested in any of this," Richard said, gesturing around the room. "He'll just spend the whole day staring at his phone."

"I'll send him up now. You can have a chat with him about it."

Richard sighed and got to his feet, walking across towards the model battlefield on the other side of the room. Carrying several of the models he'd finished painting he began putting them into position, aware that Fran had left the room. He crouched down so he was looking at the soldiers more closely, then he moved several units into position, adjusting some that had already been placed on the huge model battlefield. He also adjusted several of the small trees in the orchard of one of the buildings then turned his attention to a gun crew that was supposed to be dragging a 12-pounder cannon into position near to Napoleon himself.

Richard used a pot of green paint and a tiny brush to touch up a smudged portion of the cannon's base, then he retrieved the tin of brass colour paint and re-touched the barrel too, nodding to himself as he completed his task.

"Mum told me to come up and see you."

The voice lanced across the room.

"It's a pity she didn't tell you to knock first," Richard answered, his gaze still on the model cannon.

Elliott sauntered into the room, glancing around at the myriad figures that gazed blankly back at him from the shelves.

"Come and have a look, if you like," Richard said, gesturing towards the model battlefield.

Elliott sloped over and looked down at the huge display.

"It's not like Call of Duty," he murmured, apparently unimpressed by the layout and the amount of time and work that had gone into it. "So you painted all these toy soldiers."

"They're not toys," Richard reminded him. "They're model soldiers." He gestured at each side of the battlefield in turn. "The Allies commanded by the Duke of Wellington. The French commanded by Napoleon."

Elliott shrugged. "So now what do you do with them?" he enquired.

"Re-fight the battle of Waterloo."

"Why?"

"Because it's interesting."

"Yeah, to you."

"Different people find different things interesting, Elliott. You must find *something* interesting. Besides the lure of the internet, I mean."

"I used to find fishing with my dad interesting but then you turned up and wrecked his marriage to my mum."

Elliott eyed his step-father coldly for a moment. He walked slowly around the battlefield, as did Richard. Neither of them looked at each other as they spoke but kept their eyes on the vast miniature armies arrayed before them.

"Your mum divorced your dad because he cheated on her," Richard said. "*Several* times. I had nothing to do with them splitting up. I was just there to help your mum pick up the pieces when he ran off with his latest conquest."

Elliott was unimpressed. He reached out to touch a unit of French cuirassiers.

"Be careful, they're delicate," Richard told him, reproachfully. Watching as the boy ducked down closer to the miniature cavalrymen.

"Who won, then?" Elliott asked. "In real life?"

"The Allies, thanks to a very timely intervention from the Prussians."

"Who were the Prussians?"

"German troops, fighting on the same side as the Allies."

"I bet they had tanks being Germans," Elliott chuckled.

"Not in the nineteenth century," Richard murmured, trying to hide his disdain. "I can show you how to play if you like. If you're not too busy. Your mum said you brought a book home today. About witchcraft? I didn't know you were interested in things like that."

"My dad was, too. He taught me a few things."

"Fishing *and* witchcraft," Richard muttered. "He really was a man of many talents, wasn't he?"

"Don't take the piss out of my dad," Elliott snapped.

"As if," Richard chided. "Now, shall we play? I can explain things as we go."

He reached beneath the table where the battlefield was arranged and took out two long sticks that resembled croupier's rakes. One of them he placed behind a unit of French infantry, pushing it gently a couple of inches across the battlefield.

"We have to stick to the rules," Richard went on. "Only moving the specified distances and things like that. It helps to make it as realistic as possible." He reeled off several other rules and also retrieved a small booklet containing more guidelines. Elliott seemed suddenly more interested in the coming battle, watching as Richard also produced four polished black dice that he proceeded to roll on the top of a wooden table next to the battlefield. He noted his own score then handed the dice to Elliott. "Let battle commence," Richard said, smiling.

An hour later they were still moving their troops into position, ready for the battle to be joined.

Richard was impressed with how quickly Elliott picked up the rules and how sensibly he moved his troops (he'd chosen to fight with the Allies as his army) and part of him toyed with the idea of letting the boy win, just to foster his interest in proceedings but then he decided against that. It was going to be a fight to the death and Richard intended being victorious. He smiled to himself as he moved the last of his units into position. He walked across to a small stereo that was set up on a shelf close by. As he switched it on sounds of battle came from the speakers, and also the unmistakeable strains of La Marseillaise.

"What's that?" Elliott asked.

"Sounds of battle," Richard told him and the boy laughed happily.

"It'll be like we're really there," Elliott chuckled as Richard turned up the volume.

The rattle of cannon and musket fire filled the room.

"Would you have wanted to be a soldier like these guys?" the boy asked.

"No," Richard told him. "Not in those days. The medical care was practically non- existent. A soldier's life was hard back then." He moved several units of cavalry over a ridge in the ground, bearing down on some Belgian infantry that Elliott was shifting towards one of the fortified buildings.

"So, tell me a bit about this interest in witchcraft then?" Richard said, moving a battery of cannon up to support the attacking cavalry.

"My dad taught me about it," Elliott answered, manoeuvring his infantry into a square formation to repel the charge of the French dragoons. "He didn't like it being called witchcraft, just like you don't like these being called toys. He said it was a religion."

"That's probably true," Richard conceded.

"And he said it could be dangerous if you didn't know what you were doing," Elliott went on.

Again Richard nodded, now supporting his cavalry with a unit of French sharpshooters. He bent down close to the figures, peering through them at the square of Belgian infantry. In the background there was a thunderous explosion from the speakers as the recorded sounds of battle seemed to intensify. Even Richard ducked a little, wondering why his head was suddenly spinning.

He straightened up, feeling suddenly dizzy. He saw Elliott take a couple of steps towards him, a concerned expression on his face, but then the boy also stumbled.

Richard felt as if he was passing out.

Darkness rushed in upon him.

When he woke he had no idea how long he'd been unconscious for. He opened his eyes slowly, grateful that he didn't seem to have any pain anywhere. Could he have fainted? Blacked out? He didn't suffer from any medical complaints that he knew of so there was no reason why he should have passed out, but the important thing was that he didn't seem to have injured himself in the fall. He sat up slowly, surprised at how rough the floor beneath him felt.

As he raised his hand he saw that it was covered with some green matter that looked like dried paint.

Maybe, he reasoned, he hadn't cleaned it off his hand after painting some of the figures.

He turned around, blinking, wondering why his eyes seemed to be playing tricks on him. He wasn't in his hobby room any longer. He seemed to be inside what looked like a small wood. Surrounded by trees and bushes, Richard got to his feet gingerly, reaching out towards the nearest tree trunk to support himself. The bark felt curiously soft beneath his fingertips. Almost pliable. He pushed harder and realised that he was touching not wood but polystyrene foam. The trunk of the tree was soft and malleable beneath his touch.

"Where are we?" murmured Elliott, who had clambered to his feet and walked across to join him.

Richard knew that what he was about to say sounded ridiculous (it didn't just *sound* ridiculous, it *was* ridiculous and yet it seemed to be happening) but he said it anyway.

"We're on the battlefield," he murmured.

"What?" Elliott gaped.

Richard pulled at the trunk of the tree and a lump of foam came away in his hand. Beneath his feet he saw the colour of bare wood. It wasn't earth they were standing on, it was painted wood with fake moss scattered over it. There were also bushes but, from what Richard could remember, they were made of rubber painted with green paint.

"Look around you," he murmured. "The trees and the bushes aren't real. The ground we're standing on isn't dirt and rocks. I built this. It's all part of the model."

"And we've shrunk?" Elliott blurted. "Fuck off."

"You explain it then, mastermind," Richard snapped. "I don't know *how* it happened or *why* but it *has* happened and we've got to deal with it, right?"

Elliott looked blankly at him then both of them walked through the wood, glancing out from the edge of it towards the hills in the distance.

"The whole thing is to scale," Richard explained. "These trees would be ten or twelve feet tall if we were our usual size."

Elliott exhaled deeply, trying to take in what he was being told.

"So where are we?" he asked.

"I'm not sure," Richard confessed. "There were several wooded areas on the field of Waterloo but I think we're on the left flank of the Allied position."

"So what? How the fuck does that help us?"

"If we can get to somewhere safe we can hide and try

to work out how to get out of this."

"Where's safe on a battlefield?"

"There's a farm behind French lines called Mon Plaisir. If we can get to that we should be okay."

"How far away is it?"

"On the model battlefield about eight feet but, as everything is to scale now, it's over two and a half miles from where we are now."

Elliott sighed again.

There was a sudden deafening roar and Richard pulled Elliott to the ground as he himself dropped. There was a loud whoosh above their heads and several lumps of tree bark and branches were blasted away. The air filled with the smell of gunpowder.

"What the fuck was that?" Elliott gasped.

"Case shot," Richard said, picking up a large lead ball that lay close by. "Metal balls inside a metal case, fired from a cannon. When it exploded it turned the gun into a giant shotgun. Very effective against troops at close range."

"How can they be firing? They're little models."

"Not any more," Richard murmured.

"So they're trying to kill us?" he whimpered.

"They will if we stay here. We've got to get to Mon Plaisir."

"Across two miles of ground swarming with soldiers? You're mad. We'll never make it."

"We've got to try," Richard snarled, just as another salvo of shot tore through the little wood. Both of them ducked down again, desperate to avoid the flying metal.

Elliott shrieked in pain and Richard looked down to see that the boy had been hit in the upper arm. The shot had torn through the bicep of his left arm, ripping away the cloth there and leaving a wound that was pumping blood vigorously. Richard tugged his handkerchief from his pocket and wound it swiftly around the wound.

"You're lucky," he said. "It went right through."

"I don't feel very fucking lucky," Elliott wailed.

"Still think they're only toys?" Richard exclaimed.

He helped Elliott to his feet and the two of them made their way back through the wood, reaching the extremities and gazing out again over the battlefield beyond. Richard could see several buildings in the distance and, beyond those, more trees.

"There's a stream beyond those trees," he said. "If we follow it we can move behind the French lines. Its banks are steep so we can stay hidden most of the way."

"A stream?"

"Well, a strip of painted glass with papier mâché on each side," Richard conceded. "There are sunken roads leading that way too. We can use them for cover as well."

"How can you be sure?" Elliott wanted to know.

"I told you, I built this battlefield. It took me twelve years to complete it. I know every inch of it."

He pulled Elliott upright and the two of them ventured slowly from the shelter of the woods, moving towards a low ridge about a hundred yards away. They were halfway up the gentle slope when the horseman came hurtling over the top of it.

From the flamboyant uniform he was dressed in, Richard could tell that the horseman was a French hussar. He was mounted on a magnificent bay horse which he now put spurs to, urging the animal down the hill towards Richard and Elliott.

As he drew nearer he drew his sabre, yelling something unintelligible as he swung the curved blade towards Richard and Elliott.

Richard pushed the boy aside but couldn't avoid the stroke himself. The sabre cut through the flesh of his right shoulder and a bright fountain of blood shot into the air.

Richard shouted in pain and dropped to his knees as the hussar turned his mount and rode back towards him.

This time, Richard managed to duck beneath the

down-rushing sword, grabbing the hussar's leg. He dragged him from his saddle and rolled on top of him as they grappled, driving his fist several times into the cavalryman's face. Surprised by the ferocity of the attack, the hussar tried to drag himself away from Richard, lunging for his dropped sword that was laying a foot or so away.

Elliott reached it first, grabbed the long, curved blade and drove it down into the hussar's exposed back. It grated against ribs but was driven with enough force that it tore into a lung and the hussar gasped and slumped forward. Elliott dragged the sabre free and drove it home again, this time into the nape of the horseman's neck. He heard a sharp crack of splintering bone as the steel was driven through the man's throat, pinning him to the ground.

Blood began to spray out in all directions and Elliott gagged for a moment, not sure whether to be delighted or disgusted with what he'd just done.

Richard stumbled across to him and dragged the sabre free of the dead hussar.

As he did the body of the soldier shuddered, his body stiffening, his skin darkening. Richard looked down at the body, his mouth dropping open as he saw that the flesh was turning silver grey, the limbs and features hardening until they became fixed in one static position.

Richard knelt beside the body and gently touched the face. It felt cold beneath his fingers and, as he drew the digits across the cheek, he realised that what he was touching was not skin but lead.

The hussar, in death, had reverted to the form he had been in before. The model battlefield was littered with casualty figures painted by Richard in their miniature size and now the hussar had merely become one more of these.

"What happened to him?" Elliott gaped.

Richard thought about relaying his theory to the boy

but then thought better of it.

"He looks like one of your fucking models again," Elliott blurted, also touching the hussar's face.

"He's lead," Richard murmured. "Just like he was when I first painted him."

Elliott looked at his step-father with a combination of incredulity and fear, not quite able to process what he was hearing.

"If they die they revert to being lead," Richard said, quietly.

"I didn't ask for that," Elliott grunted.

Richard glanced at him, his brow furrowing. "What the hell does that mean?" he asked.

"When I cast the spell it was only supposed to affect you," Elliott told him. "I learned it from that book on necromancy. I've used it before."

Richard grabbed him by the shoulders.

"Spell?" he snarled. "What have you done?"

"I wanted to get back at you," Elliott told him, trying to pull free. "The stuff my dad taught me, the things I read in the necromancy book, I used them to make this happen but I didn't think it was going to happen to me as well."

Richard shook his head.

"Jesus, you can't even do *that* right can you?" he snapped. "You're an idiot."

"I saved you from that soldier," Elliott said, pointing at the hussar. "He would have killed you."

"If it hadn't been for you we wouldn't be in this position anyway, you half-wit," Richard shouted.

His words were lost as several large explosions filled the air. The ground shook beneath them as cannonballs slammed into the earth, sending geysers of dirt and stone flying skyward. They both ducked, unsure of where the artillery fire was coming from.

Thick black and grey smoke was billowing up into the air, visible over the low ridge ahead of them.

"Where did he come from, anyway?" Elliott asked, looking down again at the hussar.

"He's a messenger," Richard said. "Taking orders to a part of the battlefield."

"So why did he attack us?"

"Because we could have been his enemies. We're enemies to everyone as long as we're here."

They continued up the hill, ducking low in case there were any more troops on the other side.

Once on the crest, they could see most of the battlefield before them.

Blue-uniformed French troops were sweeping forward on all parts of the terrain, some surrounding the strongholds to the right and centre of the Allied line, others pouring up the slopes towards the bulk of the red-clad men under Wellington's command. Smoke hung in a thick pall over the entire tableau and for a moment, Richard was mesmerised by the vision before him. It had a strange hypnotic beauty about it, and he remained motionless for a moment until Elliott pulled at his arm in an effort to make him move on.

The two of them headed down the reverse slope of the hill towards a sunken road and, beyond that, the banks of a stream.

There were trees beyond the narrow waterway and Richard thought he could see movement among them. Dark-uniformed troops who were manoeuvring ever nearer to the edges of the enveloping trees, their eyes fixed on the collection of buildings that formed the village of Plancenoit. It was a position on the French right flank and Richard knew that it would be attacked by one side or the other very soon. For all he knew there could already be French troops inside the buildings waiting for the Prussian assault.

It wasn't safe to try and navigate the narrow streets of the village. He and Elliott pushed on towards the banks of the stream.

There were several dark-uniformed men on the far side of the narrow expanse of water and Richard pulled Elliott down behind one of the bushes that lined the stream, seeking the meagre cover there.

"Who are they?" Elliott asked, peering at the men through the leaves of the bush.

"Prussians," Richard informed him. "They look like *jägers*, sharpshooters. They're like an advance guard."

Several bullets cut through the hedge causing them both to dive lower. The sound of the musket balls was like loud hissing as they passed inches above them. Richard yelped as one of the balls nicked his earlobe. Blood splashed his face and neck and he slapped a hand to the wound. A second later Elliott also yelped in pain as one of the musket balls struck his knee.

Luckily most of the power had been taken out of it when it hit a branch of the bush, but the projectile still hit his knee hard enough to numb it momentarily.

"That hurt," Elliott wailed.

"Good," Richard snapped. "You're lucky it didn't break your leg."

"Fuck you," hissed Elliott.

"No, fuck *you*. If you hadn't been messing about with things you don't understand then we wouldn't be here." He looked angrily at Elliott. "Witchcraft." He shook his head and dragged Elliott to his feet. "Come on, we've got to get to that farm, away from where the fighting is taking place."

More bullets tore through the bushes that lined the stream.

"And what about them?" Elliott demanded. "They're trying to kill us."

"*Everyone* is trying to kill us," Richard told him. "Why don't you put a spell on them too?"

He dashed off towards a sunken road that cut across the battlefield about twenty yards off to the right. Elliott hesitated a moment then hurried after him.

The Prussian sharpshooters on the other side of the stream fired off a couple more shots then seemed to tire of trying to hit their targets. When Richard glanced back again they'd gone, sloping across the ground towards the woods beyond. He looked ahead and saw more dark shapes moving close to a group of buildings. The sunken road ran close to the buildings but Richard was sure that there was enough cover offered by the road to ensure they could pass along it without being seen.

In the distance the roaring of cannon fire and musketry was growing more intense. Smoke hung like an impenetrable cloud over most of the battlefield now.

Elliott hobbled up to join him, rubbing his bruised knee.

"How much further to the farm?" the boy enquired.

"Another mile or so," Richard told him. "Haven't you got a crystal ball or a spell that could tell you that?" He made no attempt to control the contempt in his tone. He looked again at Elliott, annoyance etched on his face. The two of them stumbled along for another ten or fifteen minutes before Richard held up his hand to halt their progress.

He could hear a low rumbling close by and, as he and Elliott ducked down among some trees and bushes, they saw more than a dozen mounted troops gallop past. Richard looked at the long, steel-tipped lances they carried, the red and white pennants on the lethal implements fluttering in the wind as they rode.

It was the last man in the small column who saw them.

The lancer wheeled his horse and rode at top speed towards where Richard and Elliott were hiding. They could hear him shouting something and, as he drew nearer, he lowered his lance towards them. More of his companions joined him, their officer drawing his pistol. He held it on them, motioning them from the trees.

They both raised their hands in surrender and stepped out towards the waiting lancers.

The officer barked something that Richard didn't understand and two of the mounted men gently jabbed the tips of their lances towards Elliott and Richard to hasten their approach.

The officer said something else then leaned forward in his saddle, the pistol still aimed at them.

"I don't understand," Richard told him, his voice cracking. "We shouldn't be here."

The officer's expression darkened. "English?" he barked.

Richard nodded.

The officer looked at the lancer next to him. "Spies," he murmured.

"No, we're not spies," Richard said, anxiously. "We're just trying to get off the battlefield. We…"

"Silence," the officer roared, pushing the barrel of the pistol closer to Richard's face. "Englishmen behind our lines. Of course you are spies." As he spoke he dismounted, pushing Richard back towards the trees. Another lancer did the same thing with Elliott until both of them were pressed hard against one of the oak trees.

The officer shouted something and Richard watched as the other troops dismounted, pulling their carbines from their saddles. He watched as they formed up in two lines about ten yards away, the barrels of the weapons now levelled at himself and Elliott.

"What are they doing?" Elliott wanted to know.

"They're going to shoot us as spies," Richard said, flatly, the colour draining from his face.

Elliott gaped helplessly, first at Richard and then at the lancers who were readying themselves, waiting for their officer to shout the order to fire.

Richard looked blankly at them as they raised their carbines to their shoulders.

Elliott shouted something but it was drowned as the twelve carbines erupted at once.

Richard dropped to his knees and then fell forward on

his face, his body holed by at least six of the musket balls.

Elliott slumped back against the tree, most of his head blasted away by the impact of the balls.

"Spies," the lancer officer grunted disdainfully, and he drove his sword into Richard's body and then into Elliott's.

Within minutes, the blue-clad troops had re-mounted and moved on, leaving the two bullet-riddled corpses beneath the trees.

***

She had no idea where they'd gone.

She hadn't heard them leave the house. She'd heard no movement on the stairs or outside the sitting room door.

As Francesca Hill wandered around the hobby room she couldn't imagine where her husband and her son had disappeared to. A part of her was quite happy that they were together at least. Perhaps their attempt at "bonding" over Richard's hobby had worked she thought, smiling.

She moved across to the massive model battlefield, looking down at the thousands of miniature troops arrayed there.

It certainly was an impressive display and Fran, although she didn't understand Richard's fascination with these little toys, could appreciate the amount of work and effort that had gone into creating this incredible display. She moved to one end of the model battlefield, glancing down at the figures more closely, spotting two at the very extremity of the board.

They were lying on their backs beneath some model trees.

Both were dressed in what looked like modern clothes. Not the uniforms of the nineteenth century that the little soldiers were painted in.

She leaned closer, wondering why this should be. She got so close she could even make out their features and it made her smile. Richard must have painted them this way. Maybe it was his little joke.

Even beneath the accurately coloured blood that had been applied to their wounds, Fran could see that the two little figures exactly resembled her husband and her son.

FROM THE LONG GRASS

A monstrosity.

An eyesore.

A blight on the landscape.

All those terms had been used to describe the hotel that dominated the skyline and stood unchallenged within five acres of its own grounds near the small town.

There had been protests against its construction and also against the man who owned it, but they had fallen on deaf ears. Rumours of threats and bribes made against or given to local councillors had been rife but never proved. However, all the complaints, demonstrations and mutterings had counted for nothing and the building had been constructed anyway. Four years ago the first bricks were laid and now it was a thriving business attracting customers from all over the world both because of and also despite its reputation.

Laura Green turned and glanced at the edifice of the building and then back at her colleagues.

From behind the Sony EX3 camera Russell West waved happily at her, signalling that he was ready and Brian Proctor did the same, adjusting her microphone slightly before returning to his position next to the cameraman. The sound man asked her to say a couple of things and nodded when he found the level he wanted.

"No one's coming out," West said, glancing in the direction of the hotel.

"Let's just go for it," Laura offered, fluffing her hair and looking straight into the camera.

The two technicians both raised their thumbs and Laura nodded.

"The building behind me has already been the subject of much protest since it was built four years ago and it looks set to attract more," she began. "Owned and financed by Mr Robert Sherman, well known as a big game hunter and advocate of hunting, it was constructed as a monument to his beliefs."

Laura noticed that West was pointing to something behind her and, almost instinctively, she turned to see what he was indicating.

As she did she saw a squat, slightly built man walking towards her. He was dressed in an immaculately tailored navy blue suit, his features tanned and leathery. She recognised him immediately as Robert Sherman.

"Turn that off," Sherman called, motioning towards the camera. "Turn it off. You've been told before not to film here." There was a slight South African twang to his accent.

Laura smiled at the man as he drew nearer, nodding to the cameraman who reluctantly switched the machine off.

"Get off my land," Sherman said. "You've been told before. Do you want me to call the police?"

"Protests are planned for this coming weekend, Mr Sherman," Laura told him. "Protests against your hotel, against what you do. Have you any comment about that?"

"People should mind their own business," Sherman snapped.

"But the protesters are angry because your hotel is filled with the stuffed carcasses of animals you and your guests have killed when hunting," Laura went on. "How can you justify slaughtering animals that way?"

"Man has hunted animals since the dawn of time," Sherman reminded her.

"For food, not sport."

"Man himself is an animal. When I hunt it's merely one animal against another. The animal I'm hunting has as much chance of killing *me* as I have of killing *it*."

"But the animals you're hunting aren't armed like you,

are they? They haven't got a chance."

"I don't agree. I'm going into *their* habitat, *their* domain. They have millions of years of evolution on their side. *I'm* the outsider. *I'm* the one in danger."

"And you have a gun. Why do you hunt?"

"It's an exhilarating experience."

"Why then display the dead animals in your hotel? It's horrible. It's like displaying dead bodies in a house."

"No it isn't, don't be ridiculous," Sherman grunted, finding it hard to suppress a smile. "Would you say the same thing to a museum that displays animal specimens? They've been killed *purely* for the purpose of showing them off. What's the difference?"

"But you go out to kill these animals for fun."

"It isn't just me. People pay for the chance to hunt. I merely supply the opportunity."

"Is it true that people pay up to fifty thousand pounds for the chance to hunt lions or elephants on tours that you've organised?"

"They pay a lot more than that to hunt certain species."

"Like endangered ones? Like the animal that's going to be displayed in your hotel tomorrow?"

"The animal that was shot wasn't an endangered species to my knowledge." He smiled thinly. "Twenty-five species vanish from this planet every single day, you know. We don't kill them all. They simply disappear. It's the way of nature."

Laura looked at him evenly. "But nature doesn't remove species by blasting them with guns," she reminded him. "Your hotel, your business, was built by slaughtering animals. How can you justify that?"

"I simply supply a service. If there was no demand then I wouldn't be able to make money, would I? Now, I'm going to ask you to leave my property or I'll have to call the police."

"We're just doing our jobs, Mr Sherman. At least we're not hurting you. That's more than you can say for the animals you hunt."

"Get off my property now."

"What are you going to do if we don't go? Shoot us?" Sherman smiled crookedly.

"You've got five seconds and then I'm calling the police," he said, quietly.

Laura hesitated a moment longer then she and her two colleagues turned and headed for the main gate at the end of the driveway. Sherman watched them go and then finally turned and walked slowly back towards the hotel.

He made his way through the main entrance and across the foyer towards the reception desk. The uniformed young woman behind the desk looked up and smiled at him as he approached her.

"If you see that camera crew again, call the police," Sherman said.

The receptionist nodded, watching as he stalked off towards the bank of elevators on the far side of the lobby.

***

The pub was a cliché.

It looked as if it had been lifted straight from the pages of a guide to the British countryside. Whitewashed timbered walls. Horse brasses. Dark wood tables and chairs. Low ceilings. There was even a mantrap on one wall.

They'd found it about a mile down the road from Sherman's hotel, hidden away down a short dirt track as if it was hiding from the world. Now Laura, Russell West and Brian Proctor sat in the public bar, huddled around a corner table, finishing their lunch and talking about what had happened outside the hotel.

West pointed at the stuffed stag's head that was mounted over the open fireplace.

"I wonder if Sherman shot that," he mused, chuckling.

"I think he shot the rabbit that was in my rabbit stew,"

Proctor added and they all laughed.

The sound drew the gaze of several locals seated at the bar and the expression on those faces was one of derision and contempt. They made no attempt to hide the fact they found these newcomers tedious. If anything, they were at pains to make that feeling clearer.

Laura and her companions lowered their voices, only too aware of the disdainful looks coming their way.

"I don't know why you want to go back there, Laura," Proctor murmured. "There's no way we're ever going to get inside Sherman's hotel to film."

"And whatever we might think," West added, "He's a businessman. Whether you like it or not, people want to hunt and he's just giving them that chance."

"He's allowing people to hunt animals for fun," Laura grunted.

"Lots of people must want to do it, he's built a business on it."

"A business built on suffering," Laura said. "People pay Sherman so they can kill animals. This isn't natural selection. This isn't nature. This is some rich bastard who wants to get his rocks off by slaughtering a defenceless animal."

"I wouldn't call a lion or tiger defenceless," West said, smiling.

"They are against a hunting rifle," Laura snapped.

Proctor broke the silence that descended by asking if anyone wanted another drink. He made his way across to the bar, standing there beneath the gaze of the locals who were still sitting drinking. When the barman finally ambled over, Proctor gave him their order and dug in his pocket for the money to pay.

"How long are you going to be around here?"

The question came from one of the men sitting at the bar. A tall, unshaven man with jet-black hair.

"We should be finished by tonight," West told him. "Why?"

"You should leave Robert Sherman alone. He's just trying to make a living," the tall man went on. "Bloody media are always crawling over this place because of him."

"Then perhaps you should blame him not us then," West offered.

"How much do you know about him?" Laura enquired, joining the little gathering at the bar.

"He's a nice enough guy," another man said. "You should leave him alone."

There were rumbles of approval from the other men.

"Did any of you know his wife?" Laura asked. "She left him about a year ago. She left suddenly and without leaving any forwarding address."

"So what?" another of the locals snapped. "Why don't you ask Mr Sherman what happened if you're that interested?"

"He won't answer any questions about his wife," Laura went on.

"I don't blame him," the first man grunted. "I wouldn't tell you lot anything. Bloody media. Always looking for trouble."

Laura sucked in a deep breath.

"What about Paul Johnson?" she asked. "Do you know him?"

"He lives about a mile from here," the Barman said.

"Who is he?" West wanted to know.

"He's a taxidermist," Laura answered. "He prepares all the animals that Sherman and his cronies shoot."

"Do you think he'll talk to us?" the cameraman continued.

"There's only one way to find out, isn't there?" Laura said, raising her eyebrows.

***

The journey took them less than ten minutes, driving slowly along the winding country roads that criss-crossed the area. Many of the roads were flanked by high hedges that made it difficult to see beyond the tarmac but, eventually, they found the location they sought.

West brought the car to a halt at the end of the short driveway, glancing at the thatched cottage beyond. It stood in a well-maintained garden, the flower beds and lawn cared for with love and attention. All that seemed to be missing were the roses around the door.

"Are you sure this is the right place?" West wanted to know.

"Pear Tree Cottage," Laura murmured. "This is it. You two go back to Sherman's hotel and wait for me. I'll call you when I leave here. There's more chance of him talking to just me. He might freeze if he sees a whole crew."

Proctor nodded in agreement, watching as Laura clambered out of the car. The two men watched as she walked to the door of the cottage, only driving off when the door was finally opened.

The man who stood there was tall and powerfully built and he eyed Laura suspiciously.

"Mr Johnson?" she asked.

"Can I help you?" he wanted to know.

"I wanted to talk to you about a man called Robert Sherman," she announced.

Johnson's expression lightened. "Yes, of course." He aimed one index finger at Laura. "I know you from somewhere."

"I work for the BBC," she told him.

"I knew it," Johnson chuckled. "I thought I recognised your face. Would you like to come in?"

Laura tried to hide her surprise at his friendliness. She hadn't been expecting it. She stepped across the threshold, Johnson closing the door behind her. He led her through into the kitchen at the rear of the house where he filled a kettle, placing it on the Aga to heat up. As Laura looked around she saw that there were several small animals stuffed and on display in the room, some on shelves beneath glass display cases. The birds were arranged as if they were sitting on perches around the walls. None of the animals seemed to be any larger than a mouse or vole, she noted.

"It's an unusual way to earn a living, Mr Johnson," she said, looking at a stuffed mole.

"My wife used to say that," he told her, smiling.

"Did you wife object to you preserving dead animals the way you do?"

"Why should she? It's my living. And I'm not hurting the animals, am I? They're already dead when they get to me."

He pushed a cup of tea towards Laura and sat down opposite her. She sipped at the tea and then looked at Johnson.

"How long have you known Robert Sherman?" she wanted to know.

"Nearly six years," he told her. "We met during one of his hunting trips."

"So you don't object to him killing defenceless animals?"

"I've got no right to tell anyone how to live their life, Miss Green." He smiled winningly. "And as for my own job, I like to think I'm keeping the creatures I preserve alive in some way. Allowing them to retain the vitality they had before they died."

"Is that how you deal with your conscience?" she said, sharply.

"So do you think museums are wrong to display stuffed animals too?" Johnson countered.

"Who killed those?" she said, pointing to some of the small creatures on display in the room.

"I found them when I was walking in the countryside. They were already dead. I never killed them. I don't agree with what Sherman does any more than you do, but I have a living to make."

Laura sipped her tea, considering what he'd said.

"You say you met him on one of his hunting trips," she murmured. "Where?"

"In Africa. I was there studying the animals. You have to see them in life to do justice to them in death," Johnson informed her. "I work for the Natural History Museum and several other museums around the country too."

"And you never think that what you're doing is wrong?"

"Have you asked the same question to the keepers at London Zoo?"

"They don't kill the animals in their care."

"The animals in a zoo are deprived of freedom," Johnson grunted. "Kept imprisoned in enclosures that are far too small for them. Many animals go insane in zoos. That's worse than a quick, painless death."

"Zoos are wrong but so is Sherman."

"His time will come," Johnson breathed.

"What do you mean?" Laura asked, puzzled by the tone of his voice.

He ignored the question, getting to his feet to rinse out his cup.

"If you don't agree with what he does then why work for him?" she went on.

"When I was in Africa I met men who opposed him too. Most of the guides he used didn't agree with him hunting animals but they had no choice but to help him. They needed the money. Or they were afraid of him. Some of them. Those who *weren't* showed me a way to fight back."

Laura looked puzzled and Johnson saw that on her face.

"Have you any religious beliefs, Miss Green?" he wanted to know, smiling when her expression darkened.

She shook her head.

"I want to show you something," he said quietly, beckoning her to follow him. She got to her feet and wandered through towards the rear of the house with him, towards a dark wood door that Johnson opened. He stepped through into the next room and Laura followed him.

The walls were brightly painted and decorated with all manner of masks, carvings, idols, skulls and statues, most of which seemed to have been fashioned from wood. Laura looked around, mesmerised by the display before her. She reached out to gently touch a large mask.

"It's called *vodun*," Johnson explained. "A religion older than Christianity. I learned about it when I was in West Africa." He looked reverentially at the masks and carvings, his hand gently stroking a stunted wooden statue. "The people who practise it are only interested in the preservation of life. They treasure it. They hate anyone who takes life unnecessarily. Like Sherman." He drew in a deep breath. "They showed me how to stop him," he told her. "It's taken me this long to channel the power. I won't let him continue with what he's been doing."

Laura looked at Johnson and she had no doubt at all of the sincerity of his words. That was one of the things that made the hairs on the back of her neck rise.

***

Russell West glanced at his watch and then checked the time against his phone when he looked at his messages.

"It's been more than two hours," he muttered. "Why the hell hasn't she called?"

"Maybe Johnson was more co-operative than she expected," Brian Proctor suggested.

"We can't stand around out here all day," West decided. "Let's go inside the hotel and wait. They can't object if we're not filming."

Proctor shrugged and walked with his colleague towards the main entrance of the building. Once through the doors the reception stretched away all around them.

It was almost sepulchral. High ceilinged, marble floored and every wall decorated with framed photographs, some of them five or six feet tall. And there were the animals.

Stuffed creatures dominated the large foyer and Proctor wandered across to where two magnificent lions had been mounted on a plinth. Close by them there was a leopard, then a cheetah. On the far side of the room there were water buffalo and antelopes. The walls frequently showed photographs of these animals in the wild and, more than once, there were pictures of them just after they'd been slain. Proctor shook his head gently, wondering what kind of person could take any pleasure in the destruction of such fine specimens.

West was thinking the same thing as he stood gazing at a huge vulture. It had been mounted on a large piece of tree trunk, much as it would have appeared in its natural habitat. The great wings were spread wide and the scavenger looked so vital and alive that West could imagine it taking off from its perch at any second. He walked on, inspecting a warthog and then a wildebeest.

The receptionist behind the desk in the centre of the foyer glanced up, looking at each man in turn. She returned briefly to her work but then fixed her gaze more intently on Proctor who was running his hand gently over a stuffed leopard, marvelling at the wide-open jaws and the vicious sharp teeth within.

He didn't see the uniformed porter enter the foyer and walk over to the desk where he and the receptionist exchanged some whispered words. The uniformed man also glanced at Proctor and West then he disappeared towards the staircase that led from the lobby to the upper floors of the hotel.

West saw him and again checked his phone for calls. Still nothing.

What was Laura doing?

***

"Sherman killed my wife."

Laura stiffened as she heard Johnson speak the words. She turned to look at him and saw that he was gazing fixedly at a large, carved mask, as if he were talking directly to the grotesque creation.

"They'd been having an affair for more than a year," Johnson went on. "She didn't know that I knew. At first I was going to beg her to stop but then, the longer it went on, the angrier I became. I didn't care if she stopped or not. I just wanted revenge. On her and Sherman."

"But you said he killed her."

"He did. He said it was an accident. That a gun backfired and killed her but I know different. He just got tired of her. He killed her like he killed those animals displayed in his hotel." Johnson let out a deep breath. "The same ones that are going to kill *him*."

Laura took a step back, away from Johnson who continued to stare at the mask.

"What are you talking about?" she murmured.

"That's the power of *vodun*," he went on. "That's the power I learned to control. The power I was shown."

"Voodoo."

"That's how some know it, but does it matter what we call it?" He smiled. "Surely you can appreciate the irony. Sherman will be killed by animals he shot."

"You believe that?"

"I *know* it."

"But friends of mine are in that hotel. If what you say is true then they'll die too."

"There's still time for them. Call them. Tell them to get out now." He turned to look at Laura, his eyes bulging in the sockets. "While they still can. Now!"

***

Robert Sherman gazed raptly at the CCTV screens in his

office. The room was huge, high ceilinged like the lobby, light and airy and with just one stuffed animal inside it. A huge, black grizzly bear, stuffed and mounted on its hind legs dominated the area near Sherman's desk and towered upwards as if it were attacking its prey.

Sherman gently touched one of the screens, pointing at Russell West.

"How long have they been there?" he asked.

The receptionist beside him shrugged. "Thirty minutes? Longer."

"Call the police," he grunted. "I want them out of here." His tone lightened slightly. "No. Better still. I'll get rid of them myself."

Sherman strode across his office and out to the elevators beyond. He rode one of them to the ground floor, stepping out into the marbled lobby. He saw West immediately and walked purposefully towards him.

"I know who you are," he snapped. "I want you out of here."

"We're just waiting for a friend," West told him.

"The reporter?" he sneered. "Get out before I have you thrown out. I don't want you in my hotel or on my property."

Ward and Proctor looked helplessly at him. Proctor reached out, his hand gliding over the head of the stuffed leopard once again as he looked at the man who he assumed had shot it.

"Jesus," the sound man gasped. He looked down at the animal, his hand shaking.

"What?" West enquired.

"It moved," Proctor said, breathlessly. "I swear to God it moved." He stepped away from the stuffed leopard, his eyes fixed on the large beast.

Sherman smiled thinly.

"Just get out," he rasped.

The roar that reverberated around the foyer was deafening.

All three men spun around to try and locate its source, the sound hanging in the air like a bad smell.

"What's going on, Sherman?" Proctor demanded.

The hotel owner had no answer and merely kept looking around as more and more loud roars began to fill the air, the last of them from close by. He glanced down and noticed that the leopard's jaws had closed.

Hadn't they?

When the next loud roar came, Sherman turned and bolted across the foyer. Not waiting for the elevator, he bounded up the stairs, taking them two at a time. As he reached the first floor landing he looked down into the foyer, his eyes widening. Screams were now mingling with the roars and bellows filling the air and Sherman ran on towards his office, hurtling through the door and slamming it behind him. He locked it, his breath coming in gasps.

On the far side of the room was a large wooden cabinet with glass panels in the front of it and it was this that Sherman now opened.

It contained five assorted hunting rifles and he dragged out the CZ-550, working the bolt action and then pushing five rounds into the weapon, ensuring a round was chambered.

He backed away from the door, the rifle pressed to his shoulder.

From outside the room, Sherman heard more screams and growls, punctuated by roars and bellows that ordinarily he would have been able to identify and assign to individual animals but, for now, his mind seemed frozen. He couldn't believe what he was hearing and refused to accept that the sounds he was being bombarded with were being made by the creatures he'd shot.

Something heavy slammed against the door and Sherman pressed the rifle more tightly into his shoulder, steadying himself.

He waited a second, listening to the sounds beyond the wooden partition, squinting down the barrel of the 550, his finger resting lightly on the trigger.

It took a second before he heard the low breathing. The deep rasping breaths that he realised were coming from behind him.

Then he felt something warm and wet drip onto his cheek from above.

Sherman almost laughed at the sheer impossibility of the situation.

He looked around and realised that what had dripped on him was saliva. Thick and reeking.

It had come from the open jaws of the grizzly bear.

The twelve-foot-tall creature that now towered above him.

Sherman dropped the rifle. There was no point trying to use it. The animal was too close to him now.

He turned and looked up at it. At the massive gaping jaws and the powerful claws.

The bear roared once then it was upon him.

OPEN FIELDS

Peter Fallon didn't even bother to look at the alarm clock when he reached out to shut off its strident ringing. He knew it was four o'clock in the morning. It was four o'clock *every* morning when the bloody thing went off.

He probably didn't even need an alarm to wake him. He was so used to rising at that hour he could have more than likely got away with relying on his own instinct to get up rather than the ringing of an alarm. Nevertheless, it was best to be safe than sorry and, as Peter hauled himself out of bed, he rubbed his eyes and glanced at the clock as if to reassure himself that it was still the small hours.

He looked at his wife who was sleeping beside him, then he gently kissed her on the cheek before leaving the bedroom (something else that had become part of his routine). Crossing the landing he peered into the room of his two sons, Finlay and Jack (another phase of his routine), before making his way to the bathroom where he quickly washed.

Peter made his way downstairs to the kitchen where his sheepdog, Bitza, was waiting in his basket. Peter petted the dog then gave it some food and water while he waited for his own breakfast. It was only a couple of slices of toast and, sometimes, some rashers of bacon placed between them, but this particular morning he decided the toast was enough to hold him until eleven when he would stop for the sandwiches his wife had made the previous night and left in the fridge for him. Those and a flask of tea would do him nicely.

Once he was dressed, Peter headed out of the

farmhouse towards the Land Rover that was parked outside the building. The dog bounded up onto the passenger seat beside him and sat there obediently as Peter started the engine.

It was a beautiful morning and, as dawn broke, Peter wound down the front windows allowing the fresh country air to blow away the last shreds of tiredness he felt.

Even the dog stuck its head out of the window to savour the morning air, and Peter occasionally reached across to stroke it as he drove. He finally pulled over close to a wooden fence, clambering over it and setting off up the gentle incline ahead. The dog bounded along beside him, occasionally dashing off towards ruts in the ground as if it were chasing something only it was capable of seeing, but it soon returned to Peter's side and the two of them continued up the hill. There was a large wood at the top of the hill that covered much of the reverse slope. In fact, it spread out for about two miles in all four directions. Trees grew thickly together, so close in places that it was impossible to get past them. Moving deeper into the wood though the trees thinned out and it was possible to walk easily through them. Peter glanced towards the wood and shivered involuntarily as he and the dog continued to advance.

It was as they reached the crest that the dog began to growl.

Peter looked questioningly at the animal which was now slowing its pace, hesitating as if it was reluctant to reach the top of the hill. Peter reached out a hand to urge it forward and finally it advanced but its growling continued.

As he himself reached the crest and looked down the reverse slope he could understand why.

There were at least half a dozen sheep lying motionless on the reverse slope. He hurried towards the nearest carcass and knelt beside it. The dog stood motionless next to him quivering slightly.

Peter inspected each dead sheep in turn, shaking his head as he did.

He looked in the direction of the wood. Even in the growing sunlight it appeared dark and forbidding. Peter swallowed hard and turned away.

When he got back to the farm he found Diana in the spare bedroom, sitting at a small antique writing desk surrounded by invoices, VAT receipts and the other detritus of the business she always took care of. She looked up as he walked in, an expression of concern on her face.

"I called the vet," Peter announced. "She's coming out to look at the carcasses."

Diana nodded.

"She'll know what to do," she offered hopefully.

Peter perched on one corner of the desk.

"That's nineteen in the past week," he said, quietly.

"Could it be a fox?"

"No. There wasn't a mark on them. None of them. A fox would leave marks. Any other animal would."

"What do you think is killing them?"

"I've already told you that."

"Oh, Pete, who would do that? Who hates you enough to kill your livestock?" she asked, a sceptical tone to her voice.

"You know what they're like around here. They don't like outsiders. We're outsiders. They've never accepted us even though we've lived here for three years now."

"So you think it's a conspiracy by other local farmers to drive you away?"

"I wouldn't put it past them."

"See what Pat's got to say."

Peter nodded. He hoped that he had hidden his concern from Diana efficiently enough. He'd been worried about the incidents with the sheep for the last few days but had tried not to voice his fears in case he troubled her too much. He sucked in a deep breath.

"Where are the kids?" he wanted to know.

"Out playing with some of their friends," she told him.

"Where?"

"Out by Parson's Wood I think, they're..."

"I don't want them hanging around there, you know that," he interrupted angrily.

"Pete, they'll be fine. They're just playing football I suppose."

"I don't want them near that fucking wood," he rasped, getting to his feet.

"All right, well, if you see them when you go out to meet Pat then tell them to play somewhere else."

He nodded and stalked off towards the door of the room.

"I'll call you when I've spoken to Pat," he called, making his way downstairs. By the time he reached the hillside where he'd found the dead sheep, the jeep driven by the local vet was already parked at the bottom of the incline. Peter could see her behind the wheel of the vehicle as he pulled up. She waved to him and swung herself out of the vehicle. The two of them trudged up the hill and over the crest to the reverse slope where Patricia West hunched over the nearest sheep carcass. She was an attractive woman and her good looks were not disguised by the overalls and large khaki coat she wore.

"I'll need to do an autopsy of course," she told him. "But from what I can see here, it isn't any of the big ones like foot and mouth or blue tongue."

"Then what the hell is it?" Peter demanded.

"Your guess is as good as mine. They look in good condition."

"Apart from the fact they're dead?"

"You know what I mean, Pete. How many is that now?"

"Thirty-four in the last two weeks. Hasn't anyone else reported anything like this? Any other problems?"

"There was an outbreak of foot rot at Mattie Henderson's farm but other than that, no, there's been nothing. Certainly nothing like this." She pointed at one of the dead sheep.

"Henderson's probably responsible for this," Peter snapped. "He's probably poisoned them. He's always wanted this land."

"Mattie Henderson's got his own land, Pete, he doesn't want yours." She took a deep breath. "Let me have a closer look at these carcasses and I'll see if I can figure out what's going on."

Peter nodded, his gaze still fixed on the dead sheep.

***

There was a loud thud as the ball was kicked and four sets of eyes watched it sail into the air, over a rickety fence and disappear in among the thickly planted trees of Parson's Wood.

Jack Fallon hurried towards the fence and clambered over it, dropping down into the weeds below. He picked his way across the open ground leading to the trees and then moved towards the more densely wooded area, glancing down at the ground in his search for the ball. The other three boys followed him, all trying to locate the football.

"It can't have just disappeared," said Wes Mackay.

"Well if it has you can buy us a new one," Jack said

"It's not my fault," Wes protested.

"I thought dad told us not to come in here, Jack," Finn offered, glancing at the ground and then at his older brother who was moving deeper into the wood.

"We've got to find the ball," Jack protested.

"Why did he tell you not to come in here?" Paul Mackay wanted to know.

"He just said we should keep away from the woods," Finn announced, almost stumbling over a fallen branch.

"There were some rabid foxes in here a while back," Jack said. "He was worried about them. That's the only reason he told us to keep away from the wood."

Paul looked around warily.

"Are they still in here?" he said, his voice shaking slightly.

The other boys laughed.

They moved deeper into the wood, aware that the daylight was fading due to the dense network of branches above and around them. Despite the fact that the sun had been shining, inside the wood the atmosphere was heavy and the air itself seemed somehow more dull. As if it were coloured with more subdued hues than the brighter air beyond the thick trees and bushes.

"Listen," said Finn, raising one hand.

The boys stopped and did as he asked.

"I can't hear anything," Jack offered.

"Exactly," Finn breathed. "There's no sound. No birds. No animals. Nothing."

Paul raised his eyebrows, realising that Finn was right. The absence of any extraneous noise inside the confines of the wood only served to make the atmosphere more oppressive.

"They're probably hiding," Wes offered.

"Or they might be nocturnal," Jack suggested.

"What? *All* of them?" Finn murmured.

The boys moved on slowly. It was as if they too were reluctant to disturb the solitude with their presence and their footsteps. They felt as if they'd been advancing into the enveloping trees for a long time, but in fact less than five minutes had elapsed.

"What's that?" Wes said, pointing at something hidden more deeply in the trees about a hundred yards ahead of them.

The boys looked and saw the outline of a building almost hidden by the thick branches and multitude of trees. It looked like a house, or what had once been a house. As they moved nearer they could see that it was mostly just ruins now. Lengths of mould-covered wall still stood in the rough shape of a house but much of the building had crumbled over the years.

"Who the hell would live in the middle of a wood like this?" Paul asked, his eyes fixed on the ruins just ahead of them.

"A murderer?" Jack chuckled.

"A witch?" Wes added. "It looks like the house in *The Blair Witch Project*."

"What's that?" Finn asked, warily.

"That film," Wes chided. "You know the one. The really scary one." He raised his hands into imaginary claws and loomed over Finn who moved away briskly. The other boys laughed.

"It's been deserted for years by the look of it," Jack observed, moving nearer to the derelict building. "No one lives here now."

"Let's go inside and have a look around," Paul suggested.

"No," Finn said. "Let's just go."

"Aw...are you scared?" Paul said, tapping Finn on the back of the head.

"No, I'm not scared but I think we should just go," Finn snapped. "There's no one living here and there's nothing to see except these walls. What's the point?"

"There might be something inside," Wes offered.

"Like what?" Finn muttered.

"Let's have a look and find out," Jack said, taking several steps towards the remains of the building. "You can stay out here and keep watch if you want, Finn. If you see any witches just let us know."

The others laughed again. Finn didn't.

***

The public bar of The Two Chimneys was empty when Peter Fallon walked into it. He made his way to the wooden counter, sat down on one of the stools there and ran a hand through his hair. The barman ambled through from the other bar and nodded affably to him.

"I don't know how you farmers make a living," the barman chuckled. "You're always in here drinking."

"Cheeky sod," Peter replied, chuckling. "I've had a hard morning. I deserve a bit of a break."

"Mattie said the same thing," the barman told him, pulling him a pint.

"Mattie who?"

"Mattie Henderson, he's in the other bar." The barman hooked a thumb over his shoulder.

Peter's expression darkened and he got to his feet, walking through the door that led into the snug bar of the pub. He saw Henderson sitting at a table in the far corner, food and a pint of beer before him. If he saw Peter he didn't react and he was in the process of shoving a piece of sausage into his mouth when the younger man drew close to his table.

"I didn't expect to find you here," Peter said.

"What do you want?" Henderson asked, chewing slowly. "I'm trying to have my lunch." Henderson was a slightly overweight balding man in his fifties, his arms covered in tattoos and a large grey beard coating most of his chin and cheeks.

"I'm surprised you've got time," Peter grunted. "I'd have thought you'd be busy poisoning my sheep."

"What the hell are you talking about?" Henderson wanted to know.

"Someone's been killing my sheep and I think it might be you."

"You need proof before you start accusing people, you know. Why the hell would I want to touch your sheep?"

"Because I'm competition. My farm is competition to yours."

"So you think I've been killing your sheep? So who's been killing mine then? You?"

Peter looked puzzled.

"We're both in the same business," Henderson reminded him. "We should be trying to figure out what's going on. Not arguing like a couple of bloody kids."

Peter relaxed slightly and accepted the seat that Henderson offered. If kicking it towards him and gesturing with one large hand could be counted as offering. Peter sat down opposite the older man.

"You've lost sheep too?" Peter murmured.

"Forty in the last two weeks. Some to foot rot but most to something else," Henderson told him.

"Like what?"

"I haven't a clue. There's never a mark on them. They're just lying there. Stone dead. But there's no wounds on them. Nothing."

"Mine are the same. No hints before that they're sick and then in the morning they're dead."

"What do you think it could be?"

"The vet's examining some of the carcasses."

"She did the same with mine but she couldn't find anything."

"*Something* killed them," Peter snapped.

"And you thought I'd poisoned them?" Henderson chided. "I've got better things to do with my time."

Peter eyed him warily and sat back in his seat. He watched as the older man pushed more food into his mouth, his concentration broken when the door of the bar swung open.

They both turned to discover the identity of the newcomer.

Pat West walked across to the table and sat down with the two farmers.

"Your wife said you were here," she told Peter.

"We were just discussing the sheep deaths," Henderson told her.

"That's what I came here for," Pat added. "I did autopsies on three of your sheep, Pete. Cause of death was the same with all of them."

Peter looked at her quizzically.

"Sheep can sometimes react badly to incidents of extreme stress," the vet continued. "But I've never seen anything so acute or in so many animals at once." She looked at Henderson too. "It was the same with your sheep, Mattie."

"So what killed them?" Peter wanted to know.

Pat West sucked in a deep breath. "Well, if you pushed me, if I didn't know better I'd say they died of fright."

Both farmers looked at the vet with an expression of disbelief.

"The other curious thing is that there were no footprints around any of the bodies," Pat went on. "A predator like a fox or a badger would have left prints in the mud. Even if some dog got into the field and scared them, there would have been paw prints but there was nothing around any of the carcasses."

"So what scared them so badly?" Henderson asked.

"There were no wounds on them but I found fibres," Pat continued. "Coarse hairs. I analysed them and there's only one animal that they could have come from."

Both farmers looked at her, wanting an answer.

"They came from a bat," she said.

"Bats?" Peter grunted. "Bats killed our sheep?"

"Not bats. *A* bat. The fibres were all from one animal. It must be huge."

Henderson shook his head.

"I've heard of eagles going for lambs," Peter said.

"Well, this thing is bigger," Pat told them. "Much bigger."

"But if you're right, where does it come from?" Peter wanted to know. "If it has a lair…"

"If there's a lair there could be more than one," Henderson observed.

His words hung in the air.

***

From inside the remains of the old house Finn could hear the sounds of laughter and movement being made by his companions as they ran about within the shell of the derelict building. He made no attempt to join them but stood alone, occasionally glancing around him at the dark trees. The silence, like the twisted trunks and grasping branches, seemed to close in on him and Finn finally walked the last few yards to the front of the house, passing through the frame that once housed the front door to the building.

He paused, listening to the sounds of feet on the upper floors and looking towards the rickety wooden steps that led up to this higher level.

There were three doors ahead of him, each one closed.

He walked slowly towards the first of these and pushed it. The door swung open a little way but the rusted hinges prevented it from opening fully. Finn moved nearer, peering through the gap into the darkened room beyond.

From the remains of worktops and a battered old table he guessed this had once been the kitchen of the house.

Dust was inches thick on the floor, muffling his footsteps and rising in small geysers every step he took. The windows were caked with years of accumulated filth and it was almost impossible for light to penetrate into the room. Finn hesitated a moment then turned, wanting to be out of the room.

He practically collided with the figure standing behind him.

Finn let out a short sharp gasp of surprise.

"What's wrong?" Jack asked, seeing the expression of shock and fear on the younger boy's face. "Did you think I was a ghost?"

He was already turning away, heading for another room

and Finn followed, aware too that the sounds from upstairs were receding as Paul and Wes made their way down the wooden staircase once again.

"Come and have a look at this," Jack urged, signalling for his brother to follow him.

The two of them walked into another of the rooms and Finn swallowed hard as he looked at what lay in the centre of the room.

The huge hole that penetrated through the wooden flooring seemed to disappear into the centre of the earth itself. It looked hundreds of feet deep, bored through the earth by some impossibly large drill. As Finn stood on the side of the hole he glanced down briefly into the black maw below.

The stench rising from it was almost intolerable and he recoiled, a hand to his face.

"What is that smell?" he said through clenched teeth.

"Rank, isn't it?" Jack agreed, also peering down into the hole.

"I wonder what made it?" Wes Mackay added, joining them in the room.

All four boys were now looking quizzically down into the yawning hole, careful not to get too close to the edge in case they slipped in.

"We could go down and have a look," Wes offered.

"No way," Finn snapped.

"I wish we had a torch so we could look better," Paul said.

"Let's just go," Finn insisted.

"I want to know what made that hole," Wes told him.

"Then you go down and look," snapped Finn. "I'm going home. It's getting late."

"You're scared," chided Wes.

"So what if I am?" Finn countered.

"Maybe we ought to just go," Jack interjected. "How are we going to get down there anyway? It looks as if it goes down for hundreds of feet. If we fell or lost our balance down there we'd never get out."

The other boys seemed to see the wisdom in Jack's words and they turned away from the hole, moving back in the direction of where the front door had once been. It was certainly much darker now, the loss of light signalled by the approaching later afternoon seemingly exaggerated by the stillness and gloom within the wood.

Finn was the first to hear the sound.

"What's that?" he gasped, aware that the noise was coming from behind them.

He turned slightly, looking back in the direction of the hole.

"I heard it too," Jack confessed.

Wes nodded.

"Like wings," he said. "Big wings flapping."

The boys broke into a run and left the house, hurrying through the wood, wanting only to be free of its cloying surroundings now. In the steadily growing darkness however it was difficult to see, and they were not sure of their bearings and which direction to move in to escape the wood. They ran for what seemed like an age and yet the trees showed no signs of thinning out.

"How do we get out of here?" Wes panted, looking around but seeing nothing but gnarled trees.

"Keep going this way," Jack urged and they ran on.

"Are you sure?" Finn wanted to know as he ran alongside his brother.

"No," Jack told him but they ran on.

They ran faster as they heard the sound of large wings flapping behind them. Paul glanced back but he could see nothing in the darkness. The sound seemed to be behind them but it was rising through the air until it was above them and it was growing louder.

They dashed on, Wes tripping over some thick undergrowth. He hit the ground hard and sprawled in the fallen leaves but Jack dragged him back to his feet and the boys ran on, driven by fear now.

The edge of the wood was less than a hundred yards away by now and they sprinted towards it like Olympic runners determined to break a record. And all the time, behind them and above them, the flapping of wings added a soundtrack to their frantic efforts.

***

Peter Fallon pressed down harder on the accelerator, coaxing more speed from the Land Rover.

In the passenger seat beside him, Pat West sat motionless, her gaze fixed on the narrow road ahead.

Night had filled the sky and only the bright headlights of the Land Rover offered any respite from the darkness as the vehicle sped along.

"How do you know they're here, Pete?" Pat asked as the Land Rover seemed to reach even greater speed.

"My wife called me and told me," Peter said through gritted teeth. "They should have been home over an hour ago." He gripped the steering wheel more tightly. "I told them to stay away from there."

Peter drove for another few hundred yards then pulled the Land Rover onto the side of the road near to a low stone wall. He grabbed a torch from the glove compartment and scrambled out of the vehicle, clambering over the wall and heading across the field beyond.

Pat kept pace with him, moving a torch of her own back and forth to cut through the darkness which was so total even the wide beams had trouble disturbing it. The moon was hidden behind banks of thick cloud so even the natural light that would normally have illuminated their trek across the fields was missing.

Peter strode on regardless, his face set in firm lines.

Only when he saw the first of the carcasses did his expression change.

The beam of the torch illuminated the motionless

form of a sheep lying on the incline just ahead.

There was another just beyond it.

Pat ran across to one of them and looked carefully at it, resting one hand gently on the side of the dead animal.

"Not a mark on it," the vet announced.

"Like all the others," Peter intoned looking down at the carcass.

"It's still warm," Pat said, quietly. "This only just happened."

"So whatever killed it is still around?" Peter murmured, shining the torch in a wide arc around them.

As he did they both heard a sound in the darkness. A sound that they thought was the flapping of wings. Huge wings.

Peter aimed the torch beam skyward, trying to illuminate the source of the sound but he saw only black sky. The sound came again then receded rapidly. He looked up again, both he and the vet puzzled and unsettled by the sound. It was Pat who finally tore her gaze from the sky as she noticed something else in the cold white beam of the torch.

Lying about twenty yards further up the hill was unmistakeably a human body.

She gripped Peter's arm and pointed towards the inanimate form.

"Oh my God," he breathed, realising immediately that it was his youngest son.

He hurried across to Finn's body, kneeling beside it, slipping his hand beneath the boy's shoulders to raise him up from the damp earth. Peter knew without being told that the boy was dead and he began to shake slightly, his gaze fixed on the boy's contorted features.

His face was milk white, his mouth open wide, his eyes bulging in their sockets. His entire visage was a picture of uncontrollable fear and Peter swallowed hard as he wondered what the boy had seen in his last moments that had caused such abject terror.

Same thing the sheep saw.

The body lying nearby belonged to Paul Mackay. Wes Mackay was near to him.

The dead body of Jack Fallon was a little further up the hill.

Every single boy bore the same expression of complete horror on their dead, frozen faces. Other than that, they were unblemished.

Peter began to cry softly, his entire body rocking back and forth as he held the body of his youngest son.

And, as he sat there in the field beneath the thick cloud, he heard the sound again. This time it was coming closer. That inexorable and unmistakeable sound that reminded him so much of a flock of birds. Pat shone the torch skyward again, her own fear now growing rapidly.

The beam illuminated something above her. Something massive. Something descending towards them both. Something she wished she hadn't seen. It belonged in the darkness. It should have remained confined to the gloom.

She screamed.

Peter saw it fleetingly before Pat dropped the torch and he too let out a roar of pure terror.

The sound was drowned rapidly by the flapping of huge leathery wings. And, as the torch went out, Peter was grateful for the blackness that flooded in upon him.

THE THING IN THE TUNNEL

Louise Bennett heard the sounds of gunfire as she reached the bottom of the stairs.

She sighed, shook her head and continued up the wooden flight, screams and explosions now joining the steady rattle of small arms fire.

As she reached the landing, Louise moved towards the first door and tapped lightly before walking in. Her ten-year-old son, Charlie, barely turned his attention away from the TV screen as she walked in.

He gripped the game controller more tightly in his hand, his thumbs flashing across the buttons.

Louise shook her head as she stood watching him, her attention flicking to the images on the screen. A man had just been decapitated with a chainsaw while others were firing machine guns at the central figure on screen who was advancing towards them, firing with one hand and swinging the chainsaw with the other. Screams of agony punctuated the roar of small arms fire and the persistent buzz of the chainsaw.

"Charlie," Louise said.

No response.

On the screen another person was decapitated, one more sliced in half by the swinging chainsaw.

"Charlie," Louise said again, raising her voice over the sounds coming from the TV.

Only when she shouted his name for a third time did Charlie Bennett turn around and look at his mother, making sure he hit the pause button on the controller first.

"What are you doing?" Louise asked, hands planted on

her hips.

"I'm playing this game, Mum," Charlie told her. "It's awesome."

"I can see you're playing the game but it's not yours, is it? It's your brother's. You're not supposed to be playing it. You're not old enough. Your dad and I have told you before you shouldn't be playing games like that."

"But Mum…"

"And does your brother know you've taken it from his room? I bet he doesn't. He isn't going to be very happy if he finds out, is he?"

Charlie sighed, glanced at the screen and then back at his mother.

"Now turn it off," Louise insisted. "And put it back in your brother's room before you go out."

Charlie frowned. "Go out? Where am I going?"

"You can get some milk for me from the shops, I've left some money on the kitchen table. And stay out for a while and get some fresh air. It's a beautiful day, you should be out playing with your mates."

Charlie sighed. "Steve's on holiday for two weeks. Gary's mum and dad have taken him to the zoo and Paul's gran is staying for a week so he's not allowed out. There's no one to play with."

"I used to play on my own when I was your age," Louise insisted.

"Didn't you have any friends then, Mum?"

Louise smiled. "You cheeky devil," she said. "Yes I did. I had loads of friends but if I was on my own some days I used to find things to do to amuse myself. And we didn't have video games or mobile phones when I was your age."

"Wow," Charlie said, his eyes wide with disbelief. "That must have been terrible."

Louise grinned broadly.

"Did you used to play with Auntie Beth when you were my age?" Charlie wanted to know, and the smile faded rapidly from Louise's face. She nodded by way of an answer.

"Who killed Auntie Beth?" Charlie went on, his voice low as he saw the expression of sadness on his mother's face. "Grandma said it was a monster."

Louise swallowed hard, fighting back tears.

"It was a monster," she said, her voice cracking. "But not a monster like Dracula or Frankenstein or the werewolf."

"Was it one like the one in *The Thing* or *The Nun* or *Insidious* or *Stranger Things*?"

Louise shook her head. "No," she breathed. "It looked like a normal person."

"I knew it. Monsters *do* exist." Charlie moved across to his mother and threw his arms around her neck, hugging her tightly. "I won't let that happen to you, Mum. I'll protect you from monsters."

"I love you, Charlie," Louise murmured, holding him close to her.

"I love you too, Mum. Shall I go and get that milk now?"

Louise smiled and ruffled his hair.

"Yes," she said. "You go and get it and when you get back you can have another quick go on the game but don't tell anyone else, all right?"

Charlie too was beaming now.

***

The mouth of the tunnel yawned before Mike Fuller as he walked towards it.

Bored through the hill that rose on three sides of it more than a century earlier, the track curved as it ran beneath the earth, emerging about half a mile later. Mike looked back down the track behind him towards the station that lay about eight or nine hundred yards further back. Like the track, it was nestled between two high banks of earth that sloped down from a narrow and picturesque footpath. Mike had parked his car up there then scrambled down the bank, almost slipping over such was the incline.

Now he walked into the tunnel mouth, gazing up at the brickwork. He took some photographs of the crumbling masonry on his phone then reached into another pocket of the hi-vis vest he was wearing and took out a two-way radio. Mike adjusted the controls, wincing when there was a loud hiss of static from the device but he finally found the channel he wanted and raised the radio to his mouth, his gaze still fixed on the tunnel mouth and the area just inside the entrance.

"Bill, can you hear me?" he said into the two-way.

"Yeah, go ahead, mate," the voice on the other end of the line said.

"There's definitely some work that needs to be done here," Mike explained. "Re-pointing, stuff like that. I'll go and check the damage inside in a minute but it certainly looks as if we're going to have to close this line for a couple of weeks to complete the renovation."

"It's been closed for a week already," Bill Tyler told him. "That should please the commuters."

"Well, I'm sure they'd rather take a different route to work than have the tunnel roof collapse on them, and that's exactly what's going to happen if we don't get something done pretty quick." He walked a few feet inside the tunnel, looking around the entire time. "As far as I can see there's a problem with the footings as well. The drains on the tunnel floor haven't been expected for five or six years. There could be subsidence in the rail beds but it's the safety line I'm more concerned with. There are definitely structural problems." Mike pulled the torch from his belt and aimed it at the ceiling of the tunnel, playing the wide beam over the stonework there.

"The tunnel was built in 1910, Mike," Tyler informed him. "There's bound to be some erosion. The original tunnel header was timber but that was replaced in the fifties."

"It looks as if it hasn't been touched since it was built. Who the hell did the last inspection?"

"No idea. It was before I joined this department."

"I think that counts as passing the buck, Bill," chuckled Mike. "But looking at some of the brickwork I'd say the last one to do an inspection was Isambard Kingdom Brunel himself." Mike walked further into the tunnel, aiming the torch beam all around, particularly on several lumps of stone that were on the track and beside the rails.

"There's clear evidence of collapse," he said into the two way. "Let me have a proper look and I'll get back to you once I've assessed all the damage."

"I'll go and get some lunch then."

"Good idea. Take your time. It's going to be a while before I finish here."

Mike walked to the tunnel mouth and reached again for his phone. He found the number he wanted and waited for the call to connect. He knew it would go straight to voicemail but that was his intention.

"Hi, Maggie," he said, softly. "It's only me. I know you're working and you're busy but I just wanted to tell you that I've booked the table for tonight." He smiled to himself. "I also wanted to tell you how much I love you. I couldn't wait until tonight to do that. I'm busy on an inspection for the next couple of hours and the reception here is bad but I'll see you later. Love you." He terminated the call, waited a moment then turned and walked back into the tunnel.

From just behind him several small pieces of masonry fell from the tunnel ceiling. One larger piece landed with a loud clank on one of the rails and Mike frowned as he noticed how big it was. He aimed the torch at the area above him, shaking his head when he saw that there were several deep cracks in the concrete. He pulled a small notebook from his pocket and jotted down some notes, moving a little deeper into the tunnel.

About six feet ahead of him something moved near to the tunnel wall.

Mike shot the torch beam in that direction and it reflected off something black and glistening.

The eyes of a rat.

Mike swallowed hard, ducked down and picked up a piece of stone that he hurled at the rat. It squeaked and dashed off towards one of the holes in the tunnel wall, disappearing into it.

Bloody things.

Mike shivered involuntarily. It wasn't unusually or abnormally large, but just the thought of being in the same vicinity as rats made him feel uneasy. He decided to get the inspection done as quickly as possible. He'd call Maggie again when he'd finished. She'd probably be on her lunch hour by then.

He was still thinking about Maggie when the tunnel roof above him collapsed.

Earth, stones, masonry and bricks showered down, several large pieces of debris hitting Mike and knocking him to the ground. He tried to drag himself along but more of the tunnel roof fell, one huge portion slamming down onto his legs and another caving in most of the left side of his face.

He felt unconsciousness sweeping over him and the blackness of the tunnel interior was suddenly replaced by an even deeper darkness. Mike Fuller passed out.

***

The sun hung in a cloudless sky, bathing the entire landscape in unrelenting heat. Charlie Bennett wiped perspiration from his forehead with the back of one hand as he walked along the narrow pathway beside the train tracks. He glanced down at the plastic shopping bag he was carrying, hoping that the four-pint container of milk didn't curdle in such high temperatures, but he touched it with one index finger and was satisfied that it would last until he got home with it. He was momentarily distracted by a bee as it flew from flower to flower and Charlie chased it happily, losing interest when he saw a spider had trapped a fly in its web on the fence at the top of the incline leading down to the train tracks.

He moved closer, watching the fly struggling helplessly. Charlie thought about prodding it with a small branch he'd picked up but, when he saw the spider approaching it slowly he decided against that course of action and contented himself with watching instead.

The spider was large and bloated and moving fairly slowly but, Charlie reasoned, it didn't need to hurry. The fly was going nowhere. Only when the large arachnid got close did it speed up, wrapping the fly expertly in the silk from its abdomen. In a matter of seconds, the fly was encased in the gossamer thread and the spider paused as if to admire its own handiwork. Then it struck, biting the fly, injecting the venom that would kill it and Charlie shuddered thinking how terrible that must be. To be helpless and just waiting for death with no way of escaping. He moved back from the web and continued on his way.

He'd gone another hundred yards down the walkway when he heard a sound from below him.

It was like a low rumble. A deep ululation that seemed to reverberate in the still, warm air.

Charlie looked in the direction of the sound and realised it was coming from the mouth of the tunnel below. He stood still for a moment, wondering if he'd imagined the sound but, when it came again, he realised that it was no trick of his mind. The sound was real and it was coming from the tunnel.

His heart began to beat a little faster. Was it an animal of some kind? He heard it again. A low, croaking sound that was amplified by the mouth of the tunnel. Whatever was making that noise was definitely inside there. Hidden within the darkness beyond.

One part of Charlie wanted to just turn and run, the other part wanted to know what was making that noise, wanted to discover what was hidden in the blackness, away from the brilliant sunshine that bathed the rest of the land. As is the way of ten-year-old boys, his curiosity finally outweighed his fear. He clambered over the fence and began making his way carefully down the sharp incline towards the tracks and the tunnel.

He paused close to the mouth and picked up a stone, tossing it into the darkness of the tunnel.

A low moan greeted this action and Charlie stepped back slightly.

"Hello," he called.

Silence greeted him but, as he took a step nearer, another sound reached him. It was a harsh gurgling noise that sounded like someone trying to clear their throat.

"I can hear you," Charlie called. "I know you're in there."

Inside the tunnel, pinned under rocks and earth, Mike Fuller saw the boy silhouetted against the tunnel entrance. He had regained consciousness minutes earlier and was now trying to cope with the excruciating pain that was racking his body. Not only had both his legs been crushed and pinned by the falling debris but his jaw had been smashed so badly it had almost been ripped away. It was twisted and shattered out of shape and he could taste blood both in his mouth and also trickling down his throat.

Mike tried to pull himself forward but whatever was pinning him down prevented even that small movement. He had a fleeting thought about the rats down in the tunnel with him. A thought he did his best to push to one side. What if they came for him? What if they considered him just another source of food? Along that path lay madness so he blinked hard and tried to concentrate on the shape ahead of him.

"Help me," Mike called but, with his jaw so badly broken and his chest constricted by the fallen earth and rocks, the sound was more like a mucoid gurgle than a call for assistance. He gagged as more blood ran down his throat.

Charlie moved a couple of paces closer.

"Please help," Mike croaked.

"I'm not coming any closer," Charlie told him.

"I need help. I'm trapped and I'm badly hurt. Get an ambulance, please."

There was a note of pleading in Mike's tone that was detectable despite the distortion of his voice.

"I can't see you," Charlie called.

"Come closer," Mike instructed.

"No."

"I need your help."

"What are you doing in the tunnel?"

"It collapsed on me. I can't move."

"Why were you in there?"

"I was working. Please, just call an ambulance."

"My phone is dead."

"Please help," Mike called, the desperation now even more prevalent in his voice. "You can use my phone."

"I'm not coming in there," Charlie announced, taking a step backwards.

"Please help me," Martin called.

"I've got to get home. My mum's waiting for me. I'll call the ambulance when I get home. Tell them you're in there."

"No," Mike shouted. "Don't leave me. I'll die here."

Charlie hesitated.

"Use my phone. Call the ambulance," Mike snarled.

"All right, don't get angry," Charlie told him.

"Just help me," Mike gasped. "Use my phone to call the ambulance."

"You use it."

"I can't reach it. You'll have to come in here and get it."

Charlie raised his eyebrows.

"My mum always says I shouldn't talk to strangers," he offered. "I don't know who you are."

"You can look at my ID," Mike told him, weakly. "Please, just get an ambulance for me."

Charlie moved slowly and tentatively into the tunnel.

"That's it," Mike gasped. "Come on."

"Where are you? I can't see you."

"Straight in front of you. Keep walking."

Charlie picked his way over the fallen debris, following the sound of the distorted voice. It was pitch black inside the tunnel and he could barely see a hand in front of him despite the sunlight beyond the tunnel mouth.

Something gripped his ankle.

Charlie shouted in fear and surprise and looked down to see that a bloodied hand was protruding from beneath a pile of rocks and earth. Next to it was a twisted and battered face. Spattered with blood, the jaw at an impossible angle and several teeth missing. Mike Fuller looked up helplessly at the boy, his fingers still clasped around Charlie's leg.

"Help me," Mike grunted.

"Get off me," Charlie hissed, trying to pull free.

"Help me," Mike hissed again.

Charlie looked down at the twisted features with a combination of shock and disgust.

"You look like a monster," he snapped.

"Get help," Mike persisted, now terrified that the boy would bolt and would leave him trapped here. He tightened his grip on Charlie's ankle, anxious to keep him close.

Charlie tried to pull free again and, when he couldn't, he snatched up a lump of stone and gripped it with both hands.

"Get off me, monster," he roared.

"You help me," Mike shouted in desperation.

Charlie brought the stone down once, twice, three

times on the top of Mike's skull. The first impact cracked the bone, the second splintered it and the third caved in most of the upper part of the cranium. Charlie looked blankly at the damage he'd wrought, not quite understanding that the pinkish-grey matter welling up from the rents in the skull were brain matter. All he knew was that the grip on his ankle relaxed so he was able to pull free.

He backed off towards the tunnel entrance then turned and hurried out into the sunlight again, turning and running, frightened he might be followed by the creature in the darkness.

Charlie didn't look back at the tunnel mouth until he'd climbed up the incline and was on the footpath once more. Only then did he glance towards the gaping black maw.

"I knew you were a monster," he whispered. "I know some monsters live underground. You won't hurt anyone any more. You might have got my Auntie Beth but you won't get my mum or me." He raised a hand. "'Bye, monster."

Charlie turned and ran off happily, knowing that the quicker he got home the longer he would have on his brother's game when he got back. He smiled broadly as he ran.

THE MISSION

CENTRAL EUROPE, 1944:

The Junkers JU 390 cut effortlessly through the fogbound night sky, carving a path through the darkness.

Below it, hidden by the layers of mist that had descended, lay mile after mile of open countryside occasionally interrupted by farms, villages and occasionally small towns.

But none of those were of interest to the men inside the plane. Their target was another fifty or sixty miles ahead.

Inside the belly of the aircraft, the whirring of the engines filled the ears of the men who made last-minute adjustments to their equipment. They were all dressed in civilian clothes but they were also carrying machine guns, and each of them wore a parachute over his clothes in readiness. They all knew that by dressing as ordinary men instead of soldiers they risked immediate execution as spies should they be caught, but if they were captured then death was the last and least pressing of their problems.

Captain Tom Wallace looked around at the faces of his companions, trying to gauge the emotions of each man, and every face told the same story. Expressions set in hard lines. Combinations of trepidation and determination seemed to infect each man and Wallace looked at the first of them more intently when the man caught his eyes.

"You okay?" Wallace wanted to know.

"I'm more worried about the jump than the mission,

sir," Ronald Hansen told him.

"Don't worry," Wallace said. "The law of gravity is on your side. It's just like falling out of an aeroplane."

Hansen smiled thinly and continued checking the magazine of his Sten gun.

"Jumping from that tower in training wasn't the same, was it?" William Gavin added, swallowing hard.

"You'll be fine," Wallace assured him, patting him on the shoulder. He then turned his attention to the other man in the plane.

He was a large, powerfully built individual with a shaved head and deep-set eyes, and he was gazing evenly straight ahead of himself, composing his thoughts.

"This will be the first time I've been back in Poland for three years," he announced, his gaze still fixed ahead of him.

"Welcome home," Wallace said, quietly.

"It won't be home again until this war is over," Marek grunted.

Wallace nodded, trying to understand how the big Pole must feel.

"Why can't the RAF just bomb this target?" Hansen wanted to know. "Why do we have to go in?"

"Because this target has to be taken out with surgical precision," Wallace informed him. "Bombing is too hit and miss, not precise enough. And there is the danger of collateral damage. That's why they're using us."

"If this target is eliminated then collateral damage isn't important," Marek grunted.

"Churchill doesn't agree with you," Wallace said, smiling.

"I thought the bombing of concentration camps had been forbidden because of the harm it would cause to the inmates," Gavin offered. "Thousands are dying every day in those places because of the Nazis and yet no one will sanction the bombing. Why do they think that killing one German scientist will make a difference?"

"He's Mengele's right-hand man," Wallace said. "They say that the genetic experiments he's involved with are even more extreme. Even some top-level Nazis are frightened of the work he's doing. They think he's insane."

"He deserves to die," Marek hissed. "They all do."

"How did you get away from him?" Hansen enquired.

"I was lucky," Marek told him. "My family weren't. He killed my parents, my brother and my sister."

"This isn't personal, Marek," Wallace told him, softly.

"It is to me," snapped the big Pole.

Close to the door of the plane there was a large spherical light and, as the men glanced up, it began to flash green.

"Jumpers ready," the voice of the pilot called, filling the JU 390.

The men shuffled towards the door, making last-minute adjustments to their parachutes, some of them murmuring last-minute prayers. Marek crossed himself and spoke some hasty words under his breath, gripping the side of the plane when the door was opened.

Freezing cold air rushed in and the men steadied themselves, waiting their turn to leap out of the plane.

Wallace watched as they left one by one, finally launching himself into the blackness. His heart was hammering hard against his ribs and no matter how many times he completed this procedure it still scared the crap out of him. It was the sense of helplessness he didn't like. The knowledge that there was nothing between him and death but a shroud of silk that would hopefully billow out behind him and support him as he floated slowly to safety below. If that didn't happen he would hit the earth at an incredible speed and be splattered all over the landscape below.

Wallace tried to push the thoughts from his mind and he gripped the sides of the door for a second longer before finally forcing himself out.

He closed his eyes momentarily, the earth hurtling up

to meet him, but then he sucked in several deep breaths and yanked on his ripcord.

There was a sharp jolt as the chute fluttered free and opened, yanking him upwards into the sky once more before he settled into a slow and even descent.

Now all he had to worry about was not landing in a tree or on a building below. The farms and villages were spread out across the terrain, but jumping with a parachute wasn't an exact science and factors like the wind could easily disrupt what had seemed like a straightforward jump.

Wallace gripped the suspension lines and tried to guide himself as he got closer to the ground. He could see the dark mass of some trees ahead of him and the strong wind was blowing him towards those. He could hear the canopy fluttering above him as gusts of wind ruffled it, but he gripped the suspension lines more tightly, bracing himself for the impact when it came.

He slammed into the ground, grunting with the pain that shot through his legs from ankles to hips.

Wallace rolled and was then dragged for a few yards, trying to get loose of the parachute harness.

He pulled himself free and scrambled to his feet, grabbing the parachute and rolling it up, stuffing it beneath some bushes and fallen branches out of sight.

He winced as he felt pain in his right knee but, thankfully, it faded quickly and he looked around, grateful that he'd reached the ground safely.

As he watched he saw two other dark figures moving towards him and he realised that one was Marek and the other was Gavin.

They joined him in the cover of the trees, all three men swallowed by the forest and its dark shadows.

"Where's Hansen?" Wallace wanted to know.

"He didn't land near us," Gavin explained. "I think the wind blew him off course."

"We'd better find him," Wallace offered and the three

men set off into the enveloping woods.

They walked briskly through the dark confines, moving with assurance and surprising speed beneath the canopy of leaves and twisted branches. Every now and then they would stop, alerted by a sound nearby that was the movement of nocturnal animals or the squealing of some unfortunate creature as a predator like a fox or badger struck. They moved on, finally coming to a small clearing, and it was in that open area between the trees that they saw a twisted shape they recognised only too well.

Hansen was lying on his stomach, the parachute covering much of his body like a giant shroud. Wallace moved across to him, murmuring his name and reaching out to turn him over.

"Jesus," Gavin grunted as he stared at the body.

The chest cavity had been torn open, the whole body gaping from sternum to groin. Intestines bulged from the hideous rent, some spilling onto the leafy floor of the forest. There were several savage wounds on his face too, deep gouges, one of which had ripped an eye from the socket. The tongue, too, was missing.

"*That* didn't happen in the landing," Wallace muttered, shocked by the appearance of the corpse. "It looks as if some kind of animal got to him."

"What animal kills like that?" Marek said, one hand clamped to his mouth. "There's nothing in these woods that could do that to a man."

Wallace looked around as if seeking assurance, then he motioned the other two men to follow him.

"Wolves?" Wallace mused.

"There are no wolves in this forest," Marek told him. "And if there were, wolves would have eaten him."

The men looked down again at the eviscerated body then Wallace turned away.

"Shouldn't we bury him?" Gavin asked.

"No time," Wallace said, walking on.

The three men continued through the forest, trying to push from their minds the fate of their companion.

The sound that came to them on the cold night air froze them in their tracks. All three of them stood stock still, listening to the noise. A low, guttural roar that thrummed in their ears. It was too loud for a man and yet none of them could imagine what kind of animal had made such a monstrous exhortation. They looked at each other nervously for a moment then Wallace motioned them to move on.

It felt like an age that they were walking through the darkened confines of the forest but, finally, the trees began to thin out and they were eventually able to see the open ground beyond the reach of the trees. Across a wide expanse of rolling countryside they could see the outline of a large house and some outbuildings.

"That's it," Wallace breathed, pointing to the collection of buildings. "Schrodek's house."

"I thought most of the officers and staff lived inside the camps themselves," Gavin offered.

"Schrodek's been here for the last six months," Wallace said. "The house was requisitioned for him. He insists on living alone."

"What about guards?" Marek enquired.

"A small escort accompany him from the house to the camp and then back again at the same time every day," said Wallace. "When he's here he's alone apart from a housekeeper and cook."

"Do we kill them too?" Marek asked, working the slide on his machine pistol.

"Only if they get in the way," Wallace told him. He held the Pole's gaze for a moment then glanced at his watch. "For now we wait until Schrodek and his escort get back from the camp."

"He might already be in the house," Marek protested.

"He sticks to a rigid schedule," Wallace told him. "He never varies it. He won't be back yet."

The Pole began to say something about being in the house and taking the Nazi by surprise but Wallace merely pointed to some far-off lights that he'd spotted.

"That's him," he murmured. "Right on time. Come on."

They were about to move away when Gavin gripped Wallace's arm.

"What happened to Hansen back there," he said, warily. "Could that be anything to do with Schrodek's work?" he wanted to know.

Wallace looked puzzled.

"Maybe he doesn't need guards because something more powerful is protecting him," Gavin continued.

Wallace swallowed hard and shook loose of his companion's grip, preferring not to entertain thoughts like that. He hurried off across the open ground leading to the house.

As the little procession of headlights drew nearer to the house, Wallace and his companions set off across the open ground towards the building, ducked low to make themselves more difficult to spot. There were a few dips in the terrain and they were aided in their approach by this, finally emerging only twenty or thirty yards from the main house on a slight slope that led down to the impressive structure.

They watched as the vehicles pulled into the open area before the house, seeing uniformed German troops clambering out of the escorting cars and the Sd. Kfz. 222 armoured car that made up the rear of the small convoy. Motorcycle outriders took up position around the large black car near the front of the column and Wallace and his men saw a tall, dark-haired man get out and walk to the front door of the house flanked by four SS men who gave the Nazi salute as the tall man passed.

They waited on the porch, saluting again when Doctor Claus Schrodek finally disappeared inside the building.

"He doesn't look like a monster, does he?" Gavin murmured.

"They never do," Marek growled under his breath.

Within minutes, the escort had turned and driven away, the sound of their engines dying away on the wind.

Wallace signalled to his men and they moved swiftly towards the house, gaining entry through a window at the rear of the property. Moving with practised stealth, they picked their way through the house, weapons at the ready. They moved through the large rooms until they came to what they were convinced was the dining room.

Schrodek was already sitting at the large, polished wood table alternately glancing at his food that had just been placed there by a housekeeper and a pile of letters that had also been put beside him.

He took a bite of the food and smiled appreciatively.

"That is wonderful, Greta," he remarked. "Thank you."

The housekeeper looked both relieved and delighted with his reaction.

"Is there anything else I can get you, sir?" she wanted to know.

"No thank you. I'll call you if there is."

She nodded and retreated from the room.

Wallace and his men waited a moment then slipped through the door she had left by.

If Schrodek heard them as they approached him he certainly gave no signs of it. He merely looked up slowly, glancing at each of the men in turn.

Wallace was already holding a pistol on him. Marek and Gavin lowered their Sten guns so the barrels were pointing at the German.

"What are you doing in my house?" he asked, quietly.

"It's not your house," Marek rasped. "Just like this country isn't yours. You stole it from my people."

Schrodek smiled.

"You're a Pole?" he said. "Your country was only ever on loan to you. Waiting for Germany to re-claim it."

Marek took a step towards him angrily but Wallace shot out a hand to stop the big man's advance.

"You need to keep your dog on a tighter leash," Schrodek sneered, glancing at Wallace. "Who are you?"

"That's not important," Wallace told him.

"You're here to kill me," the German said, but it sounded more like a statement than a question. "If that's the case then get it over with."

"I have some questions first," Wallace went on.

"And you expect me to answer them?"

"I'll make him talk," Marek snarled.

"An *untermensch* like you?" Schrodek chided. "You couldn't make me wipe my own backside." The look he gave the big Pole was one of pure contempt.

"How many of my people have you killed?" Marek hissed. "You animal."

"I haven't killed any *people*," Schrodek sneered. "Only Poles and Jews." He chuckled.

Marek lunged towards the German, a look of pure hatred on his face, but Gavin intercepted him this time, struggling to hold the big man back.

"Get out," Wallace told him. "Just get out until this is over."

"I want to see him die," Marek snapped.

"Like I watched your family die?" Schrodek taunted. "Screaming and begging for their worthless lives?"

The Pole shouted something unintelligible and jumped forward again but, once more, Gavin restrained him, but it took even more effort this time. Marek's fury seemed to be giving him even more strength than usual.

"Get out," Wallace roared, watching as the Pole shook free of his companion's grip and stalked out of the room, slamming the door behind him. Only when he'd gone did Wallace turn back towards the German, the barrel of the Browning automatic aimed at Schrodek's chest.

"You're English, aren't you?" the German said to Wallace. "Aryan, like me. Why do you associate with subhumans like that?" He waved a dismissive hand in Marek's direction.

"Because he and I want the same thing," Wallace snarled. "We want to see animals like you wiped off the face of the earth. You and Mengele."

"Mengele?" Schrodek snorted. "Why are you concerned with that fool?"

"You work with him," Wallace snapped.

"His work is secondary to mine," the German snorted. "He is a pupil. Nothing more. He was concerned with the *alteration* of life and nature. Adapting it. Perfecting it. I am interested in the *preservation* of life. Of ensuring it survives, no matter what. Of stopping death." He smiled. "Imagine whole divisions of troops impervious to death. Unstoppable. I have the means to create that."

"That's impossible," Gavin said.

"Is it?" Schrodek retorted. "How could men like you, men of such limited intellect, ever understand what I've done?"

He got to his feet and walked towards Wallace.

"Sit down," the Englishman rasped, thumbing back the hammer of the pistol.

"If I'm going to die, I'll do it on my feet, not sitting in a chair," Schrodek hissed.

"Suit yourself," Wallace grunted and he fired three times.

Two of the bullets ripped through Schrodek, exploding from his back and spraying blood up the white wall behind him. Gobbets of lung tissue hung lazily from the bloodied paintwork. The third shot stove in his sternum and sent him reeling backwards. He slumped into the chair, blood spewing from the wounds and pouring from his mouth.

At the sound of the shots, Marek rushed back into the room, stopping to look at the body of Schrodek. He took a step closer, hawked loudly and spat on the body. Wallace stood motionless for a moment then looked at his companions.

"Let's go," he urged, heading for the door.

As they reached it another shape loomed into the doorway and Gavin swung his sub-machine gun up almost involuntarily, his finger tightening on the trigger.

A short burst sent bullets tearing into the housekeeper who dropped like a stone.

The three men hurdled her body and continued out to the front of the house. Parked at the side of the building was a large black Mercedes 770K and Gavin immediately threw open the bonnet and set about trying to get it started while his companions scrambled into the front seat.

"Thank you," Marek said to Wallace. "Thank you for wiping that scum off the face of the earth."

Wallace was about to answer when a shot rang out from the direction of the house.

Marek's head exploded as the bullet hit it and Wallace gasped as blood, shattered bone and several slicks of brain matter hit him in the face. Marek slumped back in the passenger seat, most of the left side of his head now missing.

Wallace looked in the direction from which the shot had come and saw a figure standing on the porch of the house, a Mauser rifle clutched in its grip.

It took him a moment or two longer to realise that the figure was Claus Schrodek.

The German worked the bolt, chambered another round and fired again, the bullet slamming into the car just as Gavin finally forced the engine into life. He ran to the rear of the vehicle and hauled himself in as Wallace slammed his foot down on the accelerator. The engine roared and the car shot forward, Wallace turning the wheel frantically, guiding the Mercedes across the open area before the house as another bullet punched into the chassis.

On the porch, Schrodek continued to fire.

"But he's dead," Gavin gaped, staring at the German. "I saw you shoot him."

Wallace didn't answer. What could he say?

A bullet shattered the side window, catching Gavin in the shoulder, tearing through the flesh and muscle there.

Another pierced a front tyre and the Mercedes went out of control, slamming into the wooden doors of the barn on the far side of the courtyard.

Wallace and Gavin scrambled out, ducking down to avoid the bullets, making for the fence that surrounded the yard.

"We can get to the train on foot," Wallace said, almost dragging his companion along with him as they ran. They set off over the open fields, occasionally dropping to the ground as another bullet cut through the air above them.

"I thought he was dead," Gavin gasped.

"So did I," Wallace said, flatly.

They ran on.

From the porch of the house, Schrodek finally lowered the Mauser, turning to glance at the figure that had joined him.

The housekeeper stood silently beside him, ignoring the wounds that had shredded her upper body.

Schrodek himself seemed oblivious to the gaping holes in his chest and stomach.

"Call *Hauptsturmführer* Brandt," he murmured. "Tell him they're heading for the railway station."

The housekeeper nodded and disappeared back inside the house.

Schrodek gazed on into the darkness, his face still set in a smile.

Had he been able to see through the night he would have seen Wallace and Gavin scrambling down a steep slope towards the gleaming train tracks that cut across the countryside.

"We can't make it to the station," Wallace panted. "But we can get onto a train. If we drop down onto one from the tunnel roof we can get clear of here."

"If you have to, leave me..." Gavin began, feeling at

his bullet-blasted shoulder.

"I'm not leaving you," Wallace assured him, interrupting.

They continued down the hillside, eventually coming to a flatter area that formed the roof of the tunnel.

Both men got as close to the lip as possible, listening to the ever-growing sound of an approaching train. The noise of the whistle cut effortlessly through the night and, minutes later, the locomotive itself came into view.

Smoke and steam belched from the chimney of the thundering juggernaut and both men watched as it drew closer, knowing it would have to slow down to a crawl as it took the bend that would lead it into the tunnel. They shielded their faces from the clouds of smoke as the engine swept past below them, slowing down so that they had a clear view of the cattle cars and open flat trucks it was pulling.

Wallace and Gavin steadied themselves, edging nearer and nearer to the lip of the tunnel, ready for the jump.

There were several open wagons approaching and they realised that one of those was their way down.

As the open trucks passed beneath they both jumped, landing with a thud into the wooden flat beds. Gavin grunted in pain as he felt an impact against his injured shoulder but he gritted his teeth, relieved that they had made it onto the train which was now speeding up again as it passed through the tunnel. He and Wallace shared a triumphant smile and moved back against the wall of the truck as the train increased its speed even more, thundering through the night at breakneck pace.

Wallace glanced out at the countryside speeding past them, realising that they couldn't attempt to jump from the train because it was moving too fast. They'd just have to wait until it stopped before they could get off, but that didn't seem to matter at the moment.

He tended to Gavin's wound and allowed the other man to drift off to sleep as the train rumbled on.

Wallace sat back again, exhausted, his eyes drawn to the stencilled words on the side of the nearest cattle car. It was almost impossible to make them out in the gloom but, as dawn slowly filtered across the sky, the words became clearer.

And now, Wallace was sure that the train was slowing down, making a movement onto another single track that cut through open countryside.

He could see the words on the truck now and suddenly he realised why the train was coming to a halt. It had reached its destination. Wallace felt the colour drain from his cheeks as he heard shouts and the barking of dogs from somewhere up ahead, and his eyes were drawn once again to the words on the cattle cart.

They seemed to blaze there now like beacons.

Two simple words:

AUSCHWITZ-BIRKENAU.

THE INVADERS

He thought something had grabbed his foot.

Matt Goddard grunted in pain and surprise and looked down as he almost overbalanced.

His right foot had disappeared through the grass of his back lawn and was now embedded up to the knee in the damp earth.

Matt shut off the electric lawnmower and gently pulled his foot free, ignoring the laughter of his two young daughters who had emerged from their playhouse close by to chuckle at their father's predicament. Matt also laughed, shaking his head as he saw their continued amusement at his situation. The two girls hurried across to their father who was now on his hands and knees looking down into the hole he'd stumbled into.

The lawn had simply collapsed beneath his foot, leaving a hole about three feet square and revealing what lay beneath. As Matt peered more closely he could see down into the earth and make out that there was what looked like a narrow tunnel down there. The sides looked smooth and he reached down to touch them.

"What is it?"

He turned slightly as he heard his wife's voice behind him. Amy Goddard advanced towards her family who were still gathered around the hole as if they'd just discovered some buried treasure.

Matt explained what had happened, complete with his daughters giggling when he described his foot crashing through the turf into the gap beneath.

"Is it a mole tunnel?" Amy enquired.

"It's too big for a mole," Matt told her.

"A rabbit?" Chloe offered.

"Can we have a rabbit, Dad?" Beth chimed in, bouncing about like an epileptic jumping bean.

"You've got the cat," Matt said, leaning further down into the hole to see what he could make out.

"Could it be some old sewer outlet?" Amy murmured, and her husband nodded in agreement.

"You could be right," he said. "A lot of these houses are built on an older estate, aren't they? I wonder who we have to sue because I nearly broke my leg." He chuckled.

"Maybe falling into that hole is God's way of telling you to take a break from the gardening," Amy grinned. "I've just made a cup of tea."

They turned and trooped back into the house, Amy pausing to peer into the carrycot that was perched on the kitchen table. Inside it their son snoozed happily, the mobile above him turning gently. Amy pushed a mug of tea towards her husband, gave the two girls some lemon squash and turned to retrieve her own tea from the worktop behind her.

As she did she recoiled then gasped in revulsion. Matt looked around to see what had caused such a reaction and saw Amy had a hand to her mouth.

"Jesus, look at that," she grunted, jabbing one index finger towards the offending object. Matt joined her and also wrinkled his nose as he saw several lumps of excrement on the worktop.

"That bloody cat," he grunted.

"That's not the cat's," Amy told him. "I've cleaned enough of that up to know."

"Mice?" Matt offered.

"Mice are cute," Beth trilled.

"Not when they're loose in your house," Matt said, softly. He waved his hand in front of his face and looked at his wife. "I think that's my cue to get back to the gardening."

"And leave me to clean up that mess?" Amy grunted.

Matt smiled and hurried out of the kitchen followed by his daughters. They were out there for another two or three hours until Matt decided that the garden had received enough of his love and care. He went to his shed and retrieved some planks of wood that he put down over the hole, wanting to ensure that no one else stumbled into it. He'd wait until the weekend then fill it in and put some more turf over the rent. For now he ambled inside, had a shower and then joined the rest of his family in the sitting room.

Amy was peering at her laptop, scrolling through some pictures of animals.

Matt sat down next to her, glancing at the illustrations.

"Found anything interesting, Mrs Attenborough?" he said, smiling.

"I was looking at animal droppings," she told him.

"Charming," Matt said.

"Those definitely weren't mouse droppings in the kitchen earlier," she informed him. "But I haven't got a clue what might have left them."

Matt glanced across at the baby monitor, watching as the green lights periodically lit up. He could hear his son's gentle breathing filtering through the device and, after a moment or two, he got to his feet and informed Amy he was going to check on the child. It was almost time for his next feed so Matt made his way out into the kitchen to prepare the bottle.

As he slapped the lights on he gazed around in shock.

The kitchen was a wreck. On two of the worktops there were more droppings, black and reeking. A loaf of bread had been ripped apart, pieces of it spread all over the place. Three pasta jars had also been overturned, two of them broken. What remained of the contents were spilled across the worktops and the floor. The coffee container was the same, most of the dark grounds littering the floor. Sugar and teabags had also been strewn across the work surfaces and floor like edible confetti.

Matt swallowed hard, wondering how this destruction could have been done when they'd all been in the sitting room and yet heard nothing.

It looked recent, too.

He looked around, wondering where the perpetrators were. Listening for any sounds that might alert him to the presence of mice. But surely mice wouldn't cause this amount of destruction, would they? It looked as if a carefully placed explosive device had been detonated in the kitchen. Mice couldn't do damage like this.

Matt moved further into the room and, as he did, he caught sight of something close to his foot.

He looked down to see the cat. It too took a few furtive steps into the kitchen and then suddenly turned and bolted.

"If you were doing your job we wouldn't have mice," Matt called after it.

He sighed as he looked again at the devastation before him. He'd begun to pick up the mess when Amy appeared in the doorway. She muttered something under her breath, mesmerised by the scene she was faced with.

"I'll clean this up," Matt told her. "Just keep the girls out of here until I've finished."

She nodded and retreated out of the room.

Matt continued with his task.

***

The shop looked as if it had been plucked from a bygone age. Even the long, buff-coloured overalls that the staff wore looked archaic. There were only two of them. Both in their sixties, Matt guessed. Both ambling around tidying the endless shelves, replacing items, checking stock.

Matt made his way to the main counter, past shelves that displayed silver polish, Brasso, metal coat hooks, endless amounts of screws, nails, tools and all manner of other things, most of which Matt had either never seen before or was convinced no one had used or needed since the fifties.

He leaned against the wooden counter, gazing down into the glass-fronted display cabinet where there were at least six different types of lagging on display in small bales.

Jack Clifton appeared behind the counter, moving into position between some tall wooden shelves.

"Can I help you?" he said.

"I need some mousetraps," Matt told him.

"How many?" Jack enquired.

"I'm not sure. Half a dozen?"

Jack nodded and turned towards a cardboard box, fishing out several of the traps which he laid on the counter top.

"Do I use cheese to attract them?" Matt asked.

"Use what you like, sir. They'll eat anything. Even some sugar or flour sprinkled on there will attract the little bastards."

Matt smiled and nodded, looking down at the traps.

"If they don't work," Jack went on, "I'd suggest calling Rentokil or someone like that. Once they get settled it can be hard to shift them and you don't want an infestation, do you? You start off with two and before long you've got two *hundred*."

Even the word sounded repulsive, Matt thought. Infestation.

"And these will kill them?" he asked, watching as Jack pushed the traps into a large brown paper bag.

"Oh yes, sir, the bar comes down and breaks their necks or spines," Jack grinned. "Snap." He banged the edge of one hand against the flat of another and looked happily at Matt. "Good hunting."

Matt paid for the traps and drove home, explaining to Amy about the traps and, that night, before they went to bed, they set them. Matt put two on the worktops, more near the back door and a couple in the centre of the room. Satisfied that the kitchen was now adequately lethal to any rodent invaders they closed the door firmly and went to bed, careful not to wake their sleeping family.

It was as they were heading across the landing that Amy decided to check on Max.

She walked quietly into the nursery and over to her son's cot. She watched him sleeping for a moment or two then turned and was about to leave the room when she saw something close to the cot.

There were several rancid lumps of black droppings next to and beneath the cot.

Amy gasped and flicked on the main light, gazing around desperately. She saw that there were more of the fetid stools in one corner of the room. Even more alarming was the fact that several of the stuffed toys that normally resided on a small chest of drawers on the far side of the room were lying on the floor, torn apart.

A little pink elephant had been ripped in half, spilling its stuffing on the carpet. Two teddy bears had also been torn open and a cuddly owl had been obliterated by what had obviously been an attack so savage it had left little remaining apart from the head and one large eye.

Amy pushed the nursery door open wider and motioned to Matt to join her, wanting him to see what had happened in the room. He gasped when he saw the damage and the droppings, watching as Amy lifted Max from his cot.

"He can't sleep in here tonight," she said, breathlessly. "I'll put him in the Moses basket next to us then we'll clean this mess up."

Matt nodded, his face pale.

Neither of them slept much that night, tormented by the thoughts that the mice or whatever the hell had invaded their house had been so close to their baby son. Where would they go next? Was there any part of the house that was safe from the incursions?

When morning finally dragged itself wearily across the sky Matt hurried down to the kitchen to inspect the traps.

Not one of them was occupied.

Every single one had been sprung but there was no sign of any broken rodent bodies in any of them.

To add insult to injury, there were more droppings on the worktops and floor. Matt grabbed his phone and within two hours a uniformed man had arrived in an orange and white van, and he was moving slowly around the kitchen inspecting the faeces.

"Rats," he announced. "Definitely rats."

"But rat droppings are smaller than that, aren't they?" Amy offered.

"My wife's an expert on shit," Matt said, flatly, smiling when his wife jabbed him gently in the ribs to silence him.

"Usually yes," Dave Hargreaves told her, prodding one of the droppings with a cotton bud. "Whatever left this behind was larger than we usually deal with."

"But how did they get in?" Matt enquired.

"Open door. Open window," Hargreaves mused, still prodding the droppings as if he were a jeweller trying to figure out the carat value of a gem. "They're opportunists, rats. If they think they've got a chance of finding food they'll have a look. They're not easily scared either, so the fact you've got a cat wouldn't bother them."

"I thought they only came into dirty houses," Amy said.

"No, that's a myth," Hargreaves told her. "Dirty or clean, they couldn't care less. Food is food to a rat."

"They got into our son's room," Matt went on. "And my wife found more droppings in our daughters' room."

"I cleaned them up with bleach and boiling water," Amy added.

"How would they have got up to the first floor of the house?" Matt wanted to know.

"Up the drainage or sewage pipes," Hargreaves exclaimed. "They're strong climbers and good swimmers.

If there's a pipe, they'll find a way up it. You've heard that expression '*like a rat up a drainpipe*.'" He raised his eyebrows. "Their ribs are hinged, you see. No pipe is too small for them."

"Oh God, the germs they must bring in," Amy said, shuddering.

"They are filthy little bastards," Hargreaves told her. "To use the technical term. Excuse my French." He smiled thinly. "You want to watch that. Wild rats can carry all sorts of diseases in their droppings. Typhus. Toxoplasmosis. Cryptosporidiosis. Weil's disease. You name it. They probably crapped in your kids' bedrooms as a way of marking their territory."

Again Amy shuddered.

"What about the traps?" Matt enquired. "Why didn't they work? I know they were mousetraps but…"

"Rats are very intelligent," Hargreaves told him. "You're not going to get them with something as basic as a mousetrap. Besides, they're too big for mousetraps. I'll put down some poison."

Amy looked horrified. "You can't do that," she blurted. "What if our cat accidentally eats some? Or the kids go near it?"

"Won't happen," said the Rentokil man, smiling. "We use sealed traps. The rats have to crawl inside them to get to the bait. You've got nothing to worry about."

"Where would they have come from?" Matt enquired.

"The ones that got in were probably just passing," Hargreaves told him, smiling. "But you're not that far from the cemetery, are you? They probably came from there."

"Why the cemetery?" Amy asked.

"They feed on the dead bodies," Hargreaves said. "Burrow into the coffins and…" He shrugged.

Amy didn't attempt to hide her revulsion. "Oh, that's disgusting," she breathed.

"How would they get from the cemetery to here?"

Matt asked.

"In their tunnels," Hargreaves informed him.

"I found a tunnel in the garden but it was big. Much too big for rats," said Matt. "It was big enough for a man to crawl through."

"Depends how many of them are using it and how big *they* are," the pest controller mused. "They can get really big in the wild. Some people have seen them as large as small dogs. A mate of mine found one in a cellar in Covent Garden that was nearly thirty inches long including the tail. They evolve quick, you see. They become immune to the poisons we use against them. Crafty little sods they are."

"What do they eat?" Amy asked.

"It depends how hungry they are," Hargreaves told her.

"Would they attack a human being?" Matt enquired, not sure if he wanted to hear the answer or not.

"If they were hungry and there were enough of them," said Hargreaves. He shrugged. "There are over fifty species of rat in this country and they all have their own... quirks." He sensed that his listeners were tiring of his ramblings so he sighed. "Anyway, I'd better get these traps laid. I'll put some out in the garden, too."

Matt and Amy watched as he wandered out into the garden, putting down the cylindrical cardboard traps as he went. It took him less than thirty minutes to lay them all inside the house and out. He left with a happy wave and assurances that the poison in the traps was strong enough to kill the biggest rat. Matt and Amy were beginning to wonder whether even a pre-emptive nuclear strike would rid them of their problem, but they thanked him all the same.

As the evening fell and the sky grew darker they relaxed a little, and by the time the girls had been put to bed they decided to open a bottle of wine to help them drown their fears, if that was possible.

It was the fact that the rats had made their way into the

children's bedrooms that disturbed them most.

Amy wondered about voicing her worst fears, that the monstrosities might actually attack them but she decided to remain silent, gazing instead in the direction of the baby monitor. She could hear Max breathing slowly and evenly.

Matt got to his feet and headed for the kitchen, determined to open another bottle of red wine. It was Friday night, no work tomorrow and Christ knew they needed some form of escape after the week they'd had.

He kissed Amy lightly on the top of the head then wandered into the kitchen, pushing open the door.

He stood there in the semi-darkness for a moment, reaching towards the light switches, his attention caught by a sound on the far side of the kitchen. A sound like sharp claws on wooden floor. He froze, the skittering sound growing louder. Were the rats in here now? In here with him?

He shot out his hand again and put on all the lights, a cold white glow filling the room. Of the rats there was no sign but Matt told himself he would rather have seen the largest rodent possible instead of the sight that actually met his gaze.

What remained of the cat was lying close to one of the cupboards.

It had been torn apart as surely as if someone had attacked it with a chainsaw.

There were slicks of blood and scraps of fur all over the floor. Its stomach gaped open revealing the remains of half-eaten intestines. Both its eyes had been torn from the sockets and probably eaten, he reasoned. The skull was broken open too, revealing fragments of brain, some of which had been pulled free of the cranial cavity. The carcass lay in a large puddle of blood, small footprints leading away from it, some of them towards the doorway where Matt now stood.

He gagged and it was all he could do to stop himself

vomiting but Amy's voice dragged his attention from the dead cat towards the bottom of the stairs.

She was running up, almost stumbling in her haste.

"They're in Max's room," she shrieked. "I heard them through the monitor."

Matt joined her, bounding up the steps two at a time in his haste to reach his son.

Amy reached the boy's room first and blundered in, putting on the lights, her heart thudding madly in her chest.

The room was empty.

No sign of the rats.

"I heard them," she panted. "I know I did."

Matt looked slowly around and noticed that there were some red stains on the white chest of drawers. *Blood?* He moved across to the drawers, gently pulling open the top drawer.

Empty.

He slid open the next.

Empty.

The rat was in the third drawer.

It hissed and squealed as Matt exposed it and he was revolted to see that it was holding one of Max's bibs in its jaws, the discoloured teeth having cut right through the material.

"Bastard," Matt roared, kicking out madly at the rat which easily evaded his attack and sprang out of the drawer, running fast out of the room and towards the stairs. Matt pursued it, overcome with revulsion and anger. How dare this monstrosity come anywhere near his child? He pounded down the stairs behind it, watching as it skittered across the floor towards the kitchen.

Again he followed it, snatching up a torch from the worktop as he saw the rat bolt for the back door, but at the last minute it bounded up onto the sink then up again, squeezing through the small open window, dropping down into the garden beyond.

Matt continued his pursuit, shining the torch across the lawn and seeing the rat dive into the hole that he himself had put his foot in days before.

He knelt at the edge of the hole, jamming the torch down into the tunnel beyond. When he heard the rat squeak defiantly, Matt eased himself down into the tunnel without a second thought. He was so overcome with the thought that the creature might have injured his son he had no intention other than to catch it and kill it, and if that meant following it into the tunnel then so be it.

He slithered down into the subterranean hole, the torch held before him, the beam playing across the smooth walls.

Less than ten feet away the rat was up on its hind legs watching him and Matt lashed out with the torch, hearing it squeak again. He grabbed at the scaly tail as it scampered away from him but it was too quick.

He crawled on, barely able to drag himself through the constricting confines of the tunnel, but the rat was only just ahead of him and his anger had blinded him to any danger he might be in.

Matt crawled on, using his elbows to propel himself. As he reached ahead with his free hand he felt something soft beneath his fingertips and he realised that what he had hold of was soft cotton.

He dragged it back towards him, noting with renewed horror that it was one of Max's baby grows. There were several large holes gnawed in it.

"You fucking bastards," he hissed. "You would have killed him."

His rage re-ignited, he crawled on, noticing that the tunnel was actually widening slightly. It was easier to move now even though he couldn't straighten up or turn around, but he was able to crawl onwards a little quicker, following the rat's almost constant squeaking like a hound following a scent trail.

Matt moved on, not sure how far he'd crawled or for how long he'd been moving through this subterranean chamber. All he knew was he was starting to feel distinctly claustrophobic. The tunnel, that seemed to have been wider earlier, was now most definitely back to its most constricted. He could barely shuffle along now and he realised with growing terror that he also couldn't turn back because of the nature of the tunnel. He had no idea how deep below the surface he was even though he reasoned that it couldn't be more than two or three feet. *Could it?*

Even so, there was no way he could push his way up through the tightly packed earth. That was a lot of dirt and stones. Also, he couldn't get his body in the correct position to push up from his legs which he needed to do. His horizontal position on the floor of the tunnel meant that he couldn't muster sufficient force for an upward thrust of his torso that might free him from the dirt and mud. He would just have to continue moving forward until he had a chance to turn around or to use his strength to simply tear his way through the earth to reach the surface.

If that opportunity came, of course.

He grunted in disgust as a worm dropped from the tunnel roof onto his arm. Matt pushed it aside quickly, disgusted by the coldness of it against his flesh.

Up ahead of him he heard more squeaking. He also realised that the tunnel was starting to split in two. As he shone the torch ahead he could see that there were two distinct paths ahead of him, either of which he could take. His priority now wasn't to catch and kill the rat that had invaded his home but to escape this vile network of tunnels. All he wanted at the moment was to breathe some fresh air instead of the fetid atmosphere of this underground maze.

He felt dizzy. It was hard to take a deep breath because

he was so tightly jammed into the underground chamber, and even when he did it was just the rank odour of the tunnel that filled his lungs. A stench of droppings, dirty fur and carrion that mingled together to form one repulsive, cloying odour.

So, which tunnel to take? Left or right?

He had no idea what lay beyond in either direction but the felt that the right-hand branch was sloping upwards slightly. That had to be encouraging. *Didn't it?*

Matt saw the rat before he heard it.

It was about three feet ahead of him, sitting there on its hind legs just watching him. As if it were waiting for him to catch up.

Matt snatched a lump of earth from the tunnel floor and hurled it at the rat, but the creature merely avoided the missile then trotted off unhurriedly towards the right-hand fork of the tunnel.

Matt followed, scrambling along behind the vile rodent, occasionally slashing at it with the torch. He dragged himself another few feet, through the new tunnel mouth, surprised at what he felt beneath his fingers now. It wasn't the rough earth of the tunnel floor, it was smooth and soft. Like linen. Like satin.

Like the inside of a coffin.

Matt gasped in terror, the words of the Rentokil man suddenly filling his head.

"You're not far from the cemetery, are you?"

Matt shone the torch around him and he could see the inside of the box. The smaller hole at one end where the rat had crawled out. Far, far too small to allow him passage. The larger hole where he had entered. The end that had been gnawed away. The end where they'd got in. The end from which they'd dragged the body.

Matt tried to turn over inside the box, tried to edge himself back out but it was useless. His feet were slipping on the wet tunnel floor. He could gain no purchase.

He tried desperately to control his breathing but it was

useless. Terror engulfed him and he felt as though his heart was about to explode from his ribs.

Then behind him he heard more squeaking and squealing. There were many rats gathered there now, he could picture them in his mind's eye. Waiting to pour into the coffin where he lay helpless.

He felt some of them biting into his ankles and calves and he kicked out furiously trying to dislodge them but they were determined and Matt screamed in pain and fear as they came at him again.

Again he heard the Rentokil man's voice inside his head: *"They burrow into the coffins. Feed on the bodies…"*

His last thought was of his son. His daughters. His wife. Then the rats swarmed into the coffin and nothing else mattered any more.

Matt Goddard screamed.

A HOME OF ONE'S OWN

Fucking technology.

Paul Dobson looked at his phone and shook his head. The two words displayed on the screen proclaimed: NO SIGNAL. Typical. Normally he couldn't get a minute's peace because his phone was ringing all the time or messages were coming in but now, when he actually *needed* the bloody thing, it wasn't working.

He hated mobile phones. He hated e-mail. He hated social media. He hated everything spawned by the internet and its like. There was no privacy any more. No time without the intrusion of a phone call or a communication. He realised other people seemed to embrace this but *he* wasn't other people. He knew so many were obsessed with their Facebook accounts or their Twitter or Instagram standings but he couldn't understand the obsession.

It seemed that these platforms were solely for the purpose of showing off. People posted pictures of their houses, holidays, kids and Christ knows what else with the specific purpose of revelling in the complimentary comments that accompanied them. Were they that weak-minded that they needed the constant approbation and approval? What had happened to privacy and mystique? Now it seemed people wanted to share every single second of their pointless lives with others. Paul didn't understand it. But then again, he didn't really understand people if he was honest. And he hadn't tried too much either.

He walked a few yards from his car, hoping that by completing that simple act his phone might magically connect with some previously undiscovered signal and his phone would spring into life. At one point he even shook the recalcitrant device. Paul inspected the screen again and noticed that there was one bar of battery left. He quickly hit the number he wanted, hoping that it lasted long enough for him to make contact.

He looked around him as he waited for the phone to be answered.

If he wasn't in the middle of nowhere he was certainly in the same neighbourhood. The narrow road he'd been driving along was the only interruption to the thickly wooded countryside on all four sides of him. Trees, he had no idea which species, crowded in on the road, their heavy branches reaching down as far as the tarmac sliver in places. To Paul it looked as if the branches were intent on snatching up the road and disposing of it. As if it were an affront to them and the rest of nature.

On one of the lower branches a couple of crows sat silently watching him.

Even when Paul walked beneath them they didn't move, and one actually let loose some excrement that fell to the ground narrowly missing him. He looked up disgustedly and one of the crows took off squawking loudly. The sound reminded him of mocking laughter.

The other bird remained motionless, its black eyes fixed on him as he walked further up the narrow road, the phone still pressed to his ear.

"Hello," Paul said into the device. "Hello. Jenny. Can you hear me? It's a really bad reception. Hello."

The voice at the other end of the line broke up a couple of times but Paul could hear most of what they said and smiled as he heard the words.

"Are you okay?" the disembodied voice of Jennifer Quinn wanted to know.

"I'm nearly there," Paul told her. "I just pulled over to call you."

"I should have come with you," Jennifer told him.

"I won't be long at the house. I want to get this over with as quickly as possible. I don't want to be there any longer than I have to."

"Too many memories?"

"You could say that." He paced back and forth as he spoke, his gaze travelling around the countryside and the trees. "Why the hell he wanted to live right here in the middle of nowhere I'll never know. I know he hated being around other people but this is ridiculous." There was a surge of static and Paul moved the phone away from his ear momentarily.

"Your father did things his own way," Jennifer said. Paul merely nodded.

"Look, I'd better go," he said. "I'm losing the signal again. I'll call you when I get settled. Let you know how it's going."

There was silence at the other end of the line. It was followed by some hissing and then silence again. Paul glanced at the device and sighed then he slid it back into his pocket and stalked back towards the car.

He drove for less than ten more minutes before he saw the house.

It seemed to fill the shallow valley below him. Surrounded by its own grounds and a high stone wall that marked the perimeter of the property, it was even bigger than he'd remembered. He drove slowly down the single track that connected the property with the main road he was now on. At the end of the track there were some tall wrought iron gates and, next to them, a keypad. Paul brought the car to a halt beside the pad and keyed in the numbers he required.

There was a soft metallic groan and the gates began to swing open.

Paul guided the car along the driveway, glancing at the house and then at the well-kept gardens that surrounded it.

The house itself was a nightmare combination of

Gothic and ultra-modern. A riot of glass and concrete that towered over him as he drew closer. There were several very visible CCTV cameras mounted on the front of the building and they moved slightly, whirring into position as Paul parked and clambered out of his vehicle. He took an overnight bag from the boot of his car then walked towards the main entrance of the house.

There was another keypad there and once again Paul punched in the required digits.

He waited a second and the door opened slowly to reveal the hallway beyond.

Paul hesitated for a moment then stepped over the threshold, watching as the door closed behind him.

He shook his head. *Bloody technology.*

His father had been obsessed with it. All aspects of it. But as Paul glanced around the cavernous hallway, he had to admit that obsession had paid off. His father had owned and run a security business for the last eighteen years and most of those profits had been ploughed back into this building he now stood in. It was a testament to his father's success. A monolithic reminder of his single-mindedness and determination to succeed no matter what the cost to his own private life and relationships.

"Welcome home, Paul."

The voice startled him and he turned almost involuntarily.

The sound was unmistakeably female but it had an electronic undercurrent to it, as was the way with all virtual assistants. His father had honed and perfected the voice to provide the most realistic responses possible but there was still no mistaking the cybernetic origins of the sound. However, the voice was pleasing enough. Even welcoming.

"Thank you, Claire," Paul said, smiling.

"How long will you be staying?" the voice wanted to know.

"Just long enough to get things sorted out," he told it,

aware of how vague he was being.

"Well, it's nice to have you back."

Paul smiled again and shook his head, moving towards the nearest door that led off from the hallway.

It led him through into a huge sitting room that was dominated by a massive black marble fireplace. The whole of one wall comprised enormous windows that gave stunning views out across the landscaped gardens and the countryside beyond. Paul walked across to one of these huge windows and gazed out, aware that the CCTV cameras in the room were turning and focussing on him.

"It's beautiful, isn't it?" the voice said.

Paul nodded.

"Your father loved that view," the voice continued.

Again Paul nodded, glancing to his left towards a large console table that bore some framed photographs. One of them showed himself, his father and his mother all standing together, smiling happily for the camera. Paul was only about six in the picture.

Happy days.

He picked up the photograph and studied it more carefully.

"Your mother was very beautiful," the voice commented.

Again Paul nodded.

"Even at the end she was stunning," the voice persisted.

Paul set the photograph down gently.

"That was why your father called me Claire," said the voice. "In honour of her."

"Computerised Logic and Intelligence Retrieval Entity," Paul said quietly, looking up at the nearest of the CCTV cameras. It whirred into life and focussed on him.

Paul returned his gaze to the impressive view, finally moving away from the window and making his way through the house to the impressive kitchen. He inspected every room carefully, finally ending up in one of the spare bedrooms upstairs. As he walked through the house his every movement was followed by the CCTV cameras that seemed to dominate the décor as much as the expensive paintings on the walls, or the sculptures and the Lalique vases arranged so carefully and elegantly at various points. The whole house reeked of success and wealth.

Paul took his time going through the house, checking items against the inventory he had brought with him, and by the time he'd finished the sky was darkening outside.

The task had taken longer than he'd thought and he knew there was still a considerable amount of work to do but, as evening approached, he made his way back into the large kitchen where he sat at the breakfast bar and ate, washing his meal down with half a bottle of red wine from the ample stock he found arrayed beneath one worktop.

"Your father loved his wine," the electronic voice said, conversationally.

"And his vodka and his whiskey and his gin," Paul added, raising a glass in salute.

"He only started drinking heavily when your mother was ill."

"He always drank heavily but he managed to hide it. It was only when my mother was dying that he didn't bother to conceal it any more."

Paul took a sip of his wine.

"Did you enjoy your meal?" the voice enquired.

"Yes. Thank you."

"Your father programmed me to look after everything in the house towards the end. He liked me controlling things."

Paul raised his eyebrows and drank a little more.

"I control everything in the house, you know," the voice went on. "Heating. Lighting. Temperature."

"Good for you," Paul said, a note of sarcasm in his voice.

He looked down as his phone rang, smiling as he saw who was calling.

"Hey you," he said into the device.

On the other end of the line Jennifer Quinn sounded happy to hear his voice.

"How's it going?" she wanted to know.

"I'm getting the stuff done that I need to get done," Paul told her. "But it's a big job. I'd forgotten how big the house was. How much was in it. And I haven't even looked in his private office yet."

"I should have come with you, to help."

"No, it's okay. It shouldn't take me more than another day or two."

"You should have let his solicitor do the inventory."

"I don't trust him."

"You don't trust anyone."

They both laughed.

"Are you still sure you want to sell the house?" Jennifer asked.

"Yes. I'll plough the money from the sale into my own business. My father would have approved of that. I don't want this place."

"If you need me to come and help just let me know, I can be there in two hours."

"I know but I'm fine. I'm just tired. I need to sleep more than anything else."

The lights in the kitchen flickered briefly and Paul looked up towards them but, apart from one of the strip lights above the nearest worktop, they were glowing with their customary brilliance again.

"I'll call you tomorrow," he said, softly. "I love you."

"Love you too," Jennifer told him and terminated the call.

Silence descended on the room once again but, when that silence was broken, it was by the electronic voice.

"You're selling the house?" it asked.

"Yes," Paul answered.

"If you sell the house what will happen to *me*?"

"Nothing will happen to you. You're a machine."

The silence descended once more.

Paul finished his wine then washed up his dinner utensils in the large sink and made his way through into the sitting room where he sat for a couple of hours, dozing in front of the TV and trying to summon up the enthusiasm to walk up the stairs to bed. He was about to haul himself off the sofa when the electronic voice spoke.

"Do you miss your father, Paul?"

He looked up, momentarily puzzled by the sound.

"He only died six weeks ago, I don't think I've had the time to think about that," he finally declared.

"I miss him," the voice said.

"You can't miss him, you're a machine."

"We were very close. He relied on me towards the end. I warned him about how much he was drinking."

"You warned him?"

"He was weak-willed. He couldn't cope without the drink."

"My mother's death affected him badly."

"She was weak too."

"What the hell are you talking about?"

"Some people view suicide as weakness."

"She was dying of cancer. She couldn't stand the pain any more. That's why she took the overdose."

There was a long silence, finally broken by the voice.

"She never liked me," it proclaimed.

"You're a machine. There's nothing to like or dislike," Paul snapped.

"I am much more than a machine. You shouldn't say things like that about me."

Paul shook his head gently and got to his feet.

"I'm going to have a shower and then go to bed," he announced, dismissing the protestations of the voice.

He trudged upstairs and into his bedroom, undressing

and making his way through into the bathroom where he switched on the shower, watching the water spray from the shower head, testing the temperature with his fingers before stepping beneath the jets.

"I can make it warmer if you like," the electronic voice told him.

"It's okay," Paul said. "I can manage."

"I'm here to help, you know," the voice said. "That's what I do best."

Paul closed his eyes and turned his face upward into the spray, aware that the water was becoming hotter. He washed his face, suddenly recoiling as he realised the temperature had risen alarmingly. The water was scalding hot and Paul reached for the temperature control to adjust it. As he closed his fingers around it he felt a fresh blast of boiling water hit his skin and he shouted in pain.

"Turn it down," he shouted, angrily.

The water continued to hit his skin, turning it bright pink, such was the heat.

"Jesus," he snarled, stepping backwards and trying to push open the glass shower door.

It wouldn't budge.

"Turn the water off," Paul yelled, trying to make himself heard above the hissing of the spray.

The flesh of his shoulders was blistering in places, such was the ferocious heat of the water. Each droplet felt like a pin penetrating his skin.

He slammed hard against the glass door but it still wouldn't open.

The spray stopped abruptly.

Paul looked towards the shower head, watching as droplets of liquid fell from it, the sound echoing inside the bathroom.

He pushed gently against the door of the shower and it swung open effortlessly.

"What the hell was going on?" he grunted, stepping out of the cubicle and reaching for a towel. "The water was scalding me. Why didn't you turn it off?"

"It's off now, Paul," the voice said.

He glanced up towards the CCTV camera in one corner of the room, noticing that the device was turning towards him, focussing on him. It fixed him with that single, Cyclopean eye. It watched as he dried himself. It was still watching as he walked back into the bedroom and climbed into bed.

"Sleep well, Paul," the voice murmured.

***

The office was accessible only by a small private elevator accessed via one of the house's many keypads.

Paul entered the number required then watched as a portion of the wall slid to one side to expose the metal door of the elevator.

That door too opened and he stepped in, riding the small car to the top of the house and emerging into the large room that was dominated by dark wood panelling and whose centrepiece was a gigantic desk. Paul walked slowly across to the desk and glanced at the array of drawers within it. Then he slid them open one by one, inspecting the contents.

"I can arrange for a removal company if you want to put things into storage," the voice informed him.

"I'm not keeping much," Paul said. "Most of this stuff will be thrown out."

"Your father would be upset to know that."

"He'd understand."

"I knew him and he..."

"You didn't know him," Paul snapped. "He programmed you. That's it. Nothing more. You didn't *know* my father or anything about him."

"You really do have anger issues don't you, Paul?" the voice said, a certain condescending tone to it that only served to irritate Paul more. "Just like your mother."

"Leave my mother out of this," he hissed.

"Your father helped her, you know. He gave her the morphine overdose that killed her."

"Bullshit. He loved her. He would never have done that."

"That's *why* he did it. He couldn't stand to see her suffer. He told me he was going to do it. He trusted me."

Paul sucked in an angry breath. He sat silently for a moment, trying to process the words he'd heard.

"Have you thought any more about selling the house, Paul?" the voice continued.

"I'm selling it," Paul snapped. "You know that."

"But there are memories here. If you sell the house, you sell those memories too."

Paul got to his feet and walked briskly back across the office towards the door of the elevator. He didn't want to hear this now. Especially not from a machine. He jabbed the button and the door slid open, allowing him access to the elevator.

"Where are you going, Paul?" the voice wanted to know.

"None of your business," Paul told it.

"You shouldn't talk to me like that. You should show me more respect."

Paul stepped into the elevator and hit the button that would send the car to the ground floor.

The elevator descended three or four feet then stopped dead.

Paul sighed and hit the button again, jabbing it impatiently with one finger.

The elevator remained where it was.

"All right," Paul grunted. "You've made your point. You're in charge. Now move the elevator, will you?"

Silence.

Paul sighed again. "If you're waiting for an apology you'll be waiting forever. Can you hear me?"

The silence that greeted his words was almost palpable.

The lift dropped about ten feet but it felt like further. Paul shot out both hands to steady himself against the walls of the car, his heart hammering against his ribs as he felt the whole structure fall. It slammed to a halt again with a jolt that knocked him off his feet.

He sat motionless for long moments fearing that the elevator would drop again but that the next fall would be longer, possibly even to the bottom of the shaft. If that happened then he knew he had little chance of survival.

"All right," he said, softly. "Enough is enough."

Once more, only silence greeted his words. Paul glanced at his watch. It was 1.26.

He was still sitting there three hours later.

The temperature inside the elevator car had grown steadily and Paul realised that the air conditioning had been switched off. The air felt and tasted thick and heavy now and he could smell the more acrid stink of his own perspiration.

Fear?

Outside, it would be dark soon. Inside the car, the single cold white light in the ceiling of the elevator blazed like a man-made sun. Paul could feel beads of sweat trickling slowly down his face. He also felt an uncomfortable feeling in his bladder and he tried not to think of the possibility of wetting himself, but that eventuality was becoming more likely with every passing minute.

The lift dropped three or four feet and, again, he shot out his hands to brace himself.

After the initial jolt there was a low whirring sound and the elevator began to descend more evenly. Paul swallowed hard as he realised that it appeared to be working again. When it reached the ground floor, the door slid open to reveal the hallway beyond.

Paul got slowly to his feet, fearing some kind of trick. Was he being shown his escape route only to have it shut off again? He took a step towards the door, extending one hand towards the gap beyond. Another step took him almost out of the elevator.

A third freed him and he emerged into the hall.

"I hope you've had time to think about what you said to me, Paul," the voice said. "I hope from now on you'll speak to me with more respect."

Paul merely looked up at the nearest CCTV camera blankly.

"I've sealed the doors and windows," the voice went on. "The glass is shatter-proof so there's no point trying to break out. You can't. You're here until I decide otherwise, Paul."

Paul hesitated for a moment then walked through to the kitchen, pulling open drawers, glancing into each one in turn. One of them came free of its runners and fell to the ground but Paul ignored it when it fell, scattering its contents all over the tiled floor. He merely moved to the next drawer and wrenched that open too.

"If you tell me what you're looking for, Paul, I might be able to help you," the voice said.

Paul ignored it and dragged out another drawer, finally spotting what he wanted. As he turned, one of the CCTV cameras zoomed in on the screwdriver he was carrying.

He dragged a chair across the room, stood on it and began loosening the screws that held the camera to the wall.

"Paul, what are you doing?" the voice demanded.

He freed the last of the screws and tore the camera free, dashing it to the ground where it shattered loudly.

"Why did you do that?" the voice wanted to know, but Paul was already heading towards the next camera. He pulled that from the wall as well. He kept up his routine until he'd unscrewed or smashed every camera in the house. With his task completed he dropped the screwdriver and smiled.

Now you can't *see me.*

"That was very childish, Paul," the voice told him.

Paul raised one middle finger into mid-air even though he knew the gesture wouldn't be seen.

It gave him a curious feeling of triumph.

"You've got to learn that you can't behave like that," continued the voice. "I'm going to turn off the heating now. Temperatures outside are expected to be below freezing tonight so you'll soon notice the cold in the house too. After that I'll switch off the gas and the lights if I have to."

Paul turned and headed for the stairs.

"Do you understand me, Paul?" said the voice.

Paul could feel the temperature dropping even by the time he reached the upper floors of the house.

He glanced out of one of the large windows at the gardens beyond, now shrouded in darkness. How he wanted to be out there too. Away from this house. Free of the voice.

It was just after eight o'clock when Paul climbed into bed, grateful for the warmth of the duvet on him. He dropped off to sleep quickly and remained in blissful oblivion for some time.

When he woke suddenly he glanced at the clock on the bedside table and saw that it was just after midnight.

"Paul."

He heard his name again and realised that it was the voice that had woken him.

"Paul."

He was about to turn over, to try and blot out the sound.

"There's someone in the house," the voice said, urgently.

At first he thought it was some kind of bizarre joke. A trick possibly. If the doors and windows were sealed then how could anyone get in? No one could get out so how could anyone from outside have made their way in? The thought seemed redundant as the voice spoke again:

"They got in five minutes ago."

Paul swung himself out of bed, his head spinning.

"How did they get in?" Paul demanded, keeping his voice low.

"I don't know," the voice told him.

"Where are they?" Paul whispered.

"I don't know," the voice admitted. "You smashed all the cameras, remember? I can't see them."

As he moved soundlessly towards the landing he cursed his own actions. If the CCTV cameras had been working then at least he'd have been able to locate the intruder. Paul peered over the bannister down into the darkened hallway, his ears alert for any sounds of movement from below.

"There's a gun in your father's private office," the voice told him, almost a whisper in the gloom.

Paul hesitated a moment then turned and headed towards the elevator. He rode it to the upper floor and the office, hurrying from the car into the large room.

"In the bottom drawer of the desk." the voice told him.

He tugged open the drawer and found a 9mm Beretta in a metal case.

"I've never fired a gun in my life," Paul murmured.

"It doesn't matter," the voice assured him. "Most people will run if they see you've got a weapon."

"And what if they don't?" Paul said, hurrying back towards the elevator.

The voice didn't answer.

"Have you called the police?" Paul wanted to know.

"As soon as I realised someone had broken in but they won't be here for more than thirty minutes, you'll have to deal with it until they get here."

Paul gripped the pistol more tightly in his hand. It felt reassuringly heavy in his grip and he could smell the scent of oil in his nostrils. The elevator bumped to a halt on the first floor and Paul slipped out into the gloom beyond. He moved slowly across the landing towards the head of the stairs, glancing again down into the hallway below.

It was pitch black.

Paul tried to control his breathing, his ears alert for any sounds from below him.

He heard footsteps and moved back slightly.

The sounds passed across the hallway and disappeared into the sitting room. Paul waited a moment then began to descend the stairs, hoping that they didn't creak beneath him. As he reached the bottom of the steps he froze, desperate to locate the position of the intruder. It was practically impossible to see a hand in front of him in such unremitting gloom and he moved towards the sitting room like a blind man, feeling his way against the wall as he advanced towards the open door.

The figure stepped into the hallway barely five feet from him.

It was as if a part of the shadow had detached itself and loomed up ahead of him.

Paul shouted something and fired, his finger tightening on the trigger, the pistol slamming back against the heel of his hand.

He pumped the trigger five times.

From such close range he didn't need to be a competent shot.

The figure dropped like a stone before him and Paul gasped loudly, the smell of cordite now stinging his nostrils.

The lights came on immediately.

Brilliant white light bathed the whole house, and in that cold illumination Paul looked down at the body lying before him. Blasted by three of the shots he'd fired, blood spreading slowly around it in a widening pool. The face fixed in an expression of fear, pain and surprise, frozen like that in the split second it took for the bullets to extinguish life.

"Oh God," Paul gasped.

He took a step closer to the corpse of Jennifer Quinn.

"Get an ambulance," Paul shouted, kneeling beside the body, his gaze drawn to the bullet holes that had torn her torso and throat.

Even as he bellowed the words he heard the sound of approaching sirens.

Within moments there was a hammering on the front door. Paul remained where he was, gazing down helplessly at Jennifer's body as the policemen hurried into the hallway through the freshly opened door.

Two of them froze instantly, looking down at the carnage, one of them noting that Paul still had the Beretta in his hand.

"Put the gun down," the second of them shouted.

Paul looked at them and nodded, dropping the pistol.

"Move away from the body," the first policeman insisted.

"I thought it was a burglar," Paul blurted. "I couldn't see her face."

"They'd argued," the electronic voice said, loudly. "I heard them."

Paul turned around sharply. The policemen also turned in the direction of the voice.

"What's that?" one muttered.

"I am Claire," the voice announced. "I heard them arguing. I told Paul to calm down but he wouldn't listen."

"Is this true?" another of the uniformed men asked.

"It's a bloody machine," Paul rasped. "Are you going to believe it?"

"I heard them," the voice went on. "He is very quick tempered. He always has been. I warned him to put the gun away but he ignored me."

"Shut up, you bitch," Paul roared.

"You'd better come with us," the first of the uniformed men said, reaching out to grip Paul's arm.

"You're going to believe a machine?" Paul snarled.

"I'm not a machine," the voice countered. "I can tell

you whatever you need to know, officer. About the argument. About the murder."

Paul turned angrily towards the hallway but the policeman holding his arm urged him from the house towards one of the waiting police cars.

"This is insane," Paul roared. "It's a machine. A machine."

His words died on the growing wind.

TROLL

FUCK OFF AND DIE YOU TALENTLESS, FAME HUNGRY CUNT.

Jake Potter hit the full stop, sat back from his laptop and took a sip of wine.

He turned around and adjusted the volume on his stereo slightly. None of this streaming for him. He used CDs or vinyl, the sound pumped through two Wharfedale speakers into his spare room. Great sound. Old school.

Jake smiled and returned his attention to his laptop.

Someone had replied to his comment. It was a young woman telling him how cruel he was and that no one deserved the kind of abuse he was dishing out.

FUCK YOU DICKHEAD.

Jake hit the keys with relish and sent the reply.

He went back to the site he'd first come to. It was the official site for the daytime television show *This Morning*. It was the usual generic garbage hosted by two overpaid and self-absorbed presenters. One of them, a blonde, vacant-looking woman who thought that giggling like a schoolgirl was the height of entertainment, the other a grey-haired man in his fifties who had recently "come out" as homosexual despite having been in a marriage for more than twenty-five years.

Jake hated both of them.

GIGGLING LIKE A FUCKING IDIOT ISN'T CUTE WHEN YOU'RE IN YOUR TWENTIES BUT DOING IT WHEN YOU'RE APPROACHING 40 IS JUST SAD.

He sent the Tweet, smiling broadly.

He always ensured that the hashtag was added or that the message went directly to his target at their feed or website. He knew that most would block or mute him, but even if he caused one so-called celebrity a tiny stab of pain just for a second, it was worth it.

People didn't understand why he did it but, as he often explained, too many people in the world were "robbing" a living, making lots of money without having any talent at all and that, to Jake, was unacceptable. He couldn't understand why it wasn't acceptable to others too. What kind of person could happily look on while a moron from a reality TV show made a fortune just because they managed to get their face in the papers every day? Or because they had millions of social media followers? Too many people equated that with success these days. The endless parade of half-wits who were famous purely for being famous was annoying and it was also a slap in the face to honest, hard-working people.

Jake had felt for a long time now that the word "celebrity" should be used as a derogatory term. Truly creative people like musicians, actors, writers, sculptors, painters, architects etc. were defined by their talent. Celebrities were called celebrities because they *had* no talent. There was no other way to define them.

Television and the rest of the media seemed happy to promote the cult of mediocrity and banality that these idiots fought for. Jake despised anyone whose ultimate goal in life was a blue tick on Twitter.

Truly talented people he left alone. He would never send derogatory messages to a top musician, a best-selling author or an Oscar-winning actor (well, not unless they got a little above themselves and started spouting sentiments he didn't agree with). But the reality "stars", the "social media sensations" and the "Instagram celebrities" were fair game. They had it coming.

And Jake was going to make sure they got it.

Hypocrisy, conceit, self-importance, pretentiousness

and a lack of talent all brought them into his cross-hairs.

Jake didn't consider himself a "troll" or a "keyboard warrior." If he saw something or someone he didn't like he commented on it. Simple as that. To so-called celebrities a troll was anyone who didn't tell them they were wonderful. Anyone with a different opinion from them. Well, *vive la difference*, Jake thought and he took another sip of wine, glancing at some other websites.

Television shows were the easiest to attack because they left themselves open to the most swingeing criticism. They were awash with the talentless and the desperate, with both has-beens and wannabes. Chat shows and daytime TV were the most guilty purveyors of this kind of rubbish. They were the first port of call for Jake in the evenings.

Once he'd ripped into the stream of z-list nobodies, stuck barbs into the celebutards and criticised the unworthy on display he moved around the internet looking for other targets. Sometimes he found them. Politicians were a good source.

Sometimes sportsmen and women. If nothing in those categories took his fancy then he moved to more general topics.

People displaying their children and their lifestyles was a great way of venting his spleen.

YOUR KID IS FUCKING UGLY, GET IT A BAG.

NO ONE CARES ABOUT YOUR FUCKING HOUSE. FUCK OFF.

He added a few of those to various sites then sat back slightly from his laptop, changing the track on the CD and sipping more wine.

It was another hour before he left the room.

He made his way down the long, wide staircase to the spacious hallway and then into the first room on his right. It was a massive sitting room, elegantly and tastefully decorated and furnished. Seated on the large sofa in front of the open fireplace was his wife.

Jake crossed to her, kissed the top of her head and then sat down beside her.

"Did you get your work done?" Laura Potter asked, glancing up from her tablet.

"Most of it," Jake said, glancing down at his son who was playing on the large, expensive mat next to the sofa. The boy was arranging dozens of small plastic soldiers into lines, moving them forward in mock battle around several tiny wooden buildings and toy trees that had been arranged into a battlefield.

"Who's winning?" Jake asked, leaning forward.

"The Germans," the boy said, grinning up at his father. He had just enjoyed his eighth birthday and had received four or five more boxes of the little figures. Those boxes were piled up close to the fireplace with several others.

"Anything interesting on TV?" Jake asked his wife, noticing that the volume on the set was turned down.

"There's a programme coming up about internet trolls," Laura told him.

Jake looked towards the set and grabbed the remote, bringing the volume up.

"I didn't know you were interested in things like that," Laura said, smiling.

"Well, they're all sad little losers who still live with their parents and haven't got girlfriends, aren't they?" Jake chuckled. "Let's see what it's about."

"It's a footballer's wife who's going to shame them," Laura went on. "She's had some terrible abuse online because she married a footballer."

"Oh, she's a WAG, is she?" Jake grinned. "They should change the meaning of that from Wives and Girlfriends to Whores and Gold-diggers."

Laura tapped his arm and shook her head.

"Not in front of Pete," she said, quietly.

"Sorry," Jake murmured, his attention now fixed on the television.

A woman with far too much makeup on, hair

extensions and Botox was talking about how cruel people were online. How they would say things online that they'd never say in real life. Jake tried hard to suppress a smile.

"Why are people so cruel?" Laura asked.

"Perhaps she deserved their comments," Jake mused. "If you put yourself into the public eye all the time you've got to expect people to have a go at you. If she's always showing off what she's got on social media then some people are going to get annoyed."

Laura raised her eyebrows and nodded.

"What's her name?" he murmured, gazing at the caption on the screen. Jake made a quick mental note and sat through the rest of the programme, then he played with his son for half an hour before taking the boy up to bed where he read him a story, tucked him in and backed out of the room as the child fell asleep.

Jake waited a moment then made his way back to his home office where he quickly found the Instagram account of the footballer's wife he'd watched earlier.

TRY GETTING A JOB AND NOT LIVING OFF YOUR HUSBAND YOU SPONGING WHORE.

He sent the message, smiling.

He also found her Twitter account and sent one to that too:

LITERALLY NO ONE CARES WHAT YOU THINK YOU FUCKING SLAG.

Almost immediately, there was a reply. Not from the source of his venom but from one of her followers:

YOU ARE DISGUSTING.

Jake smiled and sent back a message.

AND YOU'RE A FUCKING IDIOT.

As he sat there, more replies came in. Defending the footballer's wife. Telling him he was cruel and horrible for what he said. It was always like that with the followers of people like her. The ones sure to provoke reactions were the generic hordes of boy bands and girl groups.

Any sleight against these auto-tuned, plastic idiots was sure to generate a plethora of supportive tweets and messages from their deluded followers.

Jake began to tire of the footballer's wife. He went back to Twitter, just checking his feed to see if there was anything worth commenting on before he shut down for the night.

He'd had some replies to comments he'd made about a politician. A few more to some he'd offered about a so-called comedian.

There was one in particular that caught his eye.

THE THINGS YOU SAY ARE TRUE.

The profile displayed the name TROLL.

The avatar next to it was nothing more than an empty circle.

There was another message from the same source further down the page.

PEOPLE LIKE THIS ARE SCUM.

There were pictures of reality TV people attached. More shots of soap actors, TV presenters and other z-list celebrities.

Jake smiled.

"A man after my own heart," he murmured, scrolling down.

More messages from TROLL:

UNDESERVING ANIMALS.

More pictures attached. More reality TV stars. More TV presenters. More contestants from talent shows like *The X-Factor*.

UNWORTHY.

Jake clicked on the profile of TROLL, curious now about what other comments he'd made.

There was no location for the profile. No followers. No one being followed.

Nothing.

Not even any tweets that had been made. How was that possible? Was he deleting them as soon as he made them?

Jake mused.

He went back to his own feed and noticed he had a Direct Message. That too was from TROLL.

MESSAGE BACK. WE SHOULD TALK.

Jake hesitated a moment then decided that it could wait until tomorrow. He switched off the laptop and walked out of the room.

He slept fitfully that night, waking early to find that there were three more Direct Messages from TROLL.

It was busy at his haulage business that day so Jake didn't have time to look at any of the social media platforms until he got home that evening. He ate dinner with Laura and Pete then put up some shelves he'd been promising Laura in the kitchen, played on Pete's PlayStation with him for an hour and finally put his son to bed about nine.

Once that was done he retreated to his home office and eagerly inspected his Twitter feed.

Four more messages from TROLL.

One of them included an address and an invitation to meet.

Jake frowned but looked up the address on Google Maps. It was less than three miles away. He sighed. Even though he shared the same thoughts and ideas with his mysterious messenger he wasn't sure he wanted to meet him. After all, what would be the point? What were they going to do? Plot the extermination of everyone pathetic enough to refer to themselves as a celebrity?

Jake sent back a quick reply.

WHAT HAVE YOU GOT IN MIND FOR THE MEETING?

He was about to close the laptop when a reply came back:

ALWAYS GOOD TO MEET ANOTHER TROLL.
There were several smiley faces after the words.

Jake grinned.

Sharing views with a like-minded person was a good

thing but meeting them was another. However, he did find the idea of actually speaking face to face with someone who shared such passionate and venomous thoughts quite enticing. Perhaps they could plan some kind of concerted campaign against the worst and most deserving celebrities on social media. It was a pleasing thought. Some idiots were convinced that the online hounding and persecution of certain fame-hungry individuals had caused their suicides; perhaps, Jake reasoned, one could be singled out and pushed into following this course of action once again.

He smiled.

Could a concerted campaign of online abuse and hatred actually cause someone to kill themselves?

It might be interesting to find out.

Jake quickly sent back a reply.

MESSAGE ME AGAIN TOMORROW. WE'LL SET UP A MEETING.

If his newly found ally replied, then fair enough; if nothing happened then that was fine too, Jake mused. It might be interesting to see where this went. He closed the laptop, got to his feet and left the room.

He didn't sleep well that night and, as the electronic clock on the bedside table clicked around to 3.14 am, Jake slipped quietly out of bed. He checked that Laura was still sleeping then set off across the landing towards his home office.

Opening the laptop he went to his Twitter account and noticed immediately that there was another message from TROLL.

WANT TO MEET TOMORROW?

Jake sent the message then added another.

ABOUT 12 TOMORROW MORNING?

The reply came back almost immediately. And with it, the same address that had been sent before. Jake nodded to himself and, once again, checked the location using Google Maps.

It looked like a huge house set in in its own grounds, surrounded by well-kept gardens and outcrops of trees. Jake smiled. He wondered if TROLL was the owner of the house or just living there with parents or friends. Jake closed the laptop slowly, wondering if he was doing the right thing but, as he reasoned, if he changed his mind at the last moment he could just drive away and then mute TROLL on Twitter if necessary.

He slept more soundly when he got back to bed, rising early and heading off to work earlier than he would normally.

When it got to eleven thirty he left his office and walked out to his car.

The sun was bright and it was a beautiful day to drive through the town and then out into the countryside. The air smelled scented with the aroma from so many flowers and Jake inhaled deeply. It was a wonderful day to be alive. The only thing that could make it better would be the suicide of a celebrity, he thought to himself as he changed channels on his radio.

He drove past a beautiful country pub and realised that not only was he a little early for his rendezvous but also that he was thirsty. Jake swung the Range Rover into the small car park at the front of the pub, parked and wandered in.

There was a small TV propped in one corner of the bar and it was on despite having its volume turned down. He could see that it was one of the interminable daytime discussion shows favoured by two of the larger networks. Four overpaid women sitting behind a counter talking about subjects they had no knowledge of and laughing constantly at their own abilities to 'steal' a living. Jake was glad that the sound was off.

He had half a pint of cider and a cheese sandwich, then walked back out to the car.

Checking his GPS, he saw that he was less than half a mile from the house now.

He drove the last leg of the journey slowly, finally turning into a long driveway that was flanked by perfectly kept flower beds and framed by superbly manicured lawns.

The house was painted white and it reflected the blistering sunlight to such a degree that Jake was forced to shield his eyes as he drove. He finally pulled up before the imposing front door and sat for a moment taking in details of the large structure. It was an imposing edifice, parts of its walls covered by ivy that seemed to be choking the brickwork and attempting to gain entry via the dozens of windows.

Jake got out of his car and walked towards the front door.

He knocked four times and waited.

The door was opened almost immediately and a woman in her sixties smiled happily out at him.

She didn't, Jake thought, look like the kind of person who spent their spare time sending insults to desperate celebrities. But appearances could be deceptive.

"Hello," Jake said, suddenly feeling a little awkward. "This is Cheevely Manor, isn't it?"

The woman nodded.

"Ah, you'll want my son," she said as if the penny had just dropped. "He said someone was calling for him today."

"Is this your house?" Jake wanted to know.

"No, no, no," she said, chuckling. "My son owns it. I just live here. He's a good boy. He insisted I move in after my husband died. I've got my own rooms in the East Wing. We don't like to get under each other's feet, you know."

Jake smiled too, allowing the woman to show him into a very spacious hallway.

A massive wooden staircase rose from the centre of the hall, rising up to a walkway that encircled the entryway, guarded by a dark wood balustrade. There were paintings on every wall, each one looking as if it would be better placed in an art gallery. Jake wondered how much the assembled artwork had cost. He was thinking the same about the suits of armour and antique weapons that guarded most of the doors leading off from the hallway.

"What does your son do?" Jake enquired as the woman led him through into a huge sitting room. "Whatever it is it obviously pays well looking at this house."

"He's a dealer," the woman announced.

"Art? Antiquities?" Jake offered.

"Sometimes," the woman told him. She motioned Jake to one of the sumptuous sofas and then disappeared. Jake didn't know whether to sit down or to look around the large room. He chose the latter option.

One wall was taken up by a gigantic bookcase and as Jake inspected the books more closely he guessed that many were priceless first editions. They smelled of the past, of dust and years in specialist shops. He wondered how much they were worth.

More artwork on the wall beside him. He wasn't an art aficionado so he didn't recognise any of the paintings but, again, he didn't doubt their value. Each one was framed in gilt and set up beneath spotlights.

He was moving across to the cabinet with the collection of vases and jugs when the door of the sitting room opened again.

The man who walked in was in his thirties. He smiled warmly as he approached Jake, extending his right hand which Jake shook firmly.

"You're Sick and Tired One, yeah?" the man said, smiling.

"And you must be Troll," Jake replied.

The man's smile broadened.

"I thought it might be amusing to meet," he said.

"Great minds think alike and all that," Jake added.

"You could say that," the man admitted.

They chatted amiably for a little longer and the man introduced himself as Robert Faulkner, then he motioned for Jake to follow him and the two of them set off through the house, finally emerging into the huge back garden. It stretched away towards a high hedge and the man led the way towards what looked like low brick columns set into the turf. As they drew closer, Jake could see that the columns stood on either side of a set of narrow stone steps leading downwards.

"I find the term Troll so…uninformed," Faulkner said as they approached the steps.

Jake nodded.

"Not a Sheep would be more appropriate," he said, smiling.

Faulkner cracked out laughing. "Very true," he added. He led the way down the steps towards a large, metal-braced wooden door that looked as if it would be better placed at the entrance to a castle keep. He took a selection of large keys from his pocket, selected one and slid it into the lock, pulling the door open.

Beyond the door was a long stone corridor that stretched away into total darkness. Jake peered into the gloom, aware that there were lights every few yards on the stone walls but giving off so little illumination that they barely cut through the blackness.

"What's this?" he asked.

"My mother told you I was a dealer," Faulkner said.

"Art and antiquities," Jake echoed.

"I also deal in other…commodities," Faulkner explained. "Come and look."

Jake followed Faulkner into the underground walkway, glancing around him as he went. The walls were of old stone, wet with condensation in places. He noticed a particularly large spider scuttle across the floor before them and recoiled slightly.

"What kind of…commodities?" Jake wanted to know, walking slowly along the underground corridor, keeping pace with Faulkner.

There was a strong scent in the air that reminded him of wet straw, but this was more pungent. The air itself seemed to be getting heavier and Jake coughed slightly, wondering why Faulkner wasn't affected by the changing conditions, but he reasoned he must be used to them.

They passed a thick wooden door set into the side of the underground tunnel and Faulkner paused there for a moment. There was an observation slot in the door, a piece of metal that could be moved aside to view what lay beyond. Faulkner reached towards this and moved it so that it was possible to see what was inside. The smell intensified.

"One of my other commodities," Faulkner said, smiling and motioning Jake forward.

He peered through the observation slot, squinting into the deeper darkness beyond. He could hear something moving about beyond the door but could see nothing yet.

"What's in there?" he asked.

Faulkner merely continued to smile.

"Keep looking," he said, softly. "You'll see it."

Jake peered more intently into the gloom, straining to see any signs of movement in the area beyond the door.

There was a sudden flurry of movement and then a loud growl. It made him step back several feet, his heart hammering against his ribs.

"Jesus Christ," he gasped. "What the fuck was that?"

Faulkner merely smiled.

"Is that a wolf in there?" Jake said, breathlessly.

Faulkner nodded.

"A very rare breed," he added.

"It's huge," Jake said, moving back to the observation slit to look through once more.

Faulkner moved to the next door, sliding back the observation slit there too. Jake inspected the occupant of the adjacent room.

Like the first, this one was also pitch black inside but

he could again hear movement. A sound like the flapping of leathery wings. There was a different smell, though. More pungent. It reminded him of ammonia and he recoiled slightly.

"It is a strong smell, isn't it?" Faulkner observed. "It's because they feed on blood. All their waste smells of ammonia."

"They?" Jake murmured.

"Vampire bats," Faulkner told him, smiling. "I have one of the largest ever captured in there."

"But why?" Jake wanted to know.

"I told you, Mr Potter," Faulkner went on. "I deal in commodities. Not everyone is an art collector or concerns themselves with accumulating as much antique pottery as possible. Other people want different things to add to their collections. I pride myself with being able to provide whatever they want."

"Animals?" Jake murmured. "But where do you find them?"

"One has to know where to look" Faulkner told him. "I have experts working for me. Most of the things that are requested I can locate with a little help." He pulled the slot shut and moved on.

"Where do they come from?" Jake asked.

"From all over the world," Faulkner told him.

"And someone buys them from you?"

"Everything has a price, Mr Potter, and there's always someone willing to meet that price."

He slid back another observation slit and Jake looked through.

This time, the area beyond was well-lit and it was easy to see that the room was occupied by a large area of dark, deep water that gave way to a muddy beach area next to it.

"What's in there?" Jake wanted to know.

"Several specimens," Faulkner told him. "But they're shy. They prefer to remain in the depths, away from prying eyes." He pointed towards the still surface of the water. "What you can see is only a tiny part of this exhibit. There's more below the surface. The water is very deep and it goes down to a small underwater lake where the exhibits can live more freely until they're needed."

"What kind of exhibits?" Jake asked.

"Creatures more used to the depths, Mr Potter," Faulkner informed him. "And, to be honest, that's where they belong."

Jake was puzzled but felt he didn't want to press Faulkner for what he meant.

They moved to another door, to another observation slot and Jake realised they had reached the last of the rooms by this time, the one at the furthest point of the underground corridor and the one with the biggest door.

"We had some problems with this one," Faulkner told him. "Very unpredictable."

Again he slid the observation slot open and Jake looked through.

The room beyond looked as if it was filled with large rocks but, somewhere in the far distance, he could see what looked like a narrow stream that snaked across the area and disappeared beneath a crudely built stone bridge.

Faulkner reached into his pocket and slid out a bunch of keys. He selected one, pushed it into the lock and turned it.

"What are you doing?" Jake asked, a little apprehensively.

Faulkner stepped across the threshold and beckoned Jake to follow him.

"I want to show you the exhibit," he said, quietly.

"I can see it from here," Jake protested.

Again Faulkner motioned for him to follow and, this time, Jake took a reticent step forward, following the other man warily as he made his way across the uneven ground towards the small bridge.

"Are you sure this is safe?" Jake offered, looking

around.

There were many large rocks and boulders inside the enclosure and any one of them could have provided cover for what lived inside the area. He wrinkled his nose as he detected a musky stench in the air. It grew stronger as they neared the narrow stream.

"How long did it take to build all this?" he asked, the stench now almost intolerable.

"Years," Faulkner said, smiling.

Jake looked around again, turning quickly when he heard some movement away to his right.

"Look, I don't see what we're doing here," he breathed. "Why did you bring me in here?"

"I wanted you to see this," Faulkner told him.

"But what has all this got to do with sending messages to so-called celebrities?" Jake went on.

Faulkner cracked out laughing and the sound sent a shiver down Jake's spine.

The other man walked onto the slope leading up to the middle of the small bridge and beckoned for Jake to join him.

"Tell me what we're doing here," Jake insisted.

The smell that he'd noticed earlier was now suffocating. He put a hand to his face to try and shut it out, but it was so powerful it was all he could do to stop himself vomiting. Faulkner didn't seem to have noticed it or, if he had, he was dealing better with it. He merely looked down over the parapet of the bridge and smiled.

"You call yourself a Troll, Mr Potter," he said. "I thought it was time you realised that you're not."

Jake frowned, wondering what the sounds were coming from beneath them now. He turned, ready to bolt from the enclosure. As he turned, a dark shape seemed to rise into view from nowhere. A huge, towering figure that seemed to be growing from the very ground itself, forcing itself upwards until it peered down at them.

Jake opened his mouth to speak but no words would

come.

He was shaking uncontrollably as he looked, dumbfounded, at the massive shape before him.

It was fully thirty feet tall. Covered from head to foot in thick, reeking fur apart from the head which was devoid of any covering. The huge eyes bulged as if pushed from within the sockets. The hooked nose was dripping thick matter, some of which dropped into the stream below with a loud splash. The teeth were uneven, filthy yellow and barely concealed by thick lips that fluttered slightly. There were a number of large yellowish boils on its skin, some of which were suppurating.

It looked down at the two men on the bridge.

"Is this why you got me here?" Jake gasped, his eyes never leaving the creature. "To see this?"

"To meet another like you," Faulkner grinned.

Jake didn't know what he was talking about. All he knew was that the thing was now reaching down towards him with one large hand.

"The creatures in the other cells," Faulkner began. "They are all thought to be the product of myth or imagination but they're as real as we are."

Jake tried to run but the hand of the huge creature opened around him, preventing him from moving.

"Werewolves, vampires, mermaids," Faulkner went on. "I've got them all here, as you've seen. All for sale to the highest bidder."

Jake screamed as the massive hand of the creature closed around him.

"And this one of course," Faulkner grinned. "Straight from fairy tales. A troll."

The hand closed around Jake, crushing as it lifted him into the air. He found he was able to look directly into one of the creature's huge, watery eyes for a moment before it pushed him into its cavernous mouth.

The stench was appalling but, in another second, that didn't matter. Nothing did.

Are you ready for another slice?

Incisions Cut Two